EMILY AND THE DARK ANGEL

Other books by Jo Beverley

The Stolen Bride
Lord Wraybourne's Betrothed
The Stanforth Secrets

EMILY AND THE DARK ANGEL

Jo Beverley

Walker and Company
New York

First published in the United States of America in 1991 by
Walker Publishing Company, Inc.
Published simultaneously in Canada by Thomas Allen & Son
Canada, Limited, Markham, Ontario

Library of Congress Cataloging-in-Publication Data

Beverley, Jo
Emily and the dark angel / Jo Beverley
        p.   cm.
    ISBN 0-8027-1159-6
        I. Title.
    PR9199.3.B424E45   1991
    813'.54—dc20   90-21526
                CIP

Printed in the United States of America

2   4   6   8   10   9   7   5   3   1

My sister and my nephew helped significantly
with the research for this book.
Thank you, Eileen and William.

1

EMILY GRANTWICH FLICKED through the pages of her leather-bound record book. "It's such an opportunity, Jonas."

"That it is, Miss Emily. Old Griswold's sheep be a rare flock. We won't see its like up for sale again in a hurry. It likely won't come up for auction for a week or two, but I know he'll sell straight out if the price is right . . ."

"There must be others interested," Emily demurred.

"Aye. It's the talk of the Beast Cross. But it's not easy to lay hand on a few hundred just like that, I reckon."

"I suspect it's not so much the price, Jonas, as the land. With the war driving crop prices up, every scrap of land is under use. Ours as well as everyone else's."

Emily and her farm manager, Jonas Claythwait, had finished their day's buying and selling and had moved a little way from the market square of Melton Mowbray. But there was no getting away from the animals that crowded the centre of the town; the air was redolent of the farm, lowing and bleating was the background music. Emily accepted it as naturally as most young ladies accepted perfume and dance melodies.

"We could always put 'em on High Burton," said Jonas, scratching his nose thoughtfully.

"Hah!" was Emily's comment. "I've no mind to chance anything until we know who old Casper's heir is and what he'll do about the property."

"It's a right shame to have that good land standing idle," said Jonas, his rugged, weatherbeaten face showing only innocence. "I hear the old man left everything to his nephew—some London dandy. He'd never know."

"He'll put in a manager," warned Emily, but she was tempted all the same.

"A stranger likely. Who's to tell him the land's contested? And what cause would a stranger have to come to killing over it? It'd be back to the courts where it's been this half century or more."

Emily smiled. It was close to a grin. It was true that since their neighbour, Casper Sillitoe, had died in September there had been no one to carry on the bloody feud over High Burton Farm, and it was a crying shame to see good pasture standing idle. . . .

"We'll do it," she said crisply. "Go back and offer Griswold his price for the flock, Jonas."

He smiled, showing his crooked, stained teeth, and touched his old-fashioned tricorn. Then he said, "What about you, Miss Emily? You shouldn't be walking about town all alone. Not this close to hunting."

"Go on with you," she said. "It's eight o'clock in the morning. If there are any bucks and dandies in Melton two weeks before hunting starts they're safe in their beds nursing their port-sodden heads. I'll wait for you at the inn."

"Right then," he said, and turned purposefully back to the cross where all the trading was done.

Emily set off for the George Hotel, where they'd left the gig, fretting slightly about her decision. It was the first time she'd made such a purchase without her father's direct instruction. There would be cash to find to pay for the flock, and these days her father was very tetchy about cash. But Griswold's sheep were too good an investment to pass up, and High Burton Farm was available . . .

It had been part of the dowry brought by Clara Sillitoe when she married Emily's grandfather. In those days the families had been close and friendly. Clara, however, though a notable beauty, was frail. She had sickened and died within a year of the marriage. Everyone admitted that old Sir Henry Grantwich had been a poor husband; he'd been neglectful and had openly kept a mistress by whom he eventually had five children. On the other hand it had been clear that Clara was delicate and her family should perhaps have opposed such a marriage.

The grieving Sillitoes had accused Sir Henry of cruelty and neglect and demanded the return of the dowry. Henry bluntly refused. The matter was placed in the hands of the men of law and had remained there ever since—to no one's satisfaction except the solicitors, who presented their accounts every quarter.

Both the Sillitoes and the Grantwiches, however, were practical country people, and good land could not be let waste. While each maintained their right to the entire property, they had unofficially divided it and used it as pasture through the years.

Until last spring.

The war was to blame, thought Emily. Which put all their problems on Napoleon Bonaparte's shoulders. Well, they should be wide enough to carry the load.

The war had caused a steep rise in prices, making land-owners rich and some of them greedy. The new and growing popularity of Melton as the centre of the hunting fraternity had created a great demand for fodder in an area which was traditionally grazing land. Casper Sillitoe, Clara's nephew, had decided to put his half of the land to the plough and plant corn. Emily's father, a new Sir Henry, had objected; it was one thing to let his opponent use the land, another to let him rip it up.

Casper had sent his ploughs to rip up Two Oak Field. Sir Henry had gone with all the men of the estate at his back to stop them. A pitched battle had resulted in injuries on both sides.

In the end it had come to a duel, man to man, across the weapons of their youth, rapiers. Emily had not been witness to the fight, but her imagination had always boggled at the thought of the two rotund, middle-aged men lunging and parrying on the hummocky grass of Two Oak Field.

It had been farce and had ended as tragedy. Her father had tripped and fallen. Casper had toppled over him, unintentionally driving his sword into his opponent's back. The

3

wound had not been deep, but it had damaged the spine. Emily's father had not walked since.

To add to their problems, when word was sent to Emily's brother, Captain Marcus Grantwich, to come home forthwith and take over the estate, the news came back that the captain was missing in action and feared dead. Which was how Emily came, somewhat reluctantly, to be managing the Grantwich properties.

After the Battle of Two Oaks, as the locals called it, Casper had abandoned his ploughing, but in the aftermath no one had dared use the land at all. The mere word of it sent Sir Henry into a paroxysm of rage. Casper had retreated into sullen misanthropy and taken to drink, so that all his affairs slid into chaos.

One night in September, Casper rode out drunk to Two Oak Field. He set his horse at the fence there, fell, and broke his neck. Sir Henry said good riddance and that he wished he'd been granted such a clean death; some in the area put it down to guilty conscience or even the hand of God; most just reckoned it to be bad luck and wondered who'd inherit from the old bachelor.

Emily was jerked out of her thoughts by a warning shout. She stepped quickly back to clear the way for a brawny man carrying an amazing quantity of bricks in a hod. He nodded his thanks as he raced towards a new house rising up where lately there had been a market garden. A cart full of the bricks stood in the road waiting to be unloaded. There was so much new building now Melton had become the Queen of the Shires. After all, the town had become the mecca for the hunting fraternity.

Fox hunting had slowly been growing in popularity over the past fifty years or so, but it was only since the turn of the century that the addicts of hunting had realised the unique advantage offered by Melton Mowbray.

There were three hunts which every man of the chase wished to follow—Hugo Meynell's famous Quorn, the Duke of Rutland's Belvoir pack and the Earl of Lonsdale's Cottesmore. Melton sat plump in the middle of them all. Each pack of hounds was out only a couple of days a week, but with a base in Melton a man could reach all three and so, with luck, follow the hounds six days a week throughout the season.

Hunter's paradise.

The people of the area were renting out every available room and new buildings, like this one, were springing up all over town. Emily shook her head and moved on. She did not entirely approve of all the changes. It was true that hunting mania had brought prosperity, but she remembered nostalgically the sleepy town of her childhood. Now it was scarce safe to walk the streets in the high of the hunting season when the town was packed with wild young bucks ripe for trouble, on or off the field.

But it was still a pleasant place, especially on such a beautiful October morning, mellow after a soft overnight rain. Many trees still held their leaf, shining in the sunlight, bronze, copper, and gold. Late roses bloomed in a nearby garden and a squirrel scurried by with an acorn in its mouth.

Emily loved the cycle of the seasons, but these days they seemed to pass so fast. She was twenty-six years old. Firmly on the shelf and virtually past her last prayers. For a long time she had not minded being the quiet daughter, the plain one, the one who would stay home and look after her father. She had certainly not envied her pretty younger sister when Anne had married Sir Hubert Keynes. Sir Hubert was a pompous young fool, and Emily wondered how Anne could tolerate him for two minutes.

These days, however, she was aware of a restless dissatisfaction, though she was not at all sure what she desired. Certainly not another Sir Hubert. Nor could she contemplate a change in her life so long as her father needed her to run the estate.

In fact, she told herself sternly, she had better apply her mind to business instead of whimsical fantasies. She opened her record book as she walked on, reviewing the purchases and sales made at the market and checking the list of supplies she had to order before returning home.

The heels of her mother's old-fashioned half-boots clipped smartly on the cobbles with each step. At only five foot two, Emily felt she needed every advantage when she went to the cattle market, but the heels on the boots made her footing precarious on the wet cobbles and she kept half an eye on the road before her.

There were people about, but only servants running errands or making deliveries and country people going to and from market loaded with purchases. As she turned into the more fashionable streets even these became fewer. As she had predicted, what society people were in town were fast in their beds.

She was pondering whether to buy some of the first crop of Seville oranges, which were expensive as yet but which would make wonderful marmalade, when a shriek made her look up. In one of the new narrow houses, a window had been pushed open and it was from there the shriek had come. A tall man came out of the house and stood looking up. Before Emily could prevent it he took a few steps backwards and collided with her.

Her reticule and book went flying, and Emily herself was knocked off balance. With the agility of a cat the man twisted and grasped her in strong hands as she teetered. There was an ominous crack from the heel of her boot.

Stunned, Emily looked up at the most handsome face she had ever seen. Lean. Unfashionably brown. Royal blue eyes shining with hilarity. Crisp glossy dark curls under a fashionably tilted beaver.

"I'm terribly sorry," he said, obviously struggling with outright laughter. "I—"

A china bowl flew past them and shattered on the cobbles. "Be damned to you, Piers Verderan!" The shriek rent the air. "Go to hell, where you belong!"

Emily gaped up over his shoulder to see a red-faced woman leaning out of the upper window with most of her body hanging out of a loose silk wrap. Tousled Titian curls massed around what had obviously been intended by God to be a pretty face.

The man began to turn, his hands still on Emily's arms. The woman reached behind her and threw. A beribboned oval box sailed through the air to knock his hat flying. The box burst open, and a pungent cloud of violet-scented powder billowed out over both of them. The woman shrieked with laughter.

The man choked and let Emily go. He stooped, ripped up a tall weed complete with muddy roots, and hurled it with deadly accuracy at his attacker. She was still laughing as it hit. She stopped and opened her mouth to start another blistering tirade, but after an alarmed look at the gentleman she shut her mouth, retreated, and slammed the window shut.

Stunned, coughing, and waving away the pungent powder, Emily still had to admire such ability to silence a harridan. When the man turned back to her his face was smoothly expressionless. He coughed again, brushed a volume of powder out of his dark curls, grimaced slightly, shook himself, and then turned his attention to Emily.

Her large plain straw bonnet had caught most of the deluge, and he deftly removed it and beat the powder off downwind. Dazedly shaking her serviceable dark pelisse, Emily felt as if she'd stepped into a violet-scented hurricane. Her bewilderment increased when an elf popped out of the half-open door of the house.

A delicate creature, shorter even than Emily, with a mass of silver-blonde curls and huge blue eyes, the elf was dressed only in a filmy knee-length smock and showed a great deal of slender, shapely leg.

The elf and Emily stared at each other blankly, and then it disappeared. Emily blinked. The tall gentleman spoke as he came to stand in front of her.

"As I was saying," he drawled as he settled the bonnet back on her head and deftly retied the ribbons, "before we were so rudely interrupted, I beg your pardon." He brushed at his sleeve and then shrugged and desisted. "I think that does more harm than good." He looked down at her, and a touch of sardonic amusement lightened his features. "We'll just have to bring powder back into fashion, won't we?"

Torn between annoyance and unwilling amusement, Emily shook out her skirts and said, "Hair powder, perhaps, if you can afford the tax, but body powder?" After a moment she realised what she had said and went red. When she looked to see his reaction, however, he was picking up his hat and her reticule and book, and paying no attention to her words at all.

Arrogant, she thought. Abominably arrogant. A typical London buck come to lord it in Melton and chase foxes—a Meltonian.

He returned her possessions to her. "Perhaps I may make amends by escorting you to your destination, ma'am."

One embarrassment subsided only to be replaced by another. It was finally dawning on Emily just what kind of scene she had interrupted. On top of that it couldn't be clearer that he had no enthusiasm for being in her company.

"No, thank you," she said as coldly as possible. They both reeked of violets to a cloying degree, and she maliciously hoped it would embarrass him even more than it would embarrass her.

Even her coldness left him unruffled. "As you wish," he drawled. He produced a card. "I'm Piers Verderan, as you may have heard. Staying at the Old Club. If your clothes prove to be unreclaimable, apply to me for recompense."

"Thank you, but that will be unnecessary," Emily said frostily, annoyed at being taken for an upper servant though she deliberately dressed very plainly for these trips. She turned to make a dignified withdrawal and almost fell as the heel of her boot snapped off.

Again he gripped her arm, though he released her as soon as she got her balance. He bent and retrieved her heel from where it was wedged between two cobblestones. He looked down with interest at her footwear and raised one elegant dark brow.

"Quaint," he remarked, and Emily's lips tightened. "If you care to raise your foot like a horse, ma'am, I'll see if I can fix it, but I doubt it will work."

"I don't have far to go, sir," Emily said, and held out her hand for the heel. "I will manage, I think."

He placed the wooden heel into her hand. "My dear lady," he remarked with an edge to his voice and an air of excruciating boredom, "I don't bite, and I only abduct women if I find them wandering on deserted moors at full moon. You will be much more comfortable if I lend you my arm as you hobble to your destination."

This was undoubtedly true, and trying to teeter her way over the greasy cobblestones would be undignified at best and dangerous at worst. Still, Emily wished heartily that she did not have to accept his assistance. She looked around, but the street offered no more suitable escort.

She glanced at him. He was clearly a gentleman of the *ton*, though not quite a dandy. Beneath their silvery powdering his dark jacket and buckskins were of the highest quality, and his top boots gleamed. He was arrogant and rude, and from the scene she had witnessed he was clearly not a gentleman of unimpeachable morals, but surely he was adequate to support her a little way down the street.

"Thank you," she said, and placed her hand upon his proffered arm. They began to walk down the street. After a moment or two, Emily glanced sideways and found she was unable to see his face because of the brim of her bonnet. She could see some of his body, though. Her demure bonnet seemed designed to make her focus on his legs, a shortcoming of the hat she had never noticed before.

They were superb legs.

Well, what did she expect? He was doubtless addicted to hunting, which developed the legs wonderfully.

What on earth was she doing even thinking such a thing? Hoping her bonnet also concealed her flaming cheeks, Emily hastily fixed her gaze upon the road ahead.

"In our circumstances," the man drawled, "are introductions not in order? I promise on my honour not to encroach. You know my name. May I not know yours?"

"Grantwich," said Emily flatly, trying for chilly dignity, which is very hard to achieve when limping and clinging to a man's arm. "Miss Grantwich."

"Delighted to make your acquaintance, Miss Grantwich," he said with audible insincerity. "And are you a resident of Melton Mowbray?"

"I reside nearby," Emily replied discouragingly.

"At Grantwich Hall, perhaps?" he queried.

Startled, Emily looked up at him—which involved a sinuous contortion of her neck. How had she never realised before that a deep-brimmed bonnet forced a lady into coquettish movements if she wished to see the face of a tall gentleman with whom she walked?

A slight glint in his cynical eyes showed he was familiar with the fact. "Came across the name somewhere," he said, "and it seemed likely. You must consider yourself fortunate, Miss Grantwich, to live in the heart of the Shires."

Emily focussed again on the road. "On the contrary, sir. The recent passion for hunting is very disruptive. As I have no taste for the chase I get no benefit from the hullabaloo and a great deal of bother from the hunt charging across our land."

"I'll go odds your father and brothers don't agree," he remarked.

Maliciously she said, "As my father is an invalid and my brother has been missing in action for four months, I think their interest in hunting down foxes is limited." Emily was immediately ashamed of herself. His arrogance was no excuse for her to be positively catty.

She swivelled her head up again and saw a trace of disdain which she knew she deserved. Quickly she said, "I do apologise. There's nothing civilised you can say to such an announcement, is there? I can only excuse myself as being out of sorts after . . ." Emily found she could not think of a way to describe the recent contretemps.

His lips twitched with what appeared to be genuine amusement. "After being barrelled into," he offered. "Screeched at by a lady of obviously loose morals and drowned in revolting *Poudre de Violettes*? A powerful excuse for any incivility, I assure you."

He stopped walking and without asking permission adjusted her bonnet so it sat further back on her head and at an angle which she feared had to be jaunty. It did, however, allow her to look at him without danger of a crick in her neck.

It was done without the slightest show of consciousness on his part that he might be being bold.

As they resumed walking he said in a far more friendly tone, "I offer you my condolences on the misfortunes which have befallen your family, Miss Grantwich. Is there hope that your brother is perhaps a prisoner?"

Flustered, and even alarmed, Emily grasped a serious topic with relief. "There is hope, yes. Marcus was a great admirer of Sir John Moore, you see, and when he died nothing would do but for my brother to join Sir John's regiment. It has been a cause of anxiety, as he is my only brother, but he has always enjoyed a charmed life. Even as a boy he would escape injury in the most amazing situations. He once fell off the roof of Grantwich Hall and contrived to land in the shrubbery and merely suffer a broken collarbone."

She was babbling, which was very unlike her.

Her listener, however, looked genuinely sympathetic. "There certainly do seem to be people favoured with good fortune. I knew a man once who was the only survivor of a terrible shipwreck. There seemed no reason for it other than the favour of the gods."

"And yet such gods are notoriously fickle," said Emily. "I am beginning to fear that we are irrational to cling to hope. But if Marcus is dead—" She broke off. She really shouldn't be discussing her family's business with a stranger.

"I assume the estate is entailed," he said. Then after a pause he asked, "Felix Grantwich?"

Emily could tell from his tone he knew her disreputable cousin. She nodded.

"You have my commiserations once more," he said dryly.

Emily felt she should object to such rudeness, but his sentiments were completely in accord with her own on this subject. "All will be well," she said, "if Marcus returns home safe. We hope that he has been taken prisoner, but even so, we hear such horrid tales of the way we treat French prisoners of war and I cannot believe our enemies are any more gentle. The death rate on the hulks from disease is terrible, I believe."

"I fear so. But the war is surely drawing to its close, Miss Grantwich. Napoleon has never recovered from his disastrous foray into Russia, and now for the first time all Europe is allied against him. Wellington has mopped up the Peninsula and is already on French soil. Surrender will soon be inevitable. Then you can expect your brother home."

If he lives, Emily added silently. She was surprised, however, to be offered rational hope by this chance-met stranger, but not too surprised to be grateful. She wondered if she could convey this feeling of optimism to her bitter father and to Marcus's affianced bride, Margaret Marshalswick.

They had arrived at the George. She turned and offered her hand, able to say with sincerity, "Thank you, Mr. Verderan."

There was a courteous curve to his fine lips as he touched his fingers to hers, but the overall impression of his features was world-weary cynicism. She remembered that when she had first seen his face, while he was still amused by his inamorata's antics, he had seemed somehow younger. It was a shame that he now looked so jaded.

Emily could not imagine why her whirling mind was throwing up such intimate notions about a stranger.

"Are you sure you can manage from here?" he asked as she hesitated. "I am willing to carry you over the threshold if it is necessary."

Emily could feel herself colour. "No," she said quickly. "I mean, yes, I can manage. I . . ." She took a grip on herself. "Thank you for your assistance, Mr. Verderan," she said, and turned to limp into the inn.

She heard him say, "The worst of it is I gave her this dratted powder. There's a lesson to be learned in it somewhere." His tone was full of wry humour.

Emily glanced back at him, able at last to see him clearly head to toe.

Sleek, elegant, beautiful as a proud thoroughbred, he was also dusted silvery-mauve from his curly beaver to his gleaming black boots and stunk of the cloying perfume. Following his lead, she'd walked through the streets of Melton in the same state without a thought for the spectacle, they must have presented.

Suddenly his lips curved in a devastating, conspiratorial smile and he winked.

Emily found herself mirroring it and on the verge of a giggle. She bit her lip to suppress such wanton weakness and hurried into the inn.

Piers Verderan looked down at himself and shook his head. He supposed all his clothes would have to be thrown out. Served him right for giving in to Violet Vane's persistent pursuit, but she could be beguiling and Melton was damned dull with the hunting season not yet properly underway.

As he turned towards Burton Road, he reflected that a more cautious man would probably have delayed telling her a night of passion did not elevate her to the position of *maîtress en titre,* but caution had never been in his nature and she'd begun to bore him with her importunities. When she'd thrown a tantrum merely because he'd had a kind word for that little protégée she had brought with her he'd lost patience with it all. It had almost been worth it just for the show.

On the whole he admired an uninhibited woman, and one thing about Violet Vane, she was not inhibited, particularly in her rages.

Not like little Miss Grantwich. It was hard to imagine her even raising her voice. What was she at Grantwich Hall, the poor relation?

As he strolled through the increasingly busy town he was bemused to find thoughts of Miss Grantwich dancing through his mind. Plain, he'd thought at first, but hers was a face that grew on one. It was an unremarkable oval with a determined chin and fine-textured skin. Her eyes were brown with pleasantly dark lashes but they were not large or "speaking." Her hair was an ordinary brown, wavy rather than curly, and she wore it in a very prosaic knot at the back.

It was her expressiveness which marked her out. When flustered she became quite fetching—it could tempt a man to fluster her often. When annoyed, the very firmness of her lips and chin had its own appeal. But when she smiled, ah, when she smiled, it lit up her whole face. Hers was a wide, generous smile that shone through her skin and sparkled in her eyes. . . .

Verderan realised he had reached Burton Street and had spent the journey in contemplation of a plain country miss.

As he entered the most prized address in Melton Mowbray—the Melton Club, commonly called the Old Club—he muttered, *"Poudre de Violettes* must addle the brain."

= 2 =

EMILY ARRIVED AT Grantwich Hall in borrowed slippers and still reeking of violets.

Her housekeeper, Mrs. Dobson, immediately declared, "Lord love us, Miss Emily, what have you been up to? I'm used to you coming home smelling of the farm yard, but now . . . Well, it wouldn't be decent to say what you smell of!"

Emily chuckled. "And there you may have the right of it. A lady of easy virtue hurled the powder out of a window and some of it hit me."

"Well, I never," was the gaunt housekeeper's comment as she eased off the pelisse and held it at arm's length. "What for would she want to do a thing like that?"

Emily caught a glimpse of herself in the old kitchen mirror. Her bonnet still sat on her head as that man had arranged it—further back than her usual style so that the waves of her hair showed, and tilted so that the elegant bow he had so casually tied nestled under her left ear. It looked quite fetching, but flighty. Definitely flighty.

She saw the colour rush to her cheeks, whipped off the offending bonnet, and thrust it at Mrs. Dobson. "This can be thrown out, I think. I never did like it anyway." As the woman dumped both coat and bonnet outside the door where the smell would do less harm, Emily suppressed a strange urge to rescue the bonnet and add it to her small collection of romantic mementos.

Her wits must be addled. That man's easy familiarity with women's garments showed what kind of person *he* was.

The housekeeper returned and put thin hands on bony

hips. "Well, Miss Emily? Are you going to explain how you got into such a state?"

Emily's mother had died when Emily was only five and Mrs. Dobson had become more foster mother than servant. The Grantwich children had always regarded her as such and took no offence at her vigilance.

The woman might look like a battle-ax, but she had the heart of a mother hen.

Emily snitched a jam tart from the cooling tray and bit into it with relish. "Delicious. I just got in the way, Dobby," she assured the woman, adding mischievously, "The target was the gentleman I had the misfortune to collide with."

"Say no more!" commanded Mrs. Dobson, raising a hand. "I can imagine the rest. It's to be hoped no one recognised you."

Emily put on a rueful expression, but didn't try to hide the amusement in her eyes as she licked delicious flakes of pastry from her lips. "Well, I had to introduce myself to him, since he was obliged to lend me his arm through half of Melton."

"And why, pray, was he so obliged?"

"The heel snapped off my boot."

Mrs. Dobson stared at the borrowed slippers as if they were the devil incarnate. "Lord have mercy, Miss Emily, you'll be ruined yet. It isn't right you going around doing estate business."

"I'm coming to enjoy it," Emily confessed. "And you know Father won't hire anyone. I think it would be to admit . . . you know."

The woman sighed. "Aye. Admit he'll never walk his land again and Master Marcus won't come home. Still and all, Miss Emily, it isn't right."

"I'm actually rather good at it," Emily pointed out. She had begun the task under protest, for she had always been a very conventional person, but over the past months she had learned the ropes and now found the challenges stimulating.

"That's nothing to do with it," said the housekeeper. "What's to become of you when Master Marcus does come home?"

"I'll go back to being a proper lady and concerning myself with household matters." Emily couldn't make herself sound truly enthusiastic. She wanted her brother home safe, but knew it would mark the end of her stimulating new life.

"And when Marcus marries Miss Marshalswick?" Dobby asked.

Emily sighed. "I will probably marry her brother and become the vicar's wife," she said. It wouldn't be the same. Hector would never let her have a say in the property, and he'd probably keep a close eye on the housekeeping too.

"If he'll still want you after all this traipsing around," Mrs. Dobson said dismally. "A vicar's wife must set an example, after all. What if this morning's faradiddle get's talked of?"

Mrs. Dobson was genuinely concerned, which gave Emily pause. She had no mind to be a scandal. "Truly, it wasn't so bad," Emily assured her. "Away from the market-crosses the town was largely deserted and my rescuer seemed—" Emily had been about to say that he seemed a very proper gentleman, which is what Mrs. Dobson needed to hear. She could not bring herself to describe him that way.

"Seemed what, pray?"

"A gentleman," supplied Emily feebly.

Mrs. Dobson's eyes narrowed in the way she had when she was hot on the trail of a prevarication. "And who was this 'gentleman,' Miss Emily?"

"A Mr. Verderan. I doubt I will ever meet him again." With that, Emily stole another tart and beat a retreat before the housekeeper could dig deeper.

She went to her room to change and to vigorously brush her hair in an attempt to reduce the smell. Mrs. Dobson had only raised concerns which had lurked in Emily's mind for some time. It was not so much that she feared she would lose her reputation by managing the estate so much as the fact that ordinary life was going to seem very dull.

If the Reverend Hector Marshalswick lived up to everyone's expectations and proposed marriage, she should surely accept. It was likely to be the only opportunity ever offered. Emily was a practical young woman; she had lived twenty-six years without any man conceiving a violent passion for her, so it was unlikely to happen now. Hector was only thirty, prosperous, well-enough looking, and had the highest moral standards. He would make an excellent husband.

Emily sat with the hairbrush dangling from her hand, wondering why such a marriage seemed a dismal prospect.

This was obviously the reason society forbade young women from taking on unusual roles. It left them unsuited for marriage. Well, until there was definite news of Marcus and he either returned or her father agreed to hire a manager, there could be no decision on a marriage.

She began to apply the brush again with a distinct feeling of relief. The brush did little good to her hair, however. She would have to bathe and wash her hair. So would Mr. Piers Verderan, she thought with satisfaction. But that conjured up an alarmingly intimate picture of that tall gentleman in his bath. What on earth was the matter with her? The violet-scented powder must have gone to her brain.

She hastily took up her record book and went down to her father's room, only stopping along the way to order water heated for a bath.

Sir Henry now lived on the ground floor in what had been the library. It still contained a wall of glass-doored bookshelves full of sermons and agricultural treatises, but now it also held Sir Henry's bed and wardrobe and the daybed upon which he was sometimes persuaded to lie.

He was not a noble invalid. He complained a great deal and refused to make any effort to resume a normal life. He claimed it hurt too much to sit in a wheeled Bath chair, and for all Emily knew he was telling the truth.

She was fond of her father and made great efforts to ease his situation, but from reality or contrariness, nothing she tried was admitted to help at all.

When she came in he was lying propped up in his bed, staring out of the window. He was pale, but with a disturbing port-wine colour in his nose and cheeks. His once solid, hearty bulk now seemed a soft mass around him. He was complaining peevishly at his long-suffering manservant, Oswald. As soon as Emily entered, he ordered the man out and bade his daughter pour him some brandy.

Emily bit back her protest. It wasn't good for him, but he was drinking more and more each day. She and Oswald had tried watering the spirit, but Sir Henry had noticed the adulteration immediately. Without voicing a protest, she gave him the glass and her record book then leant forward to touch her lips to his cheek. He did not thank her for any of it.

"What foolishness have you been up to now?" he growled as he opened the leather-bound book. "That it should come to this, having a chit out of the schoolroom do man's work."

"I'm twenty-six years old, Father," Emily said quietly.

"Old maid," he grumped and ran a finger down the page. "You paid too much for those heifers."

"The war is driving prices up, Father. We agreed we needed new stock. We got a good price for the pigs."

"So I should hope. Twenty pounds for five loads of hay!" he exclaimed. "What fool promised you that price?"

"Harvey of The Swan. You know there's a tremendous demand for stable goods during hunting, Father."

"Then you could doubtless have got more."

He continued his carping scrutiny of her records while Emily struggled to be charitable. It was terrible for him to be confined here and in pain. But would it make his pain worse if he were to give her a few words of praise for her labours? She was coming to dread the times when she had to visit this cluttered, stale room.

"Griswold's sheep?" he shouted, making her jump. He glared at her. "Who buys sheep with winter coming on? And where do you think to put them, you silly ninny?"

"Helstead's underused. And Ratherby," Emily stammered, wishing she'd thought up a better answer to this inevitable question.

"Only just," he snapped. "A harsh summer and you'll have a lot of cheap mutton. And who'll pay? Me. Damn it all, you're letting everything go to wrack and ruin!" Pettishly, he hurled the book to the floor. Emily moved quietly to pick it up.

"Perhaps it's time to give up," Sir Henry muttered, draining his glass. "Accept that Marcus is dead. Let Felix come and look after things."

Emily counted to ten.

Her cousin Felix was a lightweight wastrel. He had no interest in coming to Grantwich Hall and working the land. He merely looked forward to the day when he would own it and could milk it dry to pay his gambling debts. Apart from that, its chief appeal to him was that it would be a *pied à terre* in hunting country that could buy him some friends.

Her father seemed to forget the time Felix had invited himself to stay for the hunting season three years back. He and Sir Henry had almost come to blows.

"You know the War Office still holds out hope, Father," said Emily. "Everyone says Napoleon must surrender any day and then we will know for sure."

"If you haven't ruined the place by then," he snarled. His nose twitched. "What's got you stinking like a tart? Silly tottie. Think to catch a man, do you, at your age?" He drained his glass. "I'm not paying for those sheep," he said, and set his mouth like a rebellious three-year-old.

Emily caught her breath. Sometimes he did this, became totally unreasonable. "I've bought them, Father," she said.

"Then you can pay for them," he said with a sneer.

Emily's hands tightened on her record book and she was tempted to hurl it at him. "I don't have that much money at my command," she said, wondering for a moment whether telling him she intended to pasture the flock on High Burton would help. No, it would give him apoplexy.

"Well then," he retorted, "you're in a pretty pickle, aren't you, my girl?"

"Father, everyone has accepted me as your agent. It was you who refused to hire someone to do the job. They trust my word as yours."

"I didn't tell you to buy those sheep."

"It was a chance not to be missed. Griswold's ill and wants to go live with his daughter. He's sold the farm to a Meltonian who wants it for a hunting box and doesn't want the stock. He was willing to sell cheap for a quick sale, and someone else would soon have grabbed the bargain if I'd delayed. The shepherd comes with them."

She began to relax as she saw the petulance leave him.

Oh, it wasn't fair to any of them that it had come to this. He'd been a good landowner and a good father. A rough, bluff old-fashioned squire, he'd dealt fairly with all, but now he was all twisted by his misfortune. Another reason to wish Marcus home was that Sir Henry would deal better with another man. He'd let Marcus help him and not resent it.

Her father picked fretfully at his coverlet. "Too many sheep, too many horses . . . all eating their heads off . . . You'll have to take the hunters to market soon."

Emily looked at him with compassion. The start of the hunting season must be eating at him like quicklime. Soon they'd all be out after the hounds for glorious twenty-mile runs, and all he would have would be the distant sound of the hunting horn. If he was finally talking of selling his pride and joy—his hunters—then he was coming to accept that no one in this family would hunt again: that he was an invalid and Marcus was dead. Though she had believed herself resigned to the truth, it brought tears pricking at her eyes.

She swallowed. "We'll get nothing for them in the ordinary market, Father."

"I know that," he snapped. "They need to be out in the field, but who's going to hunt them now? Not me. Not Marcus."

Emily took a deep breath as an idea came to her. "Father, can I use the sale of the horses to finance the purchase of the sheep?"

He sneered. "There're three prime five-year-olds out in the stables, but *you'll* be lucky to get fifty guineas each."

"I've heard of hunters going for hundreds."

"One of Lonsdale's sold for a thousand once," Sir Henry reminisced, a flicker of pleasure lightening his expression. "Ah, that was a night. Drunk as monks, the lot of us . . ." He came back to the bitter present. "And that's the only way to get that kind of price. Ride the hell out of the animal all day then sell it drunk at the Old Club. Assheton-Smith sold Furze Cropper for four hundred guineas after the Billesdon-Coplow run, and he'd bought him, they say, for forty. But how're you going to do anything like that, miss?"

Emily worked at keeping calm. "I don't need to get a

thousand, Father, or even four hundred. Just a hundred or so each. Nelson at least is a top-class hunter. If you'll let me try, I think I can sell them at a fair price."

A spark of interest lit his eyes. "Oh, do you? Make it a wager, then, eh? Since you seem all set on ruling the roost here. You sell those horses to cover the cost of the sheep and I'll let you carry on running this place as long as you want. Fail, and I'll turn the whole place over to Felix."

Emily caught her breath. It was a silly, dangerous wager, but it sprang out of his frustrated boredom and was not untypical. Had he not, like other men, wagered more than he could afford on such meaningless things as how many piglets a sow would have, or whether a dog would turn left or right at a fork in the road? At least in this case she would be able to work towards making it come out well.

She wasn't quite sure yet how she was going to manage it, but she'd just have to make sure she did.

"Very well, Father," she said calmly. "A wager it is." Deliberately, she held out her hand to him.

After a momentary hesitation he took it and shook on the bet. A glimmer of genuine amusement lit in him, making him look much more like his old self. "You're becoming a saucy piece," he grumbled, but his lips twitched. "Damme, but I wish you'd been a boy."

Emily dropped another kiss on his cheek and left.

Once outside the room, she took a moment to compose herself. It really wasn't surprising that her father was so tetchy, but that didn't make it any easier to bear, particularly when it led to such ridiculous situations.

To her dismay, Emily had discovered she wasn't the stuff of which good sickroom attendants are made. Perhaps it was as well that she would not marry and have children. Instead of womanly skills and a tender heart she appeared to have a gift for administration and a head for business. Which was perhaps as well, for if she were to preserve the estate she had to find a way to get a handsome price for three hunters.

She had to do it, for she could not bear to see the estate in the clammy, greedy hands of Cousin Felix.

Under her management, Grantwich Hall was prospering as never before. It was partly the effect of the war, but she knew it was also because she was an efficient administrator. Unlike her father, she kept careful records and accounts. She was happy to listen to the local experts, and they were gratified to advise a poor young lady who was struggling to manage in difficult circumstances.

She was selling surplus stock and adjusting the animals on the land to make the best use of it. She was also beginning some planned breeding programs to improve the flocks of sheep. She had instituted some economies and used the savings to bring about improvements in the conditions of the tenants.

She longed for her bath, but it was not ready yet, so she popped into another room at Grantwich Hall, that of her Aunt Junia.

Sir Henry's older sister, Junia, had lived at the Hall all her life and had no intention of moving no matter what might happen. She also had no intention, short of the direst emergency, of becoming involved in the running of the establishment. She had occupied two rooms overlooking the gardens since leaving the schoolroom. From there she attended to a vast correspondence and painted beautiful flower pictures which she either gave away or sold, as the mood took her.

She organised her life to suit herself as arrogantly as if she were a man and was as likely to wear trousers as skirts, but when the occasional stranger would congratulate or berate her for being a "modern" woman, perhaps even a Wollstonecraftian woman, she would look at him with a blank stare.

Junia Grantwich was an original and Emily thought her delightful.

She knocked, and entered the airy parlour to find her aunt absorbed in a painting of some dried seed-heads of wild garlic.

"That's lovely, Junia."

"Think so?" asked the older woman. "Not the pretty stuff the *hoi polloi* likes. I like it."

She smiled up at Emily. She had a round face, tanned and toughened by much time spent out of doors, and creased with nearly sixty years. Her hair was short grey curls. Her smile was wide, warm, and generous.

"How was business?" she asked.

"Pretty fair. Griswold of Kettleby's sheep suddenly came on the market, so I bought them."

"Good idea. Where'll you put them?"

"If I have to, on High Burton."

Junia nodded. "Good for you. Why d'you smell like a tart?"

Emily laughed. "That's exactly what Father asked."

"Well, he would know," Junia remarked. "What's the answer?"

"I got hit by a box of *Poudre de Violettes*."

Junia cleaned and laid down her brush, then turned fully to her niece. "It was flying along the street?"

Emily chuckled. "After a fashion. Propelled by an irate lady of questionable virtue."

"A tart?" asked Junia.

"A Violet Tart," Emily declared, finally finding delight in recollection of that encounter.

Junia swung around in her chair and grabbed a pencil and her drawing paper. In a moment a caricature appeared of a blowsy female, cheeks puffed up like a zephyr's as she blew a box through the air down the street. Underneath, Junia wrote, "The Violet Tart." Emily laughed out loud. It was worthy of Rowlandson.

"I'm afraid not, Junia. She merely threw it."

"Shame. Mind, judging from the aroma still clinging to you, she showed some taste in throwing it away."

"The only taste she showed was in whom she was throwing it at," Emily replied. "An unsatisfactory lover, I suppose." Even as she said it, Emily doubted that to be the reason for the attack.

Junia turned back again, eyes atwinkle with anticipation. "Tell me the whole," she commanded.

By the time Emily had finished they were both in whoops of laughter.

"Oh," said Junia, wiping her eyes. "I wish I had seen you

promenading through town all covered with the stuff. Whatever his faults, that man must have a certain panache. Who was he?"

"A Mr. Piers Verderan." Something flickered in Junia's expression—awareness, coupled with alarm and amusement. Emily asked, "Do you know him?"

"No," Junia said bluntly. "Is he a Meltonian, then?"

"I suppose so," said Emily, wondering. For all that she stayed close to home, Junia gathered all the gossip. She may not know this Mr. Verderan, but she knew of him. Emily, however, had no intention of showing vulgar curiosity, even if she was tempted.

Really, she had disliked the man intensely, and that woman had clearly been afraid of him. But the boyish amusement she had first seen and that final devastating smile confused the picture and unsettled her.

She put the man and the incident firmly out of her mind and told her aunt of the sheep and the horses. "So now I have to get the best price for the hunters and I confess I'm at a loss. Even without the problem of the sheep it would pain me to let them go for a fraction of their worth, but you know how things are—if people realise I need to sell, the price will fall."

"You need to get someone to ride them for you," said Junia.

"But it would have to be a top rider to really make a mark, and they are largely Meltonians, not local men. If only Marcus were home."

"If Marcus were home," said Junia practically, "you wouldn't need to sell them nor would he let you, for he'd want them for his own string." She picked up the drawing and handed it to her niece. "A memento," she said.

"Of what?" Emily asked uneasily, remembering her irrational desire to keep the bonnet and the temptation to question her aunt about the Violet Tart's lover.

"Of an interesting encounter," said Junia idly.

Emily wanted to disclaim any wish to remember her day's adventure, but she wasn't sure she wanted to completely forget. The possibilities ahead for adventure seemed limited. As she had gone all her life without meeting a man like Piers Verderan it seemed likely she would go the rest of her life without meeting his like again.

A little reminder wouldn't come amiss. Emily took the picture and thanked her aunt with a kiss.

After Emily left, Junia Grantwich was thoughtful. She didn't remember when she had last seen little Emily so aglow. She'd always thought it a crime the way the family loaded whatever role they wished onto Emily, but she admired the way the girl always came up trumps. She'd been a quiet, dutiful little mother's helper, then, after Henry's wife died, quiet little mother to baby Anne.

She'd been an admiring ear to her brother and father and had soon become the ruler of the household without ever ceasing to defer to their masculine authority.

After Marcus went off to the war Emily had uncomplainingly assumed some of the role of son of the house, accompanying her father about the estate and acting as sounding board for ideas, and sometimes acting as deputy.

Now in these last few months she'd taken over the lot and was doing remarkably well. And blossoming. Perhaps it was the job, but more likely it was age. It did a woman a world of good, thought Junia, to reach the age where she stopped mooning for romantic love. Liberated her.

These days Emily had a firmness to her step and a way of meeting a person's eyes frankly and smiling with unashamed humour. It would be a shame to see all this drowned if Marcus came home.

Junia wanted her nephew to survive the war, and she knew he would have only the kindest intentions towards his sister, but he was not an original thinker. It would never cross his mind that Emily might want more of life than the role of indulged maiden aunt.

Thus far, the only escape had seemed to be Hector Marshalswick, which was not a route that recommended itself to Junia. Now, however, there was Piers Verderan, who must surely be Damon Verderan's son. Did he have a scrap of his father's Irish magic?

Her mind slipped back thirty some years to a magical summer of assemblies and rides, with Damon Verderan in the area, visiting his relative, Lord Althorpe. He'd married Helen Sillitoe, who'd had the same delicate beauty that had marked her aunt Clara, the lady who had brought such problems with her brief marriage.

At least Helen had proved more robust. She'd borne one healthy son and was still alive, one gathered, living in Ireland at her father-in-law's estate, Templemore. Damon had died in a boating accident about ten years into the marriage. Junia couldn't help feeling she would have taken better care of the man.

She gave a little laugh at such old foolishness. So, his son was among them now.

Junia had followed the career of Damon's only child. She'd heard the rumours and knew he wasn't the perfect English, or even Irish, gentleman; knew that he was excluded from the more select circles of Society. Even allowing for exaggeration, he was doubtless a rogue and could be a philanderer, but Emily's reaction showed that he must have some of his father's magic touch.

It was a chance in a million that Piers Verderan be the one for Emily or that he be free and willing, but it wouldn't do any harm to find out. And if all that resulted was a little adventure for Emily to remember, that would be something to the good.

Junia went to her writing desk to compose a few letters.

Emily also decided to write a letter as she waited for her bathwater; a letter to her old school friend, Chloe Ashby. They had not met in person since their Cheltenham schooldays at Miss Mallory's select establishment, but they had kept up a regular correspondence. Emily still felt as close to Chloe as she had when they had shared a room, and secrets, all those years ago.

Such different lives they had led, however. Chloe had eloped when seventeen and enjoyed all kinds of adventures before settling with her second husband in Lancashire. Her letters were full of her darling Justin and little Steven.

Emily felt her own letters must be dull by comparison, for apart from her schooldays she had never left Leicestershire and she had no husband, had never even been kissed with more than brotherly fondness . . .

Disgusted with her tendency to sigh over this, Emily reminded herself that at least now she could enliven one letter with a description of her encounter in the High Street with a rake and a Violet Tart.

═ 3 ═

THAT AFTERNOON, WHEN Piers Verderan left the building on Burton Street which housed his uncle's solicitor, he was a trifle bemused by the tangle in which Casper had left matters. It wasn't as if it were a grand estate. Compared to the property he had inherited from his father, and that purchased on his own behalf since, this was a mere nothing and yet someone had to sort it out. That was the trouble with inheritances. They generally brought more labour than profit.

"Ho! Verderan."

He turned and sighed slightly as he saw three young bucks making eagerly towards him. Chart Ashby, Harry Crisp, and a stranger. The three young men were dressed identically in the latest fashion—blue jackets with brass buttons, buff breeches and top boots. They all had high beavers, leather gloves, and riding crops—and an air of excitement. Three young men hopeful of making their mark during the hunting season, hopeful of becoming accepted as true Meltonians, the elite of the hunting world.

He couldn't cut them, of course. Chart and Harry were cousins to his friend, Lord Randal Ashby, and Harry had been Verderan's fag at Eton.

"Good day, Harry, Chart."

"'Day, Verderan," said Chart, his grey eyes shining with the untarnished exuberance of youth. Verderan wondered if he himself had ever been so damned youthful. "Beg to present my friend, Terance Cornwallis."

Verderan acknowledged the existence of the rather round

young man who seemed out of place with the handsome, muscular cousins. Apart from the fact that Chart had dark curly hair while Harry's was tawny they could have been twins. Chart casually informed Mr. Cornwallis, "Piers Verderan, Corny. A regular neck-or-nothing. A true Meltonian."

"Honoured," said Mr. Cornwallis, his ruddy face growing redder.

Verderan turned to stroll with the trio down the street. "In the Shires a bit early, aren't you?" he remarked. "Unless you're here for the cubbing."

"Oh no," said Harry Crisp, quickly denying any interest in such tame training work. "Come to look at Corny's place. He's inherited a bit of property between here and Oakham."

Verderan glanced at the bashful young man, at last seeing why Chart and Harry had taken him up. "Remarkable good fortune, Mr. Cornwallis."

"Old aunt," blurted Terance. "Only a small farm, really."

"Still. A place like that near Melton will save you, and your friends, a fortune. Last count, lodgings here were at least two hundred for the season and stabling costs a guinea a week. You'll be bringing, what?—at least six horses each?"

"At least," Chart said blithely. "Father would never sport the blunt for Melton, but now . . ."

"But now you'll be able to pool your resources," Verderan completed. "Excellent idea." He looked pointedly at Harry and saw his schoolday training still held.

"Of course we'll be paying our share at Corny's," Harry said quickly. "Food, fodder, and all that."

Chart looked mildly surprised, but he was a kindhearted young man, if careless, and he quickly assented. "Gods, yes. Good enough of Corny to put us up. No need to put him to extra expense."

A few incoherent mumbles came from their host and were ignored. "So what are you doing here so early, Verderan?" asked Chart.

"Business," said Verderan. "I too have inherited a place nearby. But for the moment I'm staying at the Old Club." He looked at them and found himself saying, "If you promise not to blow your noses on the tablecloth you may dine with me there tonight."

Despite their attempt at sophistication, three faces flushed with colour and three pairs of eyes shone. "I say, that's damned decent of you, Ver," said Harry.

"Yes, it is," said Verderan brusquely. "Don't make me regret it."

The trio correctly took this as dismissal and made themselves scarce while Verderan wondered if it was a sign of senility, this tendency to be so disgustingly kind to people. More likely it was a lingering effect of the morning's adventure. He was never coming within a mile of *Poudre de Violettes* again.

The three ecstatic young men ducked into the nearest inn and commanded the best October ale.

"What a piece of luck!" declared Chart. He turned to Corny. " 'Course we'd never have had a chance of dining at the Club if it was the season."

" 'Course not," said Corny earnestly.

"Dining there's only for the best. Might get in after for some drink and play, mind you, particularly if Randal were here."

"Randal won't be here," pointed out Harry. "Just married."

Chart looked shocked. "You think he'll miss the whole season?"

"Unless he brings Sophie," Harry said.

"Ladies don't take to Melton much," advised Corny.

"True enough," said Chart, "but you never know with Sophie. Besides, you wouldn't think Randal would want to be with her all the time would you? Dashed queer, if you ask me, and devilish inconvenient. We need a sponsor to be in at the best."

Chart and Harry started an analysis of their family and friends and found it singularly disappointing. They were both well connected. Chart was the grandson of the Duke of Tyne; Harry was the son and heir of Viscount Thoresby and connected through his mother to Lord Liverpool and the Tory establishment.

None of this, however, was the slightest use in Melton. Here one needed a connection to Belvoir, Lord Lonsdale or Sefton, Assheton-Smith or Pierrepoint. All of which were depressingly lacking.

"Mr. Verderan?" offered Terance tentatively.

The other two looked at him in shock. "Oh no. Too risky," said Chart. He leant forward slightly. "Word to the wise, Corny. He's a dangerous man."

Terance's look was a question.

"Dueler. Killed his man twice. Never lets anyone cross him."

Terance swallowed. "Seemed . . . seemed a pleasant sort of fellow."

"Yes," said Chart thoughtfully. "Damned strange."

"Oh, come on," protested Harry. "He can be dashed pleasant. I tell you, I was grateful to get him at Eton. Never ran me ragged, and though he's got a tongue like a knife, he never laid a hand on me."

"Had a running feud with Osbaldeston that's the talk of the school still," pointed out Chart. "Broke his arm. Went after Swallowton and flogged him when he wouldn't fight."

Harry went a little red. "Well, Osbaldeston was always a bully and Swallowton . . . that was on my account. He was . . . bothering me, if you know what I mean."

"Oh," said Chart. "Still, you can't deny our families would throw fits if we're forever in his company. Probably try to order us home. My mother almost had a spasm to have to be in the same room as him at Randal's wedding."

"Doesn't like dueling," said Corny wisely. "Mothers are all the same."

"Oh, doubt she knows about that kind of thing. Man's stuff, after all. And it never came to law or anything. Both his victims were warts on the body of society and everyone was delighted to see them go. And though Ver's not exactly accepted, he's damned rich and connected to all the right people. Even if," he added thoughtfully, "they hope he won't turn up to claim acquaintance . . ."

"But why?" asked Corny. "Rich, well-turned out, Meltonian . . ."

Chart shrugged. "Stories. There was rumour at Eton he'd

run away from home with his grandfather's strongbox. But I ask you. If *you* were going to run away from home, would you run *to* Eton?"

The other two shook their heads.

"They say he won't have anything to do with his mother. I just wish I could do the same to mine."

"I've heard," offered Harry uneasily, "that she's living in poverty in Ireland because he stole the family fortune. He's here in luxury and she's living on boiled potatoes."

"Not good," said Corny, who was actually rather fond of his mama.

"Doubtless a hum," said Harry quickly. "After all, if he was a thief, the law would have something to say, wouldn't it? People make up these stories about him and he won't bother to deny them."

"As for what turns the matrons sour," broke in Chart with a grin. "Just about everything. He's rude to anyone if it suits him, has a damnable temper, and won't tolerate fools. When the mood takes him he gambles madly, though he nearly always wins—"

"Collects exotic mistresses," broke in Harry, "and rarely just one at a time."

"Had the whole opera ballet at his Hampshire place once," came back Chart. "Can you imagine?"

It was obvious from Corny's face that he was trying hard.

"And a harem of Arabians."

"And two American Indians."

"And Swedish triplets."

"All at the same time?" asked Corny blankly, causing them all to dissolve in laughter.

"In fact," said Harry when he'd recovered, "one day I'll pluck up the courage to ask Ver the truth."

"Well," said Chart, "just don't pick tonight. He may not be the most likely prospect, but he's the only contact to the inner circle we've got as yet, so it's clean faces and charming innocence, my lads!"

That evening, Verderan found the meal at the Old Club drawing to a close without any obvious disaster having taken place. Well trained by Eton and Christ Church, his three guests had the precise blend of ease and deference which made them invisible to the lions they ate with. They listened with flattering absorption to the hunting tales of the old hands and made just sufficient contribution to the conversation to avoid being apostrophised as nodcocks.

Verderan rather thought he could see them taking mental notes for their memoirs—or for tales for their grandchildren. *"Did I ever tell you about the time I dined at the Old Club with Assheton-Smith . . ."*

Golden memories of the evening had been assured the trio when it was found that Lord Robert Manners had ridden over from Belvoir Castle and brought with him the great man himself, the legendary Thomas Assheton-Smith, who had succeeded Hugo Meynell as Master of the Quorn.

Assheton-Smith was a tall, elegant man with a quiet reserved manner, which surprised people who knew only of his daring reputation in the field. He was known to disapprove of drinking and gambling, and his very presence had exerted a moderating influence on everyone in the club this evening.

He suffered the adoring attention of the three young men with good humour, encouraging Chart Ashby to ask, "Is it true, sir, that Napoleon gave you a medal?"

Assheton-Smith laughed. "Don't put that around, young man. You'll have me under lock and key! No, no. It was during the Peace of Amiens, you know, back in eighteen-oh-two. We all thought the war was over then, and a lot of us went over. I was scarce older than yourself, but I'd been hunting a few years and had some good luck. Got myself a bit of a name, which had spread even to Paris. He sought me out to talk of the great sport."

"And called you 'Le Grand Chasseur Smit,' did he not, Tom?" asked Lord Robert.

Assheton-Smith modestly agreed that to be so and turned back to Chart. "Will I be seeing you out with the Quorn, young man?"

Chart's eyes shone. "Oh yes, sir. I wouldn't miss it."

"Good, good. You have the look of a fine rider and your

bloodline's good. Your cousin's a fine man over fences, though he fails to take my advice to the full."

Verderan saw Chart's frank disbelief at this heresy. "I think Tom refers to Randal's disinclination to take a fall unless absolutely necessary," he explained dryly.

"A failing you have too, Ver," said Assheton-Smith. "You know my dictum, 'There is no place you cannot get over with a fall.' It is only by throwing his heart over every fence that a man can keep up with my hounds."

"Have you often found me lagging behind, Tom?" queried Verderan.

The great man laughed. "You have me there! But I still maintain that the only way to ride a hunt well is to stop for nothing."

"I'm with you there," said a small-statured man with a high voice and a pointed face. "Never mind prime blood. Courage is what a man rides in the field."

Verderan felt his jaw tighten, for the comment was directed at him. He and George Osbaldeston had cordially hated each other since their first days at Eton, but had luckily rarely encountered each other since. Osbaldeston had been hunting-mad even back then, and ever since leaving Oxford he'd devoted himself to the sport, first in Yorkshire, then as Master of the Burton Hunt. Now he was Master of the Nottinghamshire Hunt, moving ever closer to his target, the Quorn. He'd even taken to calling himself "Squire" Osbaldeston.

When Osbaldeston managed to get the Mastership of the Quorn, Verderan rather thought his own hunting days in the Shires would be over. The place would become uninhabitable.

"Courage won't take a cart horse over an oxer," he pointed out, "and being brave while lying in the mud is not a game I want to play." It was well known that the "Squire" couldn't afford horses fine enough for his ambitions.

"Of course being able to afford fine horses can help anyone to make a show," retorted Osbaldeston, looking at no one in particular. "Irish horses. Or Irish money."

An uncomfortable silence fell over the company at the insinuation, and Verderan was weighing the sheer pleasure of picking a fight with Osbaldeston against the amount of effort involved—and the small matter of bringing his family skeletons to centre stage—when he discovered he had a champion.

"A good rider on a bad horse can make a show," Harry Crisp said calmly, though he looked tense. "A poor rider merely ruins a good horse, Irish or not."

Champions, in fact. Chart Ashby turned to Assheton-Smith. "I understand you rarely pay more than fifty guineas for a hunter, sir. You must be a wonderful judge of horseflesh."

"Why, thank you," said Assheton-Smith, quite kindly. He didn't much care for Osbaldeston himself. "But it's amazing," he added with a twinkle of humour, "how many wonderful horses of mine turn back into slugs when I've sold 'em. It's the right kind of horse, a rider who'll work with a horse, and the courage to take risks. All that together makes a good man for hunting. You must not ask of your mount more than it can do, but you must ask of yourself everything. No hesitation, ever."

This spun off into a lively review of the last season's runs, of the places where a daring leap had been successful, and of others where it had caused delay or even left a rider out of the running. Or, as Verderan dryly pointed out, dead.

Osbaldeston brushed this off with a sneer. "What more glorious way to die, I ask, than flying over a rasper in the Shires?"

This was greeted by a roar of approval, and even Verderan had to give his old enemy his point. He was, one gathered, a skilled huntsman and a brave rider. What shame he was such a nasty little fellow.

They had crossed each other within days of Verderan's arrival at Eton, when he'd come across Osbaldeston holding a younger, smaller boy face down in a puddle because he didn't like his boots. The fight had been brief as Verderan had a good few inches on Osbaldeston and hadn't felt it fair to continue once his man was clearly bested.

Osbaldeston had never had such scruples. A few days later, he and some cronies had cornered Verderan and beat him up, leaving him badly bruised and with cracked ribs.

They'd thought to terrorise him as they had so many others, but they hadn't realised what they were up against. Verderan had been taught endurance in a hard school, and he merely waited until he caught Osbaldeston alone and thrashed him, making a more thorough job of it than he had the first time.

Osbaldeston had realised, as many others had in time, that short of killing him there was no way of suppressing Piers Verderan. And he wasn't easy to kill.

Verderan caught Osbaldeston's eye and hoped he got the message that nothing had changed.

The covers had been drawn. Candle flames reflected in deeply polished mahogany, glowed back from buffed silver, and glinted in fine crystal. A fire burned in the grate, crackling and hissing and burnishing the room with a fine warm glow. Each man still had a port glass before him and the bottle made its lazy way around, but drinking wasn't the order of the day.

The president of the Old Club, Major-General Henry Craven, had brought the cigarillo habit back from the Peninsula and persuaded a few of the other men to join him. The aromatic smoke curled above their heads. The rest, however, were sticking to the more traditional form of tobacco, snuff. There was a pot of snuff on the table, but most men preferred their own sort and the boxes were offered around.

Verderan offered his box to his three guests. Chart and Harry took a pinch elegantly enough and managed not to have a sneezing fit. Terance Cornwallis, who seemed awestruck by his circumstances, wisely refused. The three were behaving as well as any young men could be expected to. Verderan reflected that he was but six years their senior; he felt at least a dozen.

The conversation wound down to a hiatus and Osbaldeston spoke up again. "So tell us, Verderan," he drawled. "Why, pray, were you seen squiring an upper servant through town, covered with a fine dusting of flour?"

Verderan discovered that he didn't want anyone, least of all Osbaldeston, poking around Miss Grantwich's reputation. "Good lord," he replied nonchalantly. "How came you by that tale? I hardly thought any *civilised* person was about at that hour."

The sharp little face, so like his quarry the fox, tightened at the slight. "You obviously were, Verderan."

"But I have never claimed to be civilised, Osbaldeston," replied Verderan, to a general chuckle. "And it was not flour but *Poudre de Violettes*." Violet had said the "Squire" was after her favours. From the sudden colour in his cheeks, for once she had not been lying.

Before Osbaldeston could respond, Chart Ashby exclaimed, "Violet Vane," and then went red as he realised the knowledge his words implied.

"Can you afford her?" asked Verderan with interest.

"Hardly," said Chart, recovering some of his carefully cultivated *sangfroid*. "I met her once and she asked for a gift of the stuff. I—I'd heard she was in town."

"Did you give her any?" Verderan asked, curious.

Chart coloured again as he said, "Yes."

"Well," said Verderan kindly, "I wouldn't expect too much return on the investment. She obviously only collects it to use as ammunition."

"But why was she attacking you, old man?" asked Henry Craven. "I'd—er—not thought you one to disappoint even the most demanding lady."

Verderan raised his glass slightly to acknowledge the compliment. "Perhaps I satisfied her too well. It was the fact that I did not want to make the association of longer duration that infuriated her."

"Ah," sneered Osbaldeston. "You'd found her servant more to your liking. Find yourself more suited by the below-stairs maid, do you?"

"Not at all," said Verderan. The desire to pick a fight with the man was becoming pressing, but that would only draw attention to the whole incident, which hardly seemed fair to poor little Miss Grantwich. If Osbaldeston was going to haunt Melton, there were bound to be other opportunities.

He changed the subject before Osbaldeston's vulpine nose picked up the scent of a scandal. "Care to lay odds, gentlemen, on who mounts Violet as his mistress next? And perhaps more intriguing, who's going to enjoy the tender morsel she's grooming? Ethereal little thing with a cloud of silver-blonde hair and enormous blue eyes."

"Ha!" shouted Craven with a laugh. "Now we see why Violet was so enraged. Not the below-stairs maid but her apprentice. No doubt who's already laid claim to the little vixen."

Verderan saw a flash of fury in Osbaldeston's face. So that was his quarry, not Violet at all. What a revolting thought. Such a charming morsel deserved a gentle hand.

"If you say so," said Verderan blandly. "But I assure you the covert's undrawn as yet, so who's to say in which direction the vixen will break? Lay your bets, gentlemen."

That was enough to distract the whole group from the identity of the lady seen in his company that morning. The betting book came out and hundreds of guineas were wagered on the disreputable futures of Violet Vane and her promising little protégée.

But though they joined in, Verderan and George Osbaldeston were weighing other odds and making other silent wagers.

In the cool of the next morning, Emily stood in the pleasant pungency of the stable yard and surveyed her assets.

The family stock consisted of two hacks which could also be harnessed to the gig or small carriage; Emily's own riding horse, a grey gelding called Corsair; and six hunters. Three had been bred by her father for eventual sale, the others bought as yearlings or two-year-olds. There were never enough hunters, and Sir Henry had reckoned to make a tidy profit while ensuring himself and his son fine mounts for the season.

Three of the horses were still too young to hunt; they probably would have to be sold but would bring very little. Three, however, were in their prime: Nelson, Wallingford and Oak-apple. Sir Henry had ridden Wallingford and Oak-apple, and two others that he'd sold, the year before. This would be Nelson's first time out. They could all be worth a lot of money, but the whole scheme depended on someone riding them in the field and handling the subsequent gentlemanly bargaining.

Emily went over and fed a windfall to the pride of the stables, Nelson. He was a chestnut with a deep chest, well-sloped shoulders, and strong quarters. He could jump almost anything.

"Oh, you could go like the wind, Nelson," she said as she rubbed his forehead. "If they once saw you in action, all those silly Meltonians would be bidding their all to own you."

The big chestnut gently butted her and she laughed. "Yes, of course I'll ride you today. I wish I could ride you in a hunt but it isn't done, you know. Even if I were to be so bold, I couldn't go to the Old Club and get the best price. And anyway, all those arrogant men would refuse to be impressed by a mount ridden by a female. It would be demeaning, wouldn't it, to sell you for a hundred or so as if you were just another horse?"

Nelson tossed up his head and snorted at the very idea.

Haverby, the groom, came out of the tack shed. "Want me to saddle 'im, Miss Emily?"

"Yes, please." Emily suddenly realised that soon these magnificent horses would be gone. She hadn't looked ahead so far in her plans. How empty, how ordinary, the stables would seem without them.

She went the rounds, dispensing largesse and paying particular attention to Corsair so he wouldn't be jealous, until the groom led out Nelson ready for her. "We're going to have to sell them, you know, Haverby," she said.

He was stoical. "Better so, I reckon. No life for them stuck here."

"I think I'll have to hire someone to ride them, though. Do you know of anyone?"

"You want a roughrider, miss. Dick Christian's best, they say, but I doubt you'll get him this close to hunting."

"I've heard of him. He rides for the horse-copers and sometimes for gentlemen?"

"That's right. There ain't a horse born he can't ride, and ride well. He'd make even old Venus there"—he nodded at the oldest hack—"look like prime blood."

The unlikely notion made Emily smile. "I'd like to get the best. Can you get word to him that I'd like to hire him? It does no harm to ask. And see who else may be suitable as well?"

"Right you are," he said and tossed Emily into the saddle. "Where you be off to, then, Miss Emily?" he asked. It was the only restriction put on Emily these days, to let someone know where she was heading.

"Up to High Burton," she replied and gave Nelson the office to go.

She took it slowly for a while, letting the horse stretch and settle, and then began to try his paces. They cantered over a fallow field, and she set him at an easy woven hedge. He hopped over it and tossed his head.

"Too tame for you, is it?" she chuckled. "Very well."

She let him have his head and they raced across grass towards a higher fence with a ditch behind. She collected him, then set him at it. It was like flying with a smooth, controlled landing at the end.

"Oh, you beauty!" she said, laughing, and they raced on to the next obstacle.

In a little while she reined him down to a trot, then to a walk. "You could go on for hours, couldn't you, my fine fellow? But that's enough for now. I want to look at the land."

He obediently walked along, his step as light and frisky as if he had just come out of the stable, as Emily looked over the disputed property. It needed the sheep. The grass had grown long during the wasted months. In Two Oak Field the gash in the earth was unrepaired after old Casper's attempted ploughing, but already grass and weeds had disguised the damage.

Two Oak bordered directly onto the Sillitoe estate and Emily saw that the field beyond contained a well-tended covert of gorse and ferns. She wasn't surprised, for Casper had been a great supporter of hunting, and if you wanted foxes available for the chase you needed coverts for them to hide in when their earths were stopped.

It was a bother, though. She hardly wanted to encourage

foxes to lurk next door to her flock. As she frowned over the brush fence at the covert she heard the thumping of hooves and looked up. A fine dark horse ran easily up the sloped field towards her. As it came closer she recognised with a tremor of alarm that the rider was Mr. Piers Verderan. Reacting perhaps to an involuntary jerk of her hand, Nelson jibbed and sidled away as the horse and rider drew up on the other side of the fence.

Mr. Verderan raised his hat. "Miss Grantwich. What a pleasant surprise." He sounded as if he meant it, and Emily thought the surprise part was doubtless honest. How different she must look now, dressed in a bright green habit and a small-brimmed hat with a trailing veil. And mounted on what he must recognise as a handsome bit of blood.

She had been slow to respond. His smile cooled. "I must apologise. I did promise not to encroach, didn't I? Shall we assume we have never met?"

"No, of course not," she said quickly and extended her hand over the fence. "My mind was just slow to turn away from the problem of that covert, Mr. Verderan."

To her surprise he raised her gloved hand briefly to his lips before turning to look at the large area of gorse and fern. "Problem? It looks to be in fine shape."

That out-of-place salute of her hand flustered Emily even though it clearly had no significance for him. There had been no speaking look, no lingering over the touch. So why had he done it?

The part of her mind that was still rational responded to his comment. "But the foxes will eat the lambs."

He raised a brow and gazed about at empty fields.

She smiled at her foolishness. "The lambs born to the sheep I intend to put on these fields, Mr. Verderan," she explained.

That caught his attention. "Do you indeed? You will need a good shepherd, then, to care for your flock." His elegant lips twitched. "How very pious that sounds, to be sure."

Emily knew she was smiling in return. "But I hardly expect to receive divine intervention, sir," she remarked. "Definitely a case in which God helps those who help

42

themselves. I will certainly need a good shepherd."

"Forgive my curiosity, Miss Grantwich," he said, "but is this land yours?"

"Yes, of course," she replied, seeing no point in regaling a stranger with the sorry story of the dispute. "Or, at least, my father's. I manage the estate for him."

A finely curved brow quirked. "Do you know, Miss Grantwich, you are a creature of infinite surprises. Next you will be telling me you hunt that fine beast."

His tone reminded her that she'd found this man insufferably arrogant. Emily's spirit sparked in response to the challenge she detected, and she raised her chin. "I would hunt Nelson if I had any wish to do so," she retorted, who had never considered such an outrageous thing before. "As it is, I have no taste for the sport."

"And yet presumably you like to ride."

"I can ride as much as I want, sir, without having to chase an animal to death to get pleasure from it."

"That only shows that you've never ridden in a hunt," he drawled in that tone which made her want to contradict everything he said.

Before she could think of an abrasive response, he looked out over the misty landscape stretched around them, the rolling grassland and high fences that made the Shires ideal hunting country. When he spoke, it was in a soft, thoughtful voice.

"There's a challenge in the chase, Miss Grantwich, and the greatest treasure in life—an unpredictable ending. The fox will lead where a sane horse and rider would never go of their own volition, and despite his reputation for cunning, the fox does not twist and hide. He runs straight and fast and long, and he who hesitates in his wake is well and truly lost."

He turned and looked at her. "Therein lies the challenge, Miss Grantwich, which you will never get when out hacking. The speed, the danger. And the glory of facing fears and conquering them. And," he added with a smile, "surviving."

Though Emily's head advised that he described insanity, her faster breathing and a rapid heartbeat showed she was in danger of Bedlam too. She, who had always been so sensible, so careful, so moderate, suddenly wanted to take a risk, face a terrifying challenge, and achieve a dizzy triumph.

He spoke again in a normal, offhand voice. "If you're going to condemn that horse to tame canters along bridle paths, Miss Grantwich, it will be a damn shame."

Emily stared at him, startled by the word. "I beg your pardon?"

He was coolly unmoved. "Do you expect an apology for a mere 'damn'? You must surely hear worse as you go about your father's business."

That was true, but she was nettled that he did not think her worthy of common courtesy. "Another religious reference, Mr. Verderan?" she asked tartly. "You'll have me thinking you a man of the cloth."

"You are far too intelligent to think anything so absurd, Miss Grantwich."

And that was true, thought Emily. With his crisp dark curls and sardonic features, Piers Verderan brought the devil to mind, not God. The notion of him in a pulpit exhorting the local farmers to honest labour and charitable works was totally impossible.

"Lost for words, Miss Grantwich?" he challenged.

Emily was perilously close to it. Nothing in her life had prepared her for Piers Verderan. "All I can say, Mr. Verderan," she said primly, "is that your conversation is not that of a gentleman."

"Ask anyone," he said with a slight smile. "They'll tell you it's been my life's work to avoid being anything so tedious as a gentleman."

Emily was utterly confused. "What pray are you, then?"

His smile widened into that devilishly charming one, and it was as if little flames sparked in his eyes. "Why, Miss Grantwich, haven't you guessed? I'm a rake. And I'm also Casper Sillitoe's heir. I believe this land is contested between our two estates. I'll have to consider carefully this matter of your sheep."

Before she could say a word, he turned his horse and set

it back the way he'd come at a gallop, flying over a fence with elegance. Emily felt Nelson twitch with the urge to follow and challenge that dark beauty. She felt the same urge herself, but it was not a riding challenge that called her. It was something else.

She'd never met a man who behaved quite as Piers Verderan did. Though she couldn't exactly say he offered her insult, he did not treat her as a gentleman should treat a lady. Just by a gesture or a tone of voice he seemed to suggest they were already more than that.

Surely he could mean nothing by his manner with her, even though it created in her a feeling of intimacy which was turning her giddy.

"You're twenty-six," she reminded herself, "and plain, and unromantic, and businesslike . . ."

No amount of self-debate helped. "Damn," she muttered, using just the word she'd objected to from him, as she set Nelson back towards Grantwich Hall at a good speed.

She spent the whole canter home obsessed by the man. A self-confessed rake. A libertine of the first water. Doubtless a gambler and drunkard. She had never met a rake and never wanted to. No sane and decent woman would want anything to do with a man who consorted with loose women, drank himself under the table every night, and wagered his all on a fly on the window or the parentage of some poor lady's child.

She should have guessed, however, that a rake would have skills expressly designed to set the most sensible lady's head spinning like a whirligig.

= 4 =

EMILY GALLOPED THE last mile to the Grantwich Hall stables to let Nelson have his head and to try to blow a certain man out of her own. The ride was wonderful, but thoughts of the man lingered. He was surely a Meltonian and would stay for the season, living at Hume House—Casper's old place—and therefore their nearest neighbour. How was she to avoid him? Did she want to avoid him?

And to add to her problems, as an avid hunter he'd probably set up more coverts for foxes and positively encourage the hunt to work this part of the country. That meant trouble.

Not that Emily was fond of foxes. They were vermin and an utter nuisance, but traps and guns would get rid of them more efficiently than a hundred men and twenty couple of hounds chasing one poor beast for hours. In fact it was getting to the point where people were carefully preserving the foxes to ensure good sport and heaven help anyone who destroyed one. The world was assuredly mad.

For all that, she needed the hunt to win her wager with her father and preserve the estate from Cousin Felix. The hunt would make Nelson worth a small fortune if she could only display him. His smooth, ground-eating gait, his endurance, and his agility over all kinds of obstacles made him a princely hunter.

If Piers Verderan were to ride him he'd bring a high price, said a mischievous voice in her head.

"Emily Grantwich, you are suffering moon-madness," she muttered to herself as she dismounted outside the stable.

The horse shook his head.

"You don't think so?" she queried.

The horse tossed his head up and down as if in agreement. Emily wondered if she truly were going mad.

Haverby came over to take the reins.

"Have you ever wondered," Emily asked him, "whether these horses understand everything we say?"

"Surely they do, Miss Emily," he replied. "Like 'Giddyup' and 'Whoa.' "

"Do they—er—talk back?"

The groom looked at her in concern. "You all right, Miss Emily? Nelson toss you on your head?"

Emily glanced at Nelson, who seemed to have a very meaningful glint in his big dark eyes and looked hastily away. "No, no," she said quickly. "I just wondered . . ."

"You'd be best to go and have a nice lie-down," said Haverby, shaking his head as he took the horse. "But there's company."

"Who?"

"The Reverend and Miss Marshalswick."

It was strangely early for a visit and Emily had a busy morning planned, but she would be pleased to see her friend Margaret, if less pleased to see her suitor, Hector Marshalswick. She hurried to her room and changed into a simple blue-sprig muslin. Then she went down to the morning room, where she found Junia lackadaisically entertaining their guests. As soon as Emily arrived, her aunt made her excuses.

Both Hector and Margaret were looking puzzled.

"Forgive me, Emily," said Hector bemusedly, "but is your aunt—? She talked only of toads."

Hector was a solidly handsome young man: square hands, square shoulders, square face. His dark hair curled pleasingly and his eyes were large and sensitive, though Emily wondered sometimes if that wasn't a misleading impression. His only fault was that he was rather short, but that made him well suited to her own meagre height.

After all, she wouldn't want to marry a tall man and forever have to twist her neck to look him in the eye. A picture of a certain tall man instantly presented itself.

"Oh dear," she said quickly. "I'm afraid Aunt Junia always speaks of whatever is uppermost in her mind. She did say she was reading up on toads for use in controlling garden pests. Many people round here leave out milk, you know, in the hopes of attracting a toad to their garden."

"If they're not leaving it out to appease the boglins," said Margaret with a mischievous twitch of her lips. She too was short but fortunately more delicately built than her brother. On her the curly dark hair and large dark eyes were decidedly fetching.

"That is possible," agreed Emily, and they shared a mischievous look, knowing that the superstitions of the local people greatly annoyed solid, practical Hector. "How are you both?"

"We are very well, thank you," said Hector. "We stopped by so early because we felt we must give you a warning. We have a viper in our midst."

"Snakes?" queried Emily in confusion, her mind still on toads.

"Rakes!" declared Margaret cheerfully. "Or rather one rake. You'll never guess who Casper Sillitoe's heir is, Emily. Poor Hector fears for the souls of his flock."

"Margaret," said her brother with a frown, "this is not a subject for levity. It is bad enough to have an annual influx of wild young men with nothing better to do than waste ridiculous amounts of money on a pointless sport, but to have one take up residence as our closest neighbour . . ."

"Who is this man?" asked Emily, knowing perfectly well.

"A certain Mr. Verderan," said Hector sourly. "The worst example of the type."

"Goodness," said Emily. Her scarce-acknowledged hopes that he had been teasing when he described himself as a rake crumbled. "What—what do we know about him?"

"I would not sully a lady's ears with what I know," said Hector, much to Emily's disappointment. "Suffice it to say that he is unfitted for any lady's company."

Emily remembered Mrs. Dobson's warning and wondered nervously if Hector would wash his hands of her if he discovered she had walked the length of Melton on the man's arm. Then she reminded herself that it was as yet none of his business.

"Hector," she said firmly, "I'm afraid I can't cut anyone's acquaintance without reason. If he's Casper's heir he is our neighbour and I'll doubtless have business dealings with him."

Hector stiffened. "Emily, I . . ." Emily knew he had been about to say, "I forbid it," but had realised that he did not have the right. "I will speak to your father," he said weightily and rose.

"Hector, that may not be wise," warned Emily. "Any mention of the Sillitoes upsets Sir Henry."

"Then he will be all the more anxious to keep you away from the man," he retorted. "It is time your father was brought to realise that he must hire someone competent to run the estate."

Emily watched tight-lipped as he left. It would do no good to protest further unless she wanted to alienate Hector. And apart from his status as possible husband, Margaret was her dearest friend.

Margaret moved quickly to take her hands. "I am sorry, Emily. But you know Hector."

"Yes, indeed." At times like this Emily knew she would be insane to even think of marrying him. "I do wish he wouldn't upset father though. And yet on the other hand, father seems to relish a good fight now and then."

"I don't think it will do him any harm," agreed Margaret. "But I'll be surprised if Hector sways him, which means you probably will get to meet the rake. What fun. I'm dying to see him myself."

"Why? You surely would never be interested in such a one, Margo."

"I'm only interested in Marcus," said Margaret firmly, if wistfully. "But it's like a giraffe at the zoo," she went on with determined good humour. "I just want to see what a rake is like. It will doubtless be a dreadful disappointment, just like the giraffe I saw when we went to London. Flea-bitten, and on its last legs."

Emily thought of Piers Verderan and giggled. "No, really, Margo. A flea-bitten rake?"

Margaret nodded. "Port wine nose. Gout. Corsets."

Emily had great trouble not to laugh out loud and discovered an urgent desire to share this with a certain lean, handsome, healthy gentleman of her acquaintance. "Is he old then?" Emily asked innocently.

Margaret grinned. "I haven't the slightest idea," she admitted. "Since all I have are Hector's annoyingly guarded warnings, I've been indulging in the most absurd flights of fancy. It's as good as a novel and someday I'll be able to see how close my suppositions are to the truth. After all, we're sure to at least see him in passing. He may even come to church."

"A rake at Evensong?" queried Emily.

"Old Sir Bertram comes every Sunday, and he's the greatest rascal out."

"Well, Margaret," said Emily conspiratorially. "Promise. Anything you find out, tell me."

"Of course," whispered her friend as they heard a door close rather loudly across the corridor. "And you the same?"

"Of course," Emily promised, guiltily aware that she was already concealing a great deal from her friend.

At that moment Hector returned, looking disgruntled. "Your father grows more unreasonable every day, Emily. I offer earnest prayers for your brother's safe return."

"Thank you, Hector," said Emily meekly. "So do we all. But I do wish you could give me a hint as to what this Mr. Verderan has done. To put me on my guard," she assured him.

He took a solid stance before the window, hands tucked behind the tails of his black coat. "I have made it my business to find out about the man," he said weightily. "It has been most distasteful. There are any number of sordid tales, going back, if you will believe this, even to his school days, but I will not repeat them for they are unsubstantiated gossip. It is commonly acknowledged, however, that he gambles for large sums. He—and I hesitate to say it before innocent ears—he regularly consorts with *loose women*. He is known for his violent nature and has even fought in duels."

"Oh," said Emily, unimpressed. Surely many people committed foolishness during their schooldays; if such things were the worst being said about a grown man, that told a tale in itself. A taste for gambling, women, and duels merely described the larger part of the fashionable men of England.

Hector obviously read her expression. "I see I will have to be blunter. You may think such fashionable vices as play and pistols romantic, Emily, but this man's crimes are more sordid. I spoke with a Mr. Osbaldeston, who was at school with this Verderan. He told me that Mr. Verderan swindled a large amount of money from his grandfather and as a consequence the old gentleman and Mr. Verderan's own mother live in poverty in Ireland while he idles here in luxury."

"That is hard to believe," said Emily. "The law would surely have something to say about it."

"I can only assume that his family has too much sensibility to take it to court. Perhaps they yet hope to appeal to a better nature he clearly does not possess." Hector frowned at Emily. "I have to wonder why you are so determined to act as this man's advocate."

Emily stiffened at his tone, aware that she had flushed. "Christian charity," she retorted. "You are regaling me with a great many rumours, Hector, most of them hard to believe."

He coloured slightly. "You cannot believe, Emily, that I would take any man's good name lightly. Some facts are not disputed at all. In fact, in the eyes of the men I have spoken with, they are seen as matters of some admiration. It is apparently a fact that Mr. Verderan has not only taken part in a number of duels, he has killed two of his opponents."

Margaret gasped. Emily went cold. "*Killed* two men?" she repeated. "That cannot be. He would have been charged."

"He is apparently very rich. He is also connected to some of our highest families, though his reputation is such that he is not accepted in Society. Given the lax state of the Fashionable World, I have to ask what we must think of a man even they cannot tolerate." He saw that his words were finally having an effect and nodded. "We know how these things work in this corrupt world, Emily. The poor man feels the full weight of the law for stealing a rabbit, while this rich man walks free after stealing his mother's means of sustenance and two men's lives. And I ask," he wound up, in the tone he used in his pulpit, "can such a villain, so lost to the most fundamental type of human decency, be trusted to behave correctly with a gently born lady?"

"I suppose not," said Emily numbly, exchanging a sobered look with Margaret. Such a man in the neighbourhood was decidedly not a subject for levity.

She went through the motions as her guests discussed local matters for a little longer and then took their leave. Why, she wondered, was she so deeply distressed?

Because she did not want Piers Verderan of the dry wit and smiling blue eyes to be a true, blackhearted villain.

She could dismiss Hector's stories as nonsense, as nonsensical as Margaret's picture of the decrepit libertine. Tales grew in the telling and could spring from nowhere at times. But so many tales?

And she had to be fair—Hector was not a man to spread malicious rumour.

Moreover, though Emily found it nearly impossible to believe that Piers Verderan was a thief, she could believe that he had killed two men. She was strangely certain that he was skilled with blade or pistol and would not hesitate to use them if the mood took him.

She remembered the instant, accurate retaliation he had taken against the Violet Tart and the sudden look of fear on the woman's face. No doubt she too had been fooled for a while by that glint of intimate amusement, that ridiculously charming smile, and had learned later of his evil side.

Emily shuddered and made a firm resolution to avoid Mr. Piers Verderan on all occasions in the future.

Piers Verderan, on the other hand, found himself tantalised by Emily Grantwich. On the surface she was such a conventional, quiet person, yet he sensed so much more. There was wit and spirit and, he'd go odds, passion buried beneath that conventional exterior.

It was very tempting to seek to uncover it.

The next day, as he hacked into Melton, lost in thought, he came up with another rider on a fine, though fidgety beast.

"Good day to you, Christian. A handful?"

"You could say that, sir," the young man said, laughing, ably discouraging his horse from nipping at Verderan's mount. "But we're coming to terms."

"Busy this year?"

"Busier than ever. Seems everyone wants me to ride. Give up, Fly-By-Night!" he said to his mount as the horse tried to circle. With voice and vicelike legs he held the horse steady. "You'd think he'd be ripe for a rest," he commented wryly. "We've just done a five-mile run. He'll be a fine one for a long day once he realises who's master."

"Whose is he?"

"Just a coper's, sir. I'm riding a prime piece of blood later in the season for Lord Stourbridge, though. Might be to your taste."

"I'm not looking for more horses at the moment."

"Pity. The Grantwich lot's coming up too. The old man's bedridden and the son's dead in the war they say. Sorry business, but there's a couple of fine horses there. Sir Henry had an eye for them. Had word asking if I'd ride for them. I'd like to oblige, being such a sad case, but I'm booked for most of the season."

"Word from Sir Henry?" asked Verderan, alert.

"No, from the daughter. She runs things these days."

It was a crazy impulse, but he didn't fight it. "Do you have a couple of customers you don't mind offending, Christian?"

The young man looked at him shrewdly. "A couple maybe."

"A bonus of twenty guineas to take on the Grantwich horses. Just between the two of us."

The young man's eyes widened. "Twenty! You're on, sir, and it's a pleasure."

Verderan saluted. "It's my season for mad charities. I'll send a draft to you. At the Blue Bell?"

"Aye, sir. And if you've any more such charities in mind, I'm your man."

With a laugh, Verderan rode on.

Despite her resolution to avoid Piers Verderan at all costs, the next time Emily saw him he was a sight for sore eyes.

Five days had passed since their last meeting, and Emily had done her best to put him out of her mind. She had even had some success, as she had been busy. First there had been the matter of the tranquil movement of a few hundred sheep, then the disaster threatened by deliberate damage to one of the new threshing machines, and constantly the problem of getting the best price for the hunters.

Dick Christian had come out to see her and the horses. He was a handsome, sturdy young man with the confidence of one who knows he is the best at his trade, but with no flashy airs. Nor did it seem to bother him to deal with a woman. He had agreed to ride the horses for his standard fee for "casuals"—a guinea a ride. It seemed a small enough price to pay when a horse ridden by him was certain to show its finest paces. Being naturally cautious, however, Emily had fixed for him to ride Wallingford first in case his reputation was inflated.

To balance that positive step had been the news yesterday that the fence at High Burton was weaker than it looked and the newly installed sheep were beginning to wander. The shepherd had assured her that he and his dog could control the matter for a few days but repairs were clearly needed. Emily had not yet had time to look into that.

She was crossing the long drive on foot, taking a shortcut from the home farm to the orchards to discuss pruning, when she was almost run down by a recklessly driven travelling coach which had just swung in the gates. Alarm turned to fury when the coach hauled to a halt and her cousin and a dandified crony tumbled out.

Though never a prepossessing creature, Felix was at least dressed in standard wear of dark jacket, buff breeches, and boots. His companion was a more startling sight. He was a remarkably slender young man, dressed ludicrously for the country in yellow pantaloons and cream jacket over a cream and gold waistcoat. A tall, ornate cravat of bright green held his chin up high, and his hair was a clear butter yellow.

He reminded Emily of nothing so much as a daffodil, but that was to insult the lovely flower.

The coachman climbed down from the seat. He wore a dusty, many-caped greatcoat, a slouch hat, and a Belcher. Despite his slovenly dress, the way he sauntered over to join the other two showed he was obviously a member of the party, not a servant.

When he smiled, Emily saw he had his front teeth filed to points in imitation of the professional coachmen, the better to fire globules of tobacco juice at innocent people. She knew the type; trust Felix to take up with such a rough customer. What a ludicrous trio they made.

She turned to her cousin. "What on earth are you doing here?"

Though not particularly fat, Felix Grantwich was soft and had a smooth, round face which could almost have been pretty were it not for the pouches under his eyes. He had full pink lips, and in response to her greeting he formed them into what she suspected was supposed to be a sneer. It looked like a pout.

"Why, Cousin dear. I have come to inspect my expectations." He swept his arm around to encompass the open parkland, the stands of trees, the distant house, and all the rest of the Grantwich estate.

The movement unbalanced him and he giggled slightly. Emily realised with alarm that they were all the worse for drink. "I have been in anticipation," Felix enunciated carefully, "of an invitation, but I'm sure everything must be at sixes and sevens with no man to take care of things."

"I am quite willing to show you round, Felix," Emily said, striving for a calm, authoritative voice, "but today is not convenient. And, of course, my father and I have every expectation of good news of Marcus."

Felix put on a lugubrious expression. "My dear little Emily, I fear you delude yourself. Why, I checked at the Horse Guards before leaving London. They hold out no hope, no hope at all."

Emily's chest ached and she tightened her lips against a quiver. "That is not what they have told us," she said firmly.

"Well, an invalid and a woman. They doubtless wanted to spare you further distress . . ."

"How about sparing me distress, old boy?" slurred out the coachman. He swaggered forward. "I need a drink. And a wench." He spat close to Emily's feet and his bloodshot eyes roamed over her.

She glared at Felix with such outrage that he stirred himself to object. "Now, now, Jake," he muttered nervously. "Don't ogle my cousin. I'm sure there's any number of maids who'd be honoured—"

"Not in this house," snapped Emily. "Felix, get out of here and take your revolting friends—"

Emily stopped because Jake had moved forward to loom over her. He was over six feet and of heavy build. An aura of violence, stale sweat, and brandy stole her voice. "You better watch your mouth," he said flatly. "I don't hold with uppity women."

Though an attack of the vapours was immensely attractive, Emily would not let herself back down. It was inconceivable that she be attacked here on her own driveway. "I don't care what you hold with, sir!" she declared, forcing herself to meet his horrible eyes. "This is my father's property and here you behave as he says—"

Jake hooked a sausagelike finger in the neckline of her dress and pulled her to him. "Fclix!" Emily screamed as she tried to stop her dress being pulled so far away as to reveal her breasts. "Do something!"

"Jake," protested Felix in rather a high voice. "Do give over. You don't want Emily, for heavens sake. She's an old maid."

Jake leered down Emily's bodice, then let go only to pull her into a bear hug. "Looks to have all the right bits," he said.

Struggle as she might, it was like being in a vice. As she screamed into his smelly jacket and writhed to no avail, the big man said calmly, "You don't know women, Felix, my lad. When they face up to a man like this and spit and snarl, they're just playing come-on. Your little cousin fancies me, don't you, sweetheart?"

Emily kicked and told him just what she thought of him,

but even her sensible half-boots made no impression on his top boots and her words were swallowed by the rough wool of his coat. Her heart was pounding, and she was beginning to turn dizzy. This couldn't possibly be happening!

Even in her terror she fixed the blame for this solidly where it belonged—on her Cousin Felix. She loathed him as never before in her life. Visions of bloodthirsty retaliation flashed before her eyes . . .

"Let her go."

The world suddenly went still. Emily found herself released, and she staggered out of reach, gasping for air.

She looked up at her erstwhile captor, but his attention was no longer on her but on the owner of that quiet voice. Jake appeared abruptly sobered but not a scrap less dangerous.

She turned to see Piers Verderan on his dark horse, a steady pistol aimed at the man's heart. Looking at his face she knew why the Violet Tart had quailed and slammed the window shut, and she doubted he had looked at the woman with such deadly intent. When she tore her eyes away she saw her cousin transfixed like a trapped rabbit.

"Uh . . . I'm sure . . ." gabbled Felix. The pistol moved to cover him and he fell silent.

Jake moved forward. "Come on, boyos! It's only one man laying claim to our sport. Have at him!"

"No!" shrieked Felix, grabbing his arm. "It's Verderan! The Dark Angel!"

He looked sick with terror, and Emily saw some of the same fear invade Jake, though he was less willing to give it rein.

"So?" he said, and stood wide-legged and arms akimbo to face up to the man on the horse.

"I would kill you here," said Verderan in a conversational voice, "but I hesitate to make such a mess on Miss Grantwich's driveway. You will hear from me later."

The man licked his lips but continued with his bravado. "Will I? Well, if she's your fancy dish you're welcome and I won't meet you over her, boyo. I don't fight over my pudding."

The crack of the pistol made Emily jump. Jake let out a guttural scream and fell down in the dust, but he was yelling and cursing too much to be seriously injured. She saw he was clenching the top of his thigh where blood was welling.

Verderan holstered the pistol and slid smoothly off his horse to stand by Emily. "That won't stop you meeting me," he said to Jake in a drawl, "but if you don't watch your manners I'll fire higher next time and your pudding-eating days will definitely be over."

He no longer had a weapon, but Jake and Felix were overtaken by an urgent need to depart. Felix pushed the cursing Jake into the coach and the Daffodil Dandy moved with a sigh to climb onto the seat and unwrap the ribbons. Emily realised he had stood back throughout as if the whole business had nothing to do with him.

"Pockets to let, Renfrew?" asked Verderan.

The man gave a slight smile. "As usual."

"Wits gone begging as well, to let Miss Grantwich be so insulted?"

The man smiled sweetly. "My dear Ver, I saw you coming. You're so much better at this sort of thing than I am. You know I can't be unpleasant."

Emily realised she was shaking and Mr. Verderan had put an arm around her, an arm that was too comforting to be rejected just yet. Her mind was trying to come to terms with the fact that he was talking about duels. And he killed men in duels . . .

"I should call you out too," he said sharply to the dandy, "and teach you the virtues of unpleasantness." But then he added, "I have a place here. Hume House. If you wish, you may move in."

The dandy gave a small salute. "I'll just take my erstwhile host home then. Least I can do."

With that he drove the coach skillfully around in a circle and off back towards the road.

For some reason Emily thought of giraffes. The world had turned mad, and it wouldn't surprise her to see giraffes and zebras and lions loping across the meadow . . . all wearing daffodils . . . Emily realised she was still standing in Piers Verderan's arm and pulled away.

"You've invited that—that daffodil to live with you," she accused.

He kept a supporting hand on her arm. "Daffodil? Are you all right, Miss Grantwich?"

"The Daffodil Dandy," she explained. "What peculiar people you know, to be sure. Daffodil Dandies, Violet Tarts. And of course, you are a flea-bitten giraffe."

He raised a brow. "Someday you must explain this conversation to me, Miss Grantwich, but for now, my offer to carry you over the threshold still stands."

"I am quite able to manage," Emily lied, for her legs felt like *blancmange* and her head seemed detached from her body. She looked at the security of her home and it was a discouraging distance away.

She turned her mind instead to a closer problem, her rescuer. She remembered Hector talking of his violent nature, and now she had the evidence of her own eyes. The worst thing was that he appeared perfectly calm and unruffled. "You—you *shot* that man," she said.

"Creased him. Unless he takes an infection from his revoltingly dirty garments he'll come to no harm from it."

"But you couldn't have been sure to hit him just there!" Emily objected, startled by how shrill her voice sounded. She searched his face for remorse, or even excitement, for some sign that he had done something out of the ordinary.

"Of course I could," he said. "I think we should get you to the house, Miss Grantwich, and force some hot sweet tea down you before you have the vapours." He looked up at the Hall. "I'm somewhat surprised your servants haven't appeared to assist you."

"It's the end of harvest and we've had trouble with some of the machines. All the men are out helping and some of the women too . . . If it's not one thing it's another . . ." Emily found herself unable to think straight. He swept her up into his arms and strode towards the house, saying crisply, "Come, Beelzebub." After a startled moment, Emily realised he was addressing his horse.

"Beelzebub?" she queried faintly. She hadn't been carried since she was a child.

"Second in rank to Satan in *Paradise Lost*," he explained. "I could hardly call him Satan when I'm the Dark Angel myself."

Emily remembered the horror in Felix's voice when he had said that name. She was truly in the devil's grasp. At least, she thought prosaically, he was a very strong devil and in no danger of dropping her.

As he approached the house he shouted loudly, bringing Mrs. Dobson hurrying from the kitchen to open the door. She stood in goggle-eyed silence at the sight of her mistress in the arms of a tall, dark, handsome stranger followed by a black horse that seemed to have every intention of coming into the house.

Verderan turned, and Emily saw with a giggle that Beelzebub had his front hooves on the lower steps, following his master's command to the letter.

"Stay, Bel," said Verderan, and the horse retreated to stand quietly in the drive.

"I can walk," protested Emily, beginning to recover and feeling more than a little ridiculous.

"I might as well carry you to a comfortable sofa," he said, and looked a query at the housekeeper.

"In here, sir," said the woman quickly and led the way to the morning room, where Verderan placed Emily carefully on the chaise. "Sweetened tea," he ordered. "Your mistress had an accident. I'm sure she is unhurt, but a little shocked."

It was clear to Emily that Dobby was brimming over with questions, but something in his manner sent her off obediently on her mission. Was there no one in the world willing to say boo to this man? How very strange that must be.

It brought something to mind, however. He was proposing to fight a duel over her. No, intending to *kill* the man called Jake.

"I do appreciate your assistance, Mr. Verderan," said Emily, "But I must insist—"

"What excitement!" declared Junia as she hurried into the room. She was wearing full, loose purple trousers, a fitted black spencer jacket, and at least two multicoloured shawls. A paintbrush was pushed behind her right ear, and a streak of yellow ochre ran down her cheek like Indian war paint.

"What do you mean?" asked Emily, thinking something else must have occurred.

"Why, you and Felix in the driveway. It was as good as a play, and when you shot that rogue, young man, I positively cheered! I—er—couldn't exactly see. You didn't . . . ?"

"No," said Verderan frostily. "I didn't. It didn't occur to you, ma'am, to come to Miss Grantwich's assistance?"

Junia looked up at him with her open smile. "Of course it occurred to me. But I could see you riding up and by the time I had come downstairs, found Henry's pistols, cleaned, loaded, and primed them, and got out there to do anything, it would doubtless have all been over, so I decided to watch instead. You appear to be a very competent gentleman. You are Piers Verderan, I suppose?"

He bowed slightly, and Emily could see annoyance and amusement warring in him. It was a common reaction to Junia. "I am, ma'am."

"Oh, good," said Junia as if she had just received confirmation of something wonderful. "Very good. And I'm Junia Grantwich, Emily's aunt. She's normally most punctilious about introductions and such, Mr. Verderan, I assure you. I'm sure all that was a bit of a shock for an *innocent young thing*." The last three words were issued with all the subtlety of a battering ram.

Emily winced. "Junia, please sit down. There is tea coming. Mr. Verderan, however, may wish to be about his business." She realised this sounded discourteous and hastily added, "Not that he is not welcome to stay, of course. There will surely be enough tea . . . or brandy . . . or whatever a rake drinks—" She caught herself and looked up in despair. There was distinct and warm amusement in his face.

"Tea will be delightful, Miss Grantwich," he said smoothly. "So kind of you to offer."

"Yes, indeed," said Junia severely. "It seems to me that you are insufficiently grateful to your rescuer, Emily."

"Grateful!" burst out Emily, putting a distracted hand to her head. She was beginning to remember the things Hector had said about this man, and trying to make them mesh with the reality standing before her was making her head

61

ache. "Of course I'm grateful," she said, "but he *shot* a man, an unarmed man, just because of his taste in pudding!"

"Really," said Junia, the collector of extraordinary facts. "I do know some people are of strong opinions. Personally I dislike sago intensely, but still . . . What pudding is it that so offends you, Mr. Verderan?"

"This whole conversation offends me," he said with exasperation. "Perhaps we could discuss the weather," he said, "or the war. Or," he added, looking pointedly at Emily, "sheep on High Burton Farm."

"Oh," said Emily, snapped suddenly back to business. "Were you coming here after all?"

"Yes, Miss Grantwich, I was. I was hoping to discuss the matter with your father."

Emily abandoned frailty, sat up, and swung her feet to the ground. "It has nothing to do with my father."

"He does still own this estate, does he not?"

"Yes," Emily said, "but these days he leaves the management to me. Especially Griswold's sheep."

Verderan was looking exasperated again. "Who is Griswold?"

"The man from whom I purchased the flock," Emily explained. "From over Kettleby way. Everyone knows Griswold. He's been breeding those sheep for decades, following the experiments Bakewell of Dishly did . . ." She fell silent at the glazed look in his eyes. "Well," she said defiantly, "every landowner 'round here knows these things. Or," she added formidably, "should."

Something flashed in his eyes, and she wasn't sure if it was amusement or something more dangerous. Perhaps it was fortunate that Mrs. Dobson bustled in at that point with a tray loaded with the makings of the tea, fresh scones and coconut cake.

Junia did the honours, and no one spoke as the cups and plates were passed around. Emily's head was clearing and she eyed Piers Verderan surreptitiously. Violent nature. Yes, she had to admit that to be true. On the other hand, that violent nature had rescued her, for which she must be grateful. Now more than ever she could believe that he had killed men in duels but less than before could she believe he was a sneak thief.

One thing was certain, he did not fit in her placid world. From the corner of her eye Emily watched Piers Verderan sip from his teacup. Such a beverage should be so alien to a gazetted rake that it would be like Holy Water to a demon and cause him to dissolve into a heap of brimstone.

He suffered no ill effects, however, and looked at her to say, "If I should speak to you about the sheep, Miss Grantwich, then I will. The fence has been neglected and it appears possible for them to push through and invade the adjacent field."

"I'm sorry," said Emily, disguising guilt, for she should have looked into the problem immediately. "I am aware of the situation and will see to it as soon as possible. But as you do not use that field, Mr. Verderan, I can hardly see it as a matter of urgency."

"The covert is in that field, Miss Grantwich."

"What?" queried Emily with spurious innocence. "Are the sheep scaring the foxes?"

Verderan put down his cup and saucer with a sharp clink and rose. "You will please take steps, Miss Grantwich, to mend that fence immediately and hire an assistant for the shepherd so that you don't come running to me with complaints when the foxes eat your newborn lambs, or the hunt draws that covert and scatters your flock."

Emily too rose to her feet. "It seems to me, Mr. Verderan, that if anyone is running with complaints . . ."

His eyes narrowed, but Emily found she wasn't the slightest bit afraid. In fact, she was enjoying herself tremendously.

"I still would like to see your father, Miss Grantwich," he said.

"Why?" she asked suspiciously.

"Perhaps to tell him what an unconscionable baggage his daughter is."

Emily gasped and was aware of a pang of nervousness. What would her father do if he received a complaint?

Verderan suddenly smiled, and she knew he would never

do anything so petty. "In fact, Miss Grantwich, merely to introduce myself as a neighbour. He does still receive visitors, does he not? He must welcome the diversion, and if I am to do business with his daughter I would think he would like to meet me. Of course," he added with a twitch of his lips, "we can only hope he does not know of my reputation."

All Hector's stories came back to her like an icy shower. "No hope of that," said Emily. "The vicar has probably already told him, and though father never goes to London, he's been closely involved with the hunting here for years. He probably knows more than Hector. Somehow I don't think you melt into the crowd."

Mr. Verderan picked up his hat and gloves. "I take that as a compliment and am greatly heartened thereby," he drawled. Emily's speeding heart warned her that he was doing it again, creating that closeness that could one day steal her wits entirely. She found her hand was up at her throat, which seemed a very silly place for a hand to be.

"If he's heard talk," he said as if he never troubled his head about such things, "he'll presumably have heard that I'm a fine hunter at least. If he's a true man of the chase nothing else will matter. I'm sure your housekeeper can show me to his room, Miss Grantwich, so I'll bid you good day." He bowed to Junia. "And good day to you, ma'am. Make her rest."

With that he was gone, and Emily found her knees were not as steady as she had thought. She sat down again with a bump, feeling as if she had run a race, not taken tea with a gentleman.

"How *wonderful*," breathed Junia.

"What's wonderful?" Emily asked bleakly, and repeated for Junia some of Hector's warnings. "If father knows what he is, knows he's the Dark Angel, he may forbid me to speak to him. And how am I to do business like that?"

Apart from the fact that never speaking to him again seemed a fate worse than death.

She was mad.

Junia was looking strangely thoughtful, but she merely

said, "I'll be your go-between. I like a rake. What's the Dark Angel got to do with it?"

I like a rake too, thought Emily, her brain seeming more like a dry sponge every moment. "He's called the Dark Angel," she said. "The devil. His horse is called Beelzebub. He shoots men who like sago pudding."

"Seems fair. Only the lowest form of life would admit to liking such slimy stuff," said Junia with a grin, but it faded when she looked closely at her niece. She clucked. "He was right. You really are shaken up, aren't you, my dear? Come along and have a lie-down. You work too hard anyway."

"But I should . . . He's going to *kill* that man."

"Good thing too, I should think, and fortunately the sort of matter we females are not allowed to know anything about. Come along. Bed."

Emily allowed Junia to shepherd her to her room. As she made her way up the stairs she heard a loud burst of her father's laughter. How long was it since she had heard her father laugh like that?

Could a bad man have such a good effect? But he'd shot that man in cold blood and he was going to . . .

Emily's world had been set spinning so that she didn't know up from down anymore.

= 5 =

EMILY CERTAINLY FELT the need of a quiet rest, but unfortunately lying down in a darkened room did not calm her fretful mind. She was deeply concerned about what Piers Verderan would say to her father.

If he told Sir Henry about Felix and his friends it would probably squelch any notion of Felix taking over Grantwich but could mean restrictions upon her own movements.

If he complained about the sheep, Sir Henry would find out she'd put them on High Burton and have an apoplexy.

If Sir Henry liked him he'd be made free of the house, and she could be bumping into him all times of the day and night.

If Sir Henry took against him, or found his reputation too reprehensible, Emily could be forbidden to ever speak to the man again.

It was the last two possibilities which concerned her the most, and she wasn't at all sure which of them was most to be feared.

There was also the problem that she was undoubtedly coming to like the man and he had just proved some of Hector's warnings true. How perverse could a woman be?

He was a cold-blooded killer. Certainly she had been willing to contemplate boiling both Jake and Felix in oil, or hanging them up by hooks through their skin—all kinds of fanciful tortures. But she could never have fired a pistol ball into either of them.

And, as the final straw, it hadn't even been over the assault on her, but over *pudding*.

She had run the confrontation through her head, to try to make sense of it, but it couldn't be made to appear otherwise. Certainly she had been too stunned to follow the men's words exactly, but she remembered Jake saying, "I don't fight over my pudding." And Piers Verderan had shot him.

In a very strange place.

It was clear she just didn't understand men. Could Hector have done such a thing? Assuredly not. On the other hand, he would have been as useless as the Daffodil Dandy. If Hector had come upon the scene he would have preached at Felix and Jake about the error of their ways. Emily had no faith that such an approach would have secured her release unharmed.

What of Marcus? He was more of Verderan's stamp—a man's man, a devotee of hunting and shooting and a fine shot. No, she couldn't imagine him acting so, either. He would have plunged in with his fists, then rehashed the fight for hours after as he applied steak to his black eye and cold cloths to his bleeding nose.

Thoughts of her brother made tears trickle down Emily's face, and she brushed them away. Had Felix been telling the truth? Had the government given up hope of Marcus's safe return? It was very likely. Emily knew from the newspapers what horrors were left after a battle. It was a wonder so many soldiers were ultimately accounted for. If Marcus lived they should have had word of him. It was too temptingly convenient to imagine that he might have lost his memory.

Oh, enough of this, she told herself angrily, sitting up in bed. Falling into a fit of the dismals would help no one. When the big old clock in the upstairs hall boomed out the hour for the second time, Emily abandoned all attempt to rest and plotted instead how she was to escape the house without an interview with her father. She dressed in her habit and crept downstairs, hoping to be well on her way to Somerby before she was spotted, but Mrs. Dobson was alert.

"Your father wants you, Miss Emily," the woman said brusquely but giving Emily a comprehensively searching glance to make sure she was up to any stresses and strains.

Emily sighed. "Now?"

"An hour ago," said the woman with a warning look.

Emily sighed again but made her way to her father's room.

She knocked softly and peeped around the door, hoping Sir Henry might be asleep. Her eyes met his—very much awake.

"What you creeping about for? Come on in. I want to talk to you."

Despite a tendency for her knees to knock, Emily reminded herself she was a grown woman, and walked with dignity to the bedside chair. "Yes, Father?" She sat down, back straight, hands in lap.

" 'Yes, Father. Yes, Father.' Anyone'd think butter wouldn't melt in your mouth."

Emily felt her colour flare. What had that man said? "What do you mean, Father?"

His eyes narrowed as he tutted more in sorrow than anger. "I suppose I shouldn't be surprised. You're of an age to turn silly. First you drench yourself with cheap perfume then you fling yourself at any man you see."

Emily thought she was going to faint. *He'd* said . . . "I deny it!" she declared. "How dare—"

"Oh, give over," said her father wearily. "It's my fault for not marrying you off years ago. Selfish of me. Good to have a woman around the place, and God knows, Junia's no use. I suppose I'll have to bring Marshalswick to the point."

"No!" cried Emily, leaping to her feet. Then she clamped control on herself even though she was burning with fury. "Don't you dare, Father. I wouldn't marry Hector Marshalswick if he was the last man on earth. I will never marry any man!" Her voice was shrill and she took a deep breath. "I don't care what that—that *rake* told you, Father. I am not throwing myself at men, especially not at *him*. I am not drenching myself in cheap perfume. That was all his fault. I—I—"

She fought back words which would be much better left unsaid.

"What?" said her father in blank astonishment. "You trying to tell me now *Verderan's* been sniffing at your skirts? You'll catch cold at that, my girl. I know the type of woman he favours, and you've never been that type, even when you had youth on your side."

"I said no such thing," gasped Emily from a black pit of hurt and rage. "I know he wouldn't . . . Father . . ." She put a hand over her eyes as if to press back the tears that threatened.

Her father made an embarrassed growl, then said with gruff kindness, " 'Course he wouldn't. Now stop having the vapours, girl, and sit down." Emily had herself in hand again and faced him, but remained resolutely standing. He frowned and said, "As you wish. This is what comes of letting a girl play a man's role. Addled your wits."

His tone turned kind again, however. "Oh, Emily-chick. You've doubtless fallen head over heels for the man, which ain't surprising, given his phiz. But if I let you go bothering him, you'll not thank me when you come to your senses. His tastes don't run to country spinsters. And though he's a fine man in the field he isn't husband material for any respectable woman. But if you do something foolish," he said bitterly, "there'd be damn-all I could do about it from here, would there?"

Emily's rage lessened in the face of her father's anguish. Plenty of it remained, however, stored up for Piers Verderan when next they had the misfortune to meet.

She was able to answer calmly. "There will be no need for you to do anything." She laid a hand over his. "Truly, Father, I don't know what he said, but it is all moonbeams. I've only met the man twice before today, and both times we merely conversed, with a digression into mild disagreement. You know me, Father. Would I ever look to a rake for husband?"

Sir Henry eyed her doubtfully. "Not in your right mind, no. But women tend to fall out of their wits with remarkable speed around men of his ilk, especially women past their last prayers. I could tell you stories—" He broke off and cleared his throat. "Well, let's just say you wouldn't be the first plain miss to throw her cap at a handsome rake and have it caught. But only for a brief amusement. That's all you'd be to him."

Emily was shocked by the pain his words caused her; she'd always known she was plain, and attractive only for her comfortable dowry and practical skills. Why did it hurt so to have it pointed out so bluntly? She fought to remain impassive. If the only thing she had left in the world was her pride, she would at least hold on to that.

"Father, I have no interest in the man," Emily said tightly. "You trust me with your business. Can you not trust my good sense?"

His eyes suddenly widened and he chuckled admiringly. "Oh, now I get it. Business, eh? Realised you'll need someone to hunt those horses. But you'll catch cold with Verderan, Emily. He's got his own string, every one a prime bit of blood and you're hardly likely to besot him into doing you a favour. Now this friend of Felix's may be a better bet, but from the story I've heard it's clear you don't know how to wheedle a man. You should be able to turn him up sweet and still keep the line."

Emily wasn't sure if this was better or worse. Now she wasn't a man-mad spinster, she was a failed seductress with mercenary motives. Well, she could put an end to this.

"I've hired Dick Christian to ride the horses," she said coolly, "starting with Wallingford at the first meet."

"Christian?" Sir Henry repeated blankly. "But he has his regulars." His eyes narrowed. "And what did you offer him, eh?"

Emily ignored the disgusting insinuation, though she could feel her cheeks heat. "A guinea a day," she said crisply. "His normal fee, I believe."

"And he just said yes," scoffed Sir Henry. "I don't know what deep game you're playing, my girl, but if you bring shame on us I'll wash my hands of you, damned if I don't."

Emily had had enough. She headed for the door.

"And keep away from Verderan," Sir Henry shouted. "You're not up to his weight. He's doubtless bored, and if you show your ankles once too often he'll break them for you!"

At the implication that she'd end up with a bastard, Emily gave in for once to her baser urges and slammed the door.

She stormed down to the stables. What she needed was space and time to come to terms with her pain. She stopped in the shrubbery and pressed her hands to her hot cheeks. She *had* felt warmly about Piers Verderan. Had it been so obvious to everyone? To him? Had it unconsciously translated into pathetic seductive gestures? Had she been the source of that uproarious laughter?

She wanted to die.

She'd seen women simpering and fluttering around an attractive man. Had she done that without even being aware of it? Even so, did he have to laugh?

She went on to the stables, desperate only for escape. She managed to present a calm face as she mounted Corsair and rode out, then muttered and cursed for a good two miles, berating herself for being such a ninny and him for being a conceited, arrogant swine.

Eventually she steamed herself dry and could no longer summon the passion. She wearily concentrated on her duties instead. She rode into the village to inspect some leaking roofs.

That accomplished, she found that anything was better than returning home, so she rode a slow circuit to see how the last of the harvest was coming. The dry weather would soon break, but another day should see all the crops in. All seemed well with her world, as far as estate management went, at least. But, passion was returning, accompanied by intense embarrassment, and she was torn between a desire to avoid Piers Verderan for life or to seek him out in order to drive a long sharp knife into his cold, arrogant heart.

Returning to the Hall, she gave in to an impulse and stopped at the vicarage to see Margaret.

Over tea, she soon found herself telling the whole story of the day's events and then sketching in some of the previous excitement.

"Heavens above!" Margaret exclaimed, her cup of tea cooling untasted. "I never thought things like that happened in our country backwater. Perhaps Hector is right and having

71

a rake in our midst will cause all sorts of commotions. What fun!"

Emily shuddered. "It wasn't fun at the time, Margo, I assure you."

"I suppose not," said her friend unrepentantly. "But it makes a wonderful story. Just like a novel. And," she said with a playful frown, "I haven't missed the fact that you have apparently been hobnobbing with our local viper without a word to me."

Emily looked a guilty apology. "There just didn't seem a good time."

"Now is an excellent time," said her friend implacably. "Not, I gather, flea-bitten and on his last legs."

"Definitely not."

"Seedy? Debauched? Sallow and bloodshot from constant dissipation?"

Emily shook her head.

Margaret's silence demanded an answer.

"He's very good looking," Emily said feebly.

"Details," demanded her friend.

"Tall, dark, and handsome," retorted Emily crisply. "The man's a walking cliché."

"Handsomer than Marcus?" asked that gentleman's betrothed.

"Perhaps not in your eyes, Margo, but yes, I would say so."

"Handsome is as handsome does," quoted Margo. "What of Hector's nasty stories? *Is* he a seedy reprobate?"

Emily gave this much thought. She could have given a lecture on the subject, but in the end she just said, "No."

"I thought not. So," asked her friend, bright-eyed. "Why haven't you snared him already?"

Emily broke into tears.

When Margaret had finally calmed her and got some of the story of the morning's interview with her father, she apologised. "I was only funning, dearest. You know how we've always teased about our beaux. How horrid to have your father think you've been throwing your cap at him."

"And I haven't, Margo," declared Emily with a mighty blow of her nose. "Honestly. I know he's wrong for me on all counts. It's him . . . *He* kissed my hand, which is not at all a normal thing to do to a lady one meets on horseback."

"He kissed your hand?" echoed Margo, wide-eyed.

"*He* fixed my bonnet, and smiled at me in that way he has."

"Indeed."

Emily looked up to see lively interest and distinct amusement on her friend's face. "It isn't funny, Margo. If I ended up smelling like a tart, it's because *he* gave that horrid powder to the woman and then caused her such distress she hurled it at him. And then he tells my father I'm going around throwing myself at men. Oh, if only I had him here to give him a piece of my mind!"

Prompt to her cue, the vicarage housekeeper knocked and entered the parlour. "There's a Mr. Verderan here to see the Reverend," she said. "Shall I tell him he's out?"

Margaret gave a little laugh and bit her lip.

"Margo!" Emily whispered urgently. "Don't you dare!"

"Why don't you show him in, Mrs. Findlay," Margaret said. "I will have a word with him."

Emily leapt to her feet and looked for an escape, but there was none other than the door that led to the narrow corridor down which Piers Verderan was now presumably walking.

"What in heaven's name are you doing?" she demanded of her friend, sotto voce.

"I want to meet him. And you did say you wanted to give him a piece of your mind."

Then he was in the room, looking curiously at them. Margaret immediately rose and made introductions. Emily found herself obliged to give him her hand. If he dared to kiss it, she told herself, she'd blacken his eye.

"Miss Grantwich," he acknowledged as if they were strangers. She realised he was going to allow her to dissociate herself from him.

Or was he trying to pretend they were strangers for fear she'd throw herself at him in a mad burst of passion?

"Mr. Verderan," she said, hoping the ice in her voice would give him frostbite.

A brow twitched, but he turned to speak to Margaret, merely explaining that he was making himself acquainted in the area. He asked her to assure her brother that he would keep up the contributions his uncle had made to various charities, and would probably increase them if appropriate.

"Hector will be pleased to hear that," said Margaret pleasantly. "There are many worthy causes in the parish. Won't you stay and have tea, Mr. Verderan?"

After an inscrutable glance at Emily, he agreed.

"Then I'll just go and fetch another cup," Margo said brightly, and disappeared before either of her guests could object.

He turned from watching the speedy exit, faint surprise still on his face. "Do I gather you wish to speak privately with me, Miss Grantwich?"

Emily could feel her cheeks burn. "Never!" she declared. "I never want to speak to you again!"

His expression chilled. "Then your friend's behaviour is extraordinary."

Emily emboldened herself and faced him straightly. "I did say I wished to speak to you," she admitted curtly. "I suppose I may as well take this opportunity and get it over with. You will please keep away from my house, Mr. Verderan. If there is any need for us to communicate on business matters, I'm sure it can be accomplished by letter."

She gathered up her hat, gloves, and whip and headed for the door.

He grasped her arm and stopped her.

"How dare you!" she gasped. "Release me!" His grip did not slacken.

All Hector's warnings took on new life. "I have been warned that you cannot be trusted with a lady," she snapped, pulling against his hold and only succeeding in hurting herself. "The warning is proved true!"

He swung her around, and his hands settled hard on both her shoulders. His fine features were etched sharply with cold anger and showed no trace of remorse. "I warned you myself, Miss Grantwich," he said curtly. "Be that as it may, this morning I saved you from a fate worse than death. A modicum of gratitude would be more becoming than a tirade."

"Are you lecturing me on good behaviour?" she demanded. "How absurd."

"I am lecturing you on common decency."

She gave a brittle laugh. "That is even more absurd!"

His eyes flashed a warning, and Emily's instincts told her she was in dangerous waters. His lips were tight as he said, "I am doubtless going to have to kill a man on your behalf, you little termagant—"

"No choice of mine, sir! I abhor violence."

His hands tightened and he smiled unpleasantly. "You desire to further your acquaintance with the estimable Jake?"

She would have hit him if his hands had not still confined her. He probably felt the twitch. "I merely demand that you give up any idea of duelling over me."

Abruptly he let her go and moved away, appearing quite relaxed. "Very well. When shall I tell Jake Mulholland that you expect a call? I fear you will have to wait a day or two until he's mobile again."

"He won't bother me again," she said, but heard the uncertainty in her voice.

"That sort never take no from a woman, Miss Grantwich. His pride is on the line."

Emily felt a chill. "He wouldn't dare—"

"He won't dare not to. He'll be a laughingstock once the tale gets out, and your cousin is a notorious blabbermouth."

"But— but won't he be afraid of someone taking action?"

"You are very unprotected, Miss Grantwich, and used to going about unaccompanied. Whom is he to fear?"

Emily wouldn't say it, but she looked up at him. He raised a brow. "Am I to kill him for you, then?"

Emily turned away from his taunting. "This is terrible. This can't be true! Are you saying that I have to sign that man's death warrant or go in fear?"

She looked back and saw distinct, teasing amusement come into his face. It worried her rather more than his anger. "There is a third choice," he drawled. "If I made it clear you were of particular interest to me, Miss Grantwich, your attacker could probably save his pride on the grounds of not poaching on another man's preserve."

"What kind of interest?" Emily whispered.

He laughed briefly. "I hardly think I should set it about that you're my mistress, but I'm afraid I'm not willing to go so far as to engage myself to marry you." Emily felt her colour flare and hated it.

"Let us just say," he drawled, "that I could show a flattering interest—"

"It would not flatter me," retorted Emily.

"It should," he replied coolly. "It will make you unique."

Emily smiled equally coolly. "I suppose by that you mean you have only previously connected your name with ladies of low repute, Mr. Verderan. I fear some will think it more likely that I have joined their company than that you have entered the number of the elect."

He gave a sharp crack of laughter. "I knew we couldn't avoid the religious for long, especially not in the vicar's parlour. I'm certain your spotless reputation can withstand a brief brush with my sooty one. Well, Miss Grantwich?"

Brief. The word was both reassurance and a stab of agony. Emily took a brisk turn about the small room, then faced him again. "What exactly will this charade involve?"

"Nothing too unbearable," he assured her. "I'll drop a few hints. After all, despite my reputation, it will not be seen as impossible that I have a mind to marry. I have considerable properties and I'm heir to a viscountcy, though merely an Irish one."

"A viscountcy," Emily echoed. Ireland. Stolen money and impoverished relatives.

"Yes. My grandfather holds the title at present. But I wouldn't get your hopes up. The old man will live to be a hundred just to keep me out of his shoes."

The insinuation that she was chasing him, and not only him, but a *title*, blew all other thoughts out of Emily's mind. She projected loathing at him with all her might. "My only hope, sir, is that you and this whole debacle will prove to be a singularly nasty dream."

His eyes narrowed. "You know, I don't have the faintest idea why you're ripping up at me, Miss Grantwich. You were not so heated this morning."

"I find your intrusion into my life extremely distressing," she said straightly. "I have not had a moment's peace since I first encountered you, Mr. Verderan. You and your Violet Tart!"

All anger fled and he looked at her with delight. "I think your way of describing people is utterly delightful. Poor Renfrew is a Daffodil Dandy and Violet is a Violet Tart. Do you have a name for me, I wonder? Ah yes, for some reason, I'm a Flea-bitten Giraffe. Do you care to explain that? I never thought my neck to be extraordinarily long."

Emily had no intention of being diverted into whimsical sidetracks. "I was a little confused," she said discouragingly. "I do not need to christen you, Mr. Verderan. You are already called the Dark Angel, which sums you up very well."

He managed to look hurt. "I think I prefer to be thought of as a flea-bitten giraffe. At least you might be sorry for me. Would you believe me if I told you I am not as bad as I am painted?"

The honest answer would be yes, but Emily hardened her heart and retorted, "You forget, I am witness to the truth, sir. You consort with loose women. You are a self-confessed rake. You manhandle women and you shoot unarmed men merely because they like sago pudding."

"I do not—" He took a breath and looked at her with a shake of the head. "As a matter of fact, I can think of worse reasons. It's a revolting dish." Then he smiled at her with boyish mischievousness. "Frog spawn."

Emily chuckled. "Did you used to call it that, too?"

Then she realised he was bamboozling her again and wiped the smile off her face. It was no laughing matter. Still, she could not resist an attempt to bring him to his senses. "Mr. Verderan," she said gently, "no matter how much you dislike it, it is not rational to shoot someone over sago. It is not rational to become disturbed about any kind of pudding."

"Not at all?" he asked dubiously, but hilarity still twinkled in his eyes.

He was mad. How terrible. "Not at all," she assured him patiently. "You should try not to be so stirred up about it."

"I will try, Miss Grantwich," he said soberly. "But it will be hard in some situations. And with some kinds of pudding." The twinkle had returned to his eyes, and now it conquered his lips and he laughed. "Do you know, dear Emily, I find the notion of sharing some pudding with you extraordinarily appealing."

She took a step back. "I fear you are deranged."

He shook his head. His voice was unsteady as he said, "I fear so, too. I'd better escape before this situation gets any worse . . ." He turned at the door. "By the way, your father invited me to dine with him tonight. Do I now have your permission? It would further our appearance of having a particular relationship."

"As you will," Emily said grudgingly. "The alternatives seem to be worse. But I wish to make it clear that I have absolutely no interest in you as a husband and therefore cannot pledge myself to give even a passable appearance of fondness."

He stopped to look at her for a moment, and Emily felt as if she had issued an unwise challenge. "In other words, I am definitely sago," he murmured.

"What?"

He smiled slightly. "I just wondered if we were likely to have sago tonight."

And he kills people who offer him sago pudding, Emily thought wildly. She really should warn her father just what kind of man this was. "Of course not," she assured him. "That is a nursery dish."

He nodded, appearing quite normal except for a wild glint in his eyes. "And we want something much more suitable for adults. Tart, perhaps?"

"Yes," she said warily, wondering if he expected to have the Violet Tart served up for dinner. He was a rake, after all, and he and her father would be eating alone. She'd heard rumours of these bachelor dinners. She looked him firmly in the eye. "I believe we are to have *apple* tart, Mr. Verderan. With cream."

His lips twitched, but his face was straight as he responded, "Always a tasty dish, Miss Grantwich." With a slight bow he took his exit. Emily was sure she heard the sound of laughter as he walked down the corridor.

Margaret bounced into the room with suspicious alacrity. "I waited until he left. Did you give him a piece of your mind? I could hear you shouting at one point."

"Margo, if you ever pull a trick like that again—"

"Oh, come on. You're alive, aren't you? And judging from the flush in your cheeks, you're not in the dismals as you were before. He's utterly gorgeous, isn't he?"

"He's impossible!" Emily declared. "Margo," she added in a whisper, "I fear he's insane. He was going on again about pudding, and laughing. Was he laughing when he left?"

Margo nodded. "I thought you'd parted on a great witticism. Perhaps you should learn more of his family."

"Since I have no intention . . ." Emily stopped this disavowal when she remembered their strange arrangement. "The thing is, Margo," she explained uneasily, "he's persuaded me the only way to deal with that horrid man who assaulted me—other than killing him, that is—is for me to appear to be . . . well, Mr. Verderan's friend. Close friend."

Margo's mouth fell open. "Emily! *Are* you going to marry him?"

"No!" Emily shrieked, then shook her head. "Margo, it is all pretence. But you can put it about, if you like, that he's . . . oh, paying me attentions, I suppose. He's dining with father tonight. Not with me," she hastened to point out. "With father. But the gossips won't know that."

Margo was giving her a bright-eyed, speculative look. "Did he kiss you?"

"Of course not!"

"Pity. Before this is all over, Emily, you should see if you can arrange that he kiss you at least once. I'm sure he's very good at it."

So was Emily, and she pokered up against temptation. "Margo, I think you are lost to all decency."

Margo suddenly looked bereft. "The trouble is that I'm all too decent. I *miss* Marcus," she suddenly cried. "And one of the things I miss is the way he kissed me."

As her friend burst into tears, Emily hurried over to comfort her, wondering whether men were really worth all the trouble they caused poor females.

= 6 =

IN A CHARMING HOUSE in North Audley Street, Mayfair, Lady Randal Ashby and her husband, were sitting on a striped-silk sofa, reading their post. Eighteen-year-old Sophie looked up from her own correspondence to see her handsome husband of only two months puzzling over two letters, one held in each hand.

"Is someone writing to you in anagrams, Randal?"

He grinned. "Not precisely, though they do present a curiosity. This," he said, waving a long letter much covered by flowing handwriting, "is from Cousin Chloe. She's in a pother because her sweet, shy, demure little school friend, Emily Grantwich of Melton, has had a run-in with Ver. Apparently he showered her with perfumed powder—"

"In public or private?" interrupted his fascinated wife. "And were they . . ."

He touched her auburn curls gently with the letter. "You have a naughty mind, minx," he said with that special smile which was guaranteed to encourage such a feature. "I confess Chloe's secondhand telling of the tale is a little incoherent, but since the incident took place in the street I doubt your more lurid imaginings are possible."

"With Ver one never knows," said Sophie darkly. "Why is Chloe telling you this story?"

Randal shrugged. "She seems to think I can control Ver and prevent him from having his evil way with little Emily."

"How?"

"God knows," he said with a laugh. "She admits she hasn't seen this woman for nearly ten years. For all Chloe knows she may be the boldest piece in Leicestershire by now."

Sophie frowned. "Let me see the letter." He passed it over and she scanned it. "Chloe certainly was in a state when she wrote it, wasn't she?" she chuckled. "All blotches and squiggles. But she says here that she and this Emily have been corresponding regularly. I would have thought she knows her friend's character. *Would* Ver try to seduce a country spinster?"

"Seems unlikely," admitted Randal. "Chloe's always been excitable and she took a dislike to Ver at the wedding. Do you remember how that little hellion of hers would follow him everywhere? Ver is in Melton, though," he added thoughtfully. "He was going to look into some property he's inherited. If you need proof, he also has written to me." He waved the other letter, rather brief and with clear, disciplined handwriting.

Sophie looked intrigued. "Let me guess. To say he was attacked by a desperate spinster throwing scented powder, and begging you to protect him?"

"Not at all," said Randal. "If the incident occurred, Ver ain't mentioning it. His reason for writing," he said, pausing for effect, "is to ask me to make enquiries about the health and welfare of one Captain Marcus Grantwich of the Forty-third Light Infantry, supposedly missing in action after a minor engagement near Pamplona."

Sophie looked at him blankly for a moment and then consulted Chloe Stanforth's letter. "Grantwich!"

"Precisely."

"What do you think's going on?" Sophie demanded, bright-eyed.

"I don't know," said Randal, equally tantalised, "but I intend to find out. If Ver has a house there, he'll put us up. Are you willing to risk roughing it in the Shires?"

"Of course," said Sophie, always ripe for adventure. "May I ride the hunt?"

"No."

Sophie cocked her head. "Why not?"

Randal pulled his wife to him and slid his hands up to the base of her skull. "You're an old married lady now and should take heed to your reputation. And, little flame, I value your neck too much."

She raised her arms around his neck. "I value yours too, you know. Rather a lot."

"Then I won't hunt either."

Sophie leaned back and studied him. "Truly? But you love hunting."

"I love you more," he said simply.

Tears pricked Sophie's eyes. "Randal Ashby, you've told me your devotion a hundred times or more, but never with such depth of meaning. I'm overwhelmed."

"Good," he said. "I like you overwhelmed. Let's work on it."

Piers Verderan walked into Hume House in the late afternoon and went in search of his unplanned guest. He found Kevin Renfrew, as he expected, in the library reading a book. It appeared to be a treatise on hound breeding. He'd discarded his waistcoat, jacket and cravat, which made his excessive thinness more obvious, but diminished any likeness to a daffodil.

Verderan couldn't help smiling at Emily Grantwich's names for people. He rather wished, however, he'd been able to resist the conversation about pudding. One of these days she was going to discover what it meant and be after him with a hatchet.

On the other hand, he thought with a chuckle, it would be a memorable encounter. How had he ever thought her a meek little mouse?

"Oh, hello," said Renfrew, looking up. "Fascinating library. I never knew people put such effort into breeding dogs."

"It's a lamentable library," said Verderan bluntly. "I doubt old Casper read anything except the papers and a couple of hunting books in his life."

Renfrew looked around with childlike fascination. "But there're hundreds of books I've never read," he said.

"Because they're the sort of books anyone with sense would throw out. What the devil were you doing with a character like Grantwich?"

"London was boring." said Renfrew simply. "Grantwich

said he was coming to Melton so I asked for a ride. Damned bad driver."

Ver sighed, went over to a table, and poured two glasses of claret, wondering what he'd done to the fates to cause this influx of dependent young gentlemen. Renfrew had been another of his Eton fags, but at least not one needing protection. Kevin Renfrew could slide through any situation by simply ignoring it. His charming simplicity in the face of life's trials was both endearing and infuriating.

It wasn't that he was a lack-wit. He was in some ways brilliant but seemed to have a philosophical objection to ordering his studies in any way that made sense to the rest of the human race. Since obtaining a modest degree at Oxford he had been floating along on a small allowance from his bemused family and the endless goodwill of nearly everyone else.

He had once explained to the Prince Regent that he wore yellow because it was like sunshine and brightened even the dullest day.

Verderan had to admit that Renfrew's entrance into Casper Sillitoe's dusty, dirty old house was already brightening it. He passed the young man his glass of wine just before he drifted back into the book.

"I have to warn you, Renfrew, there's only three indoor servants, including my man. The food is plain, and the whole place is damp and dirty. I shan't do anything much to improve it until I decide what to do with it. If it's to be lived in, it needs extensive repairs."

"Oh, that's all right," said Renfrew and took a sip. "The claret's rather good, anyway. I already had a word with your housekeeper, Mrs. Greely. Very warmhearted lady and makes an excellent loaf of bread. She sent that maid to air a bed for me. That's all that matters."

Ver considered the run-ins he'd had with the said lady, who always claimed crippling rheumatism or the maid's bad feet when asked for anything beyond the minimum. He also realised the bread in the house was good and he'd taken it for granted.

"Excellent," he said. "I put you in charge of ensuring we

have a modicum of decent food and clean dry beds. If you can persuade the surly gardener to rake the drive as well, I'd be eternally grateful."

"Of course," said Renfrew with amiable vagueness. "But Whistler has too much to do, you know."

"Another friend, is he? Of course he has too much to do, but I haven't asked him to do much. He can let the gardens, such as they are, go to wilderness as far as I'm concerned, but one of these days someone's going to break an axle in the driveway."

"But he likes gardens and doesn't like driveways," Renfrew pointed out. "Why not hire a couple more men? You can afford it."

Verderan could feel Renfrew's universal goodwill creeping around him like a miasma. "Because then Mrs. Greely will want a couple more maids. It'll be bad enough when my horses and grooms turn up. Soon I'll have a household of servants in a place I may leave or sell in weeks."

"Very nice hunting box," said Renfrew, gazing round and almost investing the smoke-blackened walls and gap-planked floors with the elegance he saw in them.

"Next door to Grantwich Hall," said Verderan, and then was surprised by his own words. He had been seriously thinking of keeping Hume House as a hunting box . . .

"Not like you to run from Felix Grantwich," said Renfrew, and then smiled. "Oh, of course. The beautiful damsel in distress. Are you running from her?"

"Of course not," said Verderan, determined not to be thrown off balance by Kevin Renfrew. "In fact," he added dryly, "we're as good as engaged to be married." He drained his glass and put it down. "You can stay here as long as I'm living here and make yourself at home. You can take your pick of the stables—Casper had a few good horses—so long as you don't touch Beelzebub. Now, I have work to do."

As he left the library, he heard Renfrew murmur, "Right-o," and knew the young man would, as always, do as he pleased.

Verderan went into the small room Mrs. Greely designated as the estate office, though this merely seemed to mean that assorted estate records and publications had been left to moulder there for the last fifty years. He might as well do a further stint at sorting through it all until it was time to ride over to Grantwich Hall for dinner.

The solicitor assured him that it was merely necessary to sweep the contents of the estate office out the door and burn them, and it would certainly be possible to hire someone to undertake the task, but Verderan had come to regard sorting the documents as a way of keeping out of trouble. Once the hunting started he'd abandon it, but in the meantime, idleness increased the likelihood of taking up with someone like Violet Vane or hanging around the Old Club, drinking and gambling.

Or giving in to the temptation to search out Emily Grantwich.

It was perhaps as well that she had finally seen his true colours and taken him in aversion. After all, she'd make no kind of wife for him.

Wife? Where had that notion come from.

For God's sake, if he was going to marry, the only sane choice, probably the only choice open to him, was a hardened sophisticate like himself. Little Emily would have a fit if even half the rumours about him reached her ears, never mind the evidence of her own eyes. She doubtless thought that after Violet and Jake she'd seen his worst colours when she'd only seen their palest shades.

And that was without all the stories that crept across from Ireland. What would Emily think when they came to her ears, as they were bound to? He'd thought he'd long since armoured himself against all that, but now he felt as if he were stripped down to his nerves, sensitive to everything.

And all because of a woman, a rather ordinary woman . . .

He picked up a pile of yellowed, mouse-nibbled pamphlets and coughed as dust billowed up. It turned into a laugh as he remembered their conversation about pudding. The temptation to pull her into his arms and give her a "sweet" lesson had been almost overwhelming, but of course one couldn't do something like that with Miss Emily Grantwich of Grantwich Hall, particularly in the vicar's parlour.

Why not?

Well, the vicar's parlour would not be a good location, but . . .

He dropped the pamphlets back unconsidered and went to look out at the autumn garden. He realised for the first time that it was in tolerable order and rather attractively laid out in a casual style. What was the gardener's name? Whistler. Trust Renfrew to have got to the heart of the matter there. It was a genius he had. Pity there wasn't a way to make it paid employment.

But then again, perhaps it was. Why else did everyone in the world welcome him when he moved in and keep him happily until he decided to wander elsewhere?

What had he said? He'd described Emily as "the beautiful damsel in distress." Verderan thought few people had seen the beauty in Emily Grantwich's unspectacular face. Then he'd said, "Are you running from her?"

An interesting question.

Was he being chased?

If so, Verderan didn't want to run. He realised with blinding suddenness that he wanted Emily Grantwich for himself. And Emily, he suspected, was more a fish out of water in this quiet corner than even she knew.

Visions filled his mind of setting Emily free and showing her the world, and adventures, and the many varieties of pudding . . .

He reviewed their few encounters and saw reason to hope. Of course, their most recent one might daunt a less resolute gentleman, but Emily had at least agreed to their charade.

And a gentleman couldn't expect a woman to do all the chasing, after all. The least he could do was woo her a little and put the question. Hope that in her eyes he was something better than sago on the dessert menu of life . . .

Renfrew came wandering through the door. "I thought I heard you choke."

"Dust," said Verderan, maintaining a straight face with difficulty.

Renfrew looked around. "Nasty stuff," he said, but immediately began to riffle through a nearby pile of papers, driving up a cloud of it. "Here's someone claiming a guaranteed cure for disturbances of the mind. Sounds fiercesome stuff. Was your uncle batty?"

Verderan came over and took the sheet. "It runs in the family," he said. "Either that or it's *Poudre de Violettes*. Beware, young Renfrew, beware. That stuff has terrible effects. And they're permanent."

"Then the only thing to do is to enjoy them," said Renfrew simply, moving on to another pile.

Verderan looked up at the cracked ceiling and smiled. "Precisely what I had decided."

Emily went back to Grantwich Hall and first tried to explain the situation to Junia.

"Are you saying you're going to marry the man?" Junia asked.

"No," said Emily, repressing the desire to scream. "Do listen, Junia. He says he'll have to kill that Jake if I don't belong to someone like him. Mr. Verderan, I mean."

"I thought he was going to kill Jake," Junia remarked. "It seemed like an excellent idea."

"Junia, you *can't* approve of such a thing."

"What use is Jake? And I'll go odds he goes around attacking women, few of whom have protectors able to stand up to such a bully."

Emily blinked. "But still . . . it's not right."

"As you wish," said Junia with a shrug. "Mr. Verderan's solution seems to solve your problem, at least."

"Except that it puts me in an awkward position," Emily complained. "Do I explain to father, or do I let him think I'm continuing to chase after—Ooh!" she said, leaping to her feet. "When I think of the position I'm in, and none of it my fault at all, I could *kill* someone!"

"Then *you* kill Jake," said her pragmatic aunt.

Emily flung up her hands. "Everyone in the world's run mad! You want me to shoot someone. Margaret, the vicar's sister no less, is advocating improper behaviour. And that man was talking about pudding again and laughing. Dark

Angel, indeed. He belongs in the dark house. He's fit for Bedlam."

"Oh, that reminds me," said Junia, and looked through her drawings. "Ah, here." She whipped out a sheet of paper and gave it to Emily. "A Dark Angel."

Emily looked, transfixed, at the drawing of Piers Verderan. It was not a caricature but an ink-wash sketch. It showed him as an angel, fiery sword in hand. Despite a flowing gown and wings there was nothing feminine or even androgynous about him. He looked like a warrior capable of any act in defence . . . of what? Right or wrong?

That was the only question the drawing left in question.

Did it portray Michael or Lucifer?

Piers Verderan approached Grantwich Hall that evening in a state of considerable anticipation. Though he was supposedly dining with the invalid, there would be some opportunity to speak with Emily. He would make sure of it.

He had not, however, expected to be accosted by her before he had even plied the door-knocker, and dragged off into a private room.

When she quietly but firmly closed the door, he said, "My dear Emily. Am I going to have to defend my virtue?"

The ready colour flared in her cheeks and she looked delicious. If he was to keep his sanity he must keep his mind off food. "Mr. Verderan," she said sternly, "you do not have leave to use my name, and ladies do not attack gentlemen."

"Miss Grantwich, then," he said agreeably. "And what a very sheltered life you've led, to be sure."

She was wearing a blue wool dress with lace trim that would have looked dowdy on anyone else. Her soft brown hair was simply scooped back into a knot and her only ornament was a circle of rather paltry pearls. Even as he instinctively imagined her in more becoming outfits he knew it didn't matter. She could dress as she wished. She could dress like her eccentric aunt if that was her taste.

"I have led a *normal* life, sir," she said. "I'm sure your raffish companions are capable of any sort of strange behaviour . . ."

"Did you drag me in here just to tear a strip off me?" he asked, enjoying every minute. "I'm desolated."

"I dragged you in here—" Emily caught herself. "No, I did not! You really are an infuriating man."

"I know," he admitted. He had to at least touch her. He took her hand and led her to a small sofa, sat her down, and took the space beside her. What would she do if he kissed her? He told himself firmly to remember that she was a shy country creature.

"Now," he said. "Why do you need to speak to me?"

Emily had the feeling matters were slipping out of control. She had merely wanted to discuss their arrangement before he went into her father and said something to make her life even more difficult. Now, however, she was sitting beside him, very close beside him, and her hand was still tingling from when he had held it. And more than that, it was just something in the air, like the electricity before a summer storm.

Why did she want to speak to him? She couldn't remember.

With what sounded like a small sigh he leant forward and brushed his lips against hers.

Electricity.

Emily jerked away. "What are you doing?"

"I was kissing you," he pointed out. "Now I'm thinking of kissing you again."

"Why?"

"Because I want to."

"You can't just go through life doing whatever you want," Emily said as if it were gospel truth.

He smiled. A simple smile of pleasure. "Why not? I usually do."

It was unfair that he be so handsome. She'd never known eyes could be so clear and deep a blue, lips so beautifully shaped. Emily couldn't think. She certainly couldn't think of an answer to whatever question he'd asked.

"Of course," he said, and took her hand in his again, his thumb rubbing gently against her fingers, "if you don't like it I would have to take that into consideration."

Emily looked down at his long brown hand, warmly

tantalising hers, and remembered Margaret's outrageous advice. "I suppose you're very good at it," she whispered. "Kissing, I mean." She looked up to see a singularly sweet smile.

"I don't think," he said softly, "expertise is really what counts."

He raised her hand and brushed his lips across her fingers, making her heart tremble. Then he drew her a little closer. His other hand came up to lie along her cheek, threaded slightly into her hair. He brought his lips to hers again.

Emily tried to decide if he was good at kissing or not, but having nothing to compare this kiss with, it was a pointless exercise. Kissing was certainly an extraordinary thing—like a toasty warm fire in the winter, and an icy fountain in the summer; a crisp golden day of autumn and the first snowdrops of spring . . .

She could see why Margo had burst into tears if she was used to doing this with Marcus and hadn't seen him for a year, and he was very likely dead . . .

Verderan was telling himself he had to stop his gentle exploration of Emily Grantwich's soft, shy lips before he got completely carried away, when she burst into tears and buried her head on his shoulder.

It was the most alarming thing that had ever happened to him.

"Emily? Miss Grantwich . . ." He pushed her away slightly so he could look at her, and demanded, "What the devil's the matter?"

She looked up, eyes swimming with tears, and appearing utterly bereft. "Marcus!" she wailed.

He felt a death-chill go through him. For God's sake. Marcus was her brother! Surely to heaven—

"You were kissing me," she hiccupped, "and I thought of him. And he's probably dead." She pulled out a handkerchief and blew into it. "It's so sad."

"Why did you think of him when I was kissing you?" he asked, knowing his voice was razor sharp but unable to alter it. If Marcus Grantwich was still alive, he wouldn't be for long.

She looked up at him in alarm, clutching the handkerchief tightly. "I'm sorry," she said nervously. "I don't suppose that's what a lady is supposed to do when being kissed, is it, think of her brother?"

"No," he said baldly.

"Well, there's no need to snap," Emily replied with spirit, pulling back. She belatedly remembered that he was wicked and violent and probably mad. She mustn't allow the fact that he was so good-looking and could bring the wonders of earth and heaven through a kiss to erode plain good sense.

It was rather hard to be so resolute.

"You may be an expert at this," she said firmly, retreating to the furthest corner of the sofa, "but I've never been kissed before in my life, Mr. Verderan! How was I to know it would be so . . . so *nice* and make me think of poor Margo and how she misses Marcus and his kisses, and make me sad . . . why are you laughing?"

He leant over and dropped a gentle kiss on her lips before she could avoid it. "Because you enchant me," he said lightly. "Or perhaps it's the *Poudre de Violettes* again. Tell me, has life become very strange for you too since we were showered with the stuff?"

"Yes," said Emily, feeling hollow. So his desire to kiss her was ridiculous and he knew it. Because she'd sought this interview he'd probably put this whole episode down as her fault and see it as more evidence of her spinsterish desperation.

Utterly miserable, she stood up and moved away. "I only wanted to speak to you," she said briskly, "about father. I don't think you need to say anything to him about our little arrangement."

"I would have thought your father should be the first to know," he said, rising lazily.

"Not since it is all pretence," she retorted. "Which reminds me—" She fixed him with her fiercest look. "What exactly did you tell father about this morning's incident?"

"Why?" When she didn't answer, he said, "I told him your cousin's friend forced unwelcome attentions on you and your cousin did nothing about it. I felt he should know the sort of man Felix Grantwich is, and the sort of company he keeps."

"He already knows," said Emily with a frown. He must have said more than that. "But none of us can ignore the fact that Felix is heir after Marcus. If father doesn't know the whole, however, there's no need to tell him of our supposed relationship."

"As you wish," he said agreeably. "Should we perhaps, then, cut short our time in this room? If we're discovered it will certainly give fuel to any rumours, but it could push matters further than you wish. Your father might send for a special licence."

There he was, hinting again that she was trying to trap him into marriage. Emily darted over and flung open the door. "No such thing," she said sharply. "I am, after all, twenty-six years old, Mr. Verderan, not a green girl. No one would suppose anything other than that we were discussing business."

"How true," he said sharply and came towards her. "Doubtless your advanced age protects you from the very idea that you might be a wild, passionate woman."

He almost sounded angry. He was turning mad again. Wild and passionate had never been applied to Emily Grantwich. "Mr. Verderan . . . ," she said as he took her in his arms.

"Yes?"

"The door's open!" she squeaked.

"I know. But you're such a dried-up old thing that no one would care even if they did see us, would they?"

"Mr. Verderan!" Emily protested, but it was too late, for he had her firmly in his arms and his lips were on hers again, but more fiercely. She was held tight to his hard body, cradled in his arms, and melded with him as he slanted his head and carried her into a dizzying spiral of wild and passionate sensations.

It was outrageous.

It was scandalous.

It was delicious.

Just as she resigned herself to her fate, he released her and shook his head.

"My dear Miss Grantwich," he said, "you'll undoubtedly be the death of me."

Blaming her again. It simply wasn't fair. And, she thought emptily, it wasn't at all fair that he'd stopped . . .

Before she could express her feelings, he focussed one of his devastating smiles on her and added, "I look forward to such a demise immensely."

He was assuredly mad. Still bound by a lifetime of training, Emily muttered a polite "Excuse me!" before fleeing the room.

On the upstairs landing she almost collided with Junia. "What is it, Emily? You look as if there's an emergency."

"No, no," said Emily with some control, then blurted out, "He's here and he's dangerous!"

"Oh good," Junia said and continued downstairs. "Aren't you coming to dinner?"

"In a minute," said Emily.

As an afterthought, Junia asked, "How, dangerous?"

"In every way," gasped Emily and hurtled into her room.

Verderan had to take a few minutes to recover his composure after his interview with Emily. He was wondering if there was any way of being locked up in a cellar with her for a few days—it would be a wonderful experience—when Emily's aunt Junia entered the room. She too closed the door firmly but quietly, and he awaited new developments in amused anticipation.

"So pleasant to see you again, young man," she said and extended her hand.

He kissed it, despite the strong aroma of linseed oil. "My pleasure entirely, Miss Grantwich."

"Call me Junia," she said airily, head on one side like a robin. "You're very good at that."

"At what?"

"Hand kissing. It's an art and not as much practised as it was."

"Thank you. I strive for perfection in all the manly arts."

She chuckled and gave him a surprisingly roguish look. "I'll go odds you do," she said.

94

She was dressed quite conservatively in a high-waisted dress over a silken slip, but he had never seen such fabric before. It was a coarse, heavy twill printed with large leaves in blue and orange. He rather liked it, though it was distinctly barbaric. That was probably why he liked it. That was probably why he was coming to like Junia Grantwich.

"Young man," she said straightly, "I have a number of things to say to you, and I'd appreciate it if you did not distract me with flummery."

"I am all attention," he responded warily. Few people ever addressed him as "young man" but with Junia Grantwich he felt just that—a little wet behind the ears.

Junia sat in a plain straight chair and waved him to a seat. He took the sofa again, simply because it held pleasant memories.

"I have spent nearly sixty years," said Junia, "watching people make damn fools of themselves. I confess to having generally found it amusing, but in the case of Emily I cannot merely be an observer. The common advice is to leave well enough alone and keep out of other people's business, but if Emily is unhappy it will cut up my peace, so I think it *is* my business."

" 'No man—or woman—is an island,' " said Verderan. "Emily is fortunate in her family."

"No, she ain't," Junia said implacably, startling him. "I am a very selfish woman. Henry is a very selfish man, but that is less surprising as men are raised to be selfish. He is also a fool. He preferred simpering little Anne to Emily. Though I have to admit," she added thoughtfully, "that was to Emily's advantage or she might have ended up married to Sir Hubert. Do you know Sir Hubert Keynes?"

Having begun to get the measure of his companion, Verderan confined himself to a monosyllable. "No."

Junia nodded. "Thought not. If you'd come across him you'd probably have shot him out of simple irritation."

Verderan burst out laughing. "Miss Grantwich," he said at last. "Junia. Truly. I very rarely shoot people."

"Most people *never* do," she pointed out, "but that's neither here nor there. My point is that Emily has been put upon by a thoroughly selfish lot all her life and deserves better. She's falling in love with you. You are falling in love with her and I think it's a good thing."

"Thank you," said Verderan, startled again and feeling decidedly off-balance.

"Henry said something to upset her," continued the amazing woman. "Probably warned her of your wicked reputation. Now I find her rushing upstairs as if the devil himself were after her. I don't know what you had been up to, but she is convinced you're mad, largely because of your obsession with sago pudding. If you could avoid . . . Now why are you in whoops?"

Verderan had his head in his hands, wondering if it might not be simpler to commit himself to Bedlam immediately and have done with it all. He collected himself enough to say clearly, "I am not obsessed with sago pudding. I have never eaten the stuff since my nursery days."

"Hardly surprising," Junia pointed out, "if you have a reputation for shooting anyone who offers it."

"I do not—" He'd had this conversation before. "Miss Grantwich," he said firmly, "I promise never to mention pudding again in my life if only everyone else will agree to do the same."

"But there you are, dear boy," she said, leaning forward to pat his knee kindly. "It's not normal. How are we supposed to get along? What if you marry Emily? Is she to be scared to ask such a simple question as, 'What kind of pudding would you like tonight, dear?' There you go laughing again . . . but you're not mad," she said. "I did make enquiries, you know."

Verderan snapped himself out of his amusement. "What?"

"I wrote to a few friends. No one has heard of insanity in your family, or in you."

This was going beyond the limit. Verderan stood. "Miss Grantwich, I do not relish you poking around in my personal affairs."

She faced him calmly. "I'm not surprised in view of some of the things I turned up."

He instinctively sheathed himself in the cool arrogance

which had been his protection for so long. "Then I'm surprised you want your niece to marry me."

"You forget," said Junia quietly. "I knew your mother as a girl."

He stilled as if hit. He had forgotten that Casper Sillitoe was his mother's brother and that Helen Verderan had grown up here.

"I got a fine tale from Irene Devenish," Junia said. "She's always been one of your mother's bosom-bows. She had plenty to say of your wicked ways and arrant cruelty to poor Helen—Where are you going?"

"I'm leaving. You will make my excuses to Sir Henry."

"Coward."

The word stopped him at the door, and he swung round. "And you are a meddling old bitch!"

"Of course," said Junia, finding it surprisingly hard to keep her voice level. Her enquiries had told her he could be dangerous, but she hadn't quite believed it. As he put his hand to the doorknob she added, "If you want Emily, you're going to have to stay and listen to what I have to say."

Verderan went no further, which was as much of a concession as he was willing to make. He could feel anger growing, and he'd made a resolution not so long ago never to allow his temper free range again. "If you've been digging," he said quietly, "then you know I don't deserve Emily."

"Don't you? It seems to me you deserve some good fortune in life."

He did turn then and look at her. She appeared to care and that was positively demoralising. He should leave. His hand tightened on the doorknob.

"I can read between the lines, you know," the woman said. "As I understand it, your grandfather is an old tyrant who tried to keep his son within rigid lines and lost him. When your father died, he persuaded Helen, who was always a clinging ninny, to take you to Ireland and tried again, but with considerably more ruthlessness. You were eight when your father died and somehow you survived until you went to Eton at twelve. I'm not sure why he let you go."

Verderan looked down at his fingers, white on the porcelain doorknob, and relaxed them. "It was in my father's will," he heard himself say woodenly. He had never spoken of this, except perhaps to Randal, in bits and pieces. He wasn't sure why he was doing so now except that he clearly was mad. "It was a haphazard document, but it spelled that out clearly, at least."

He left the door and walked around the small room. "My father was"—he sought for a word that conveyed the largely forgotten magic of Damon Verderan—"eccentric, at the very least. But he had a flair for business, and when he ran away from home he made his fortune. He left my mother and my grandfather handsome annuities if they obeyed his instructions as to my upbringing. Unfortunately those instructions were very vague, except that I was to go to Eton and Christ Church."

"And once you left you refused to go back."

Verderan didn't answer. He was amazed at how painful he found all this, and deeply resented the woman who was stirring the old ashes into flame.

Junia looked at him and saw the angel she had drawn, but a tortured one. She wondered if for once she had grasped more than she could handle. "How did you support yourself?" she asked, but gently. "Even if your grandfather was compelled to pay your various fees, that is hardly enough on which to survive, and you were no more than a boy."

He turned to face her, and it was as if he wore a mask. Junia realised she was a foolish old woman. Thinking only of Emily, she had not considered that all this might still hurt a grown and hardened man.

"Didn't the rumour mill tell you?" he asked. "My grandfather is a miser. When I left home I took his hoard."

There was nothing for it but to get to the end. "I heard the story. He still gives it today as his excuse for scrimping and saving."

"You don't believe him?" he asked with superficial amusement.

Had no one else ever doubted that tale? "My assessment of his character, albeit hasty, doesn't grant him a forgiving nature. He would have had you clapped in jail."

"He would, wouldn't he?" His smile widened, and there was a trace of genuine warmth behind it. "I did take his money, but he'd been stealing from my inheritance for years. He boasted of it to me all the time. If he'd prosecuted me, it would all have come out. He made up for it by continuing to swindle me until I came of age; my foray into larceny made it unwise for me to look into matters too closely then. I think we ended up about even, and he still receives the annuity my father left him. If he's counting the candles and hoarding string it isn't for want of the ready."

There was one other thing to be raised, and Junia found herself strangely reluctant. "What of your mother? It's said Helen's in dire straights and you refuse to aid her."

The mask was back, but it couldn't quite hide the anguish. "My mother chooses to live at Templemore with my grandfather," he said in a voice as flat and hard as ice. "If she is in dire straights it is her own fault. I have offered her a comfortable home on this side of the water, but I'll give no money where my grandfather might get his hands on it. She prefers to cling to the old man."

Junia nodded. "As I said, I knew Helen. She always swayed towards the most commanding presence. If you went there, you could sway her to your side."

He faced her coldly, but a flame was burning in his eyes. "If I went there, I would kill him." It was all the more terrible for being uttered with quiet certainty. "That's one crime I do not need on my record. As for my mother . . ." He took a deep breath and said in a clipped voice, "You are exceeding your brief by a large margin. What has this to do with Emily?"

She had what she wanted. It had been more painful for both of them than she had ever intended, but life frequently was. Junia stood and smoothed her skirts, smearing one of the orange leaves. She looked at it with a frown. "Oh dear. I thought they were dry." She looked at the chair, which was splotched with blue and orange. "How fortunate I didn't sit on an upholstered one." She returned her attention to Verderan, who was staring at her printing experiment, dumbfounded.

"Emily," she reminded him. "Emily should be freed from this cage before she's too old to fly. Henry's accident has let her exercise her wings a little, but I fear she'll regress if Marcus returns home. Heaven knows what would happen if Felix took over . . . It really wouldn't be such a good thing for her to carry on being her father's deputy until Henry dies, one, ten or thirty years from now. And, of course, she shouldn't marry Hector Marshalswick."

"I haven't met the man. He seems to minister to his congregation conscientiously, which is more than can be said of many."

"True, but he's a domestic fowl." Junia wondered for a moment what species precisely. "Goose?" she mused. "Pullet . . . ?" She looked for an opinion and saw that he appeared dazed. People frequently did. Most people had such linear minds.

"Emily needs an eagle," she explained, "not a caged cock-sparrow. Now you have confirmed my suppositions about your history, you seem a very satisfactory eagle to me. Persuade her to fly. I'm sure you are capable of it, and I will stand your friend."

"Your faith is extraordinary," he said with a frown. "Despite any whitewash you may have applied to it in your mind, my reputation is unsavoury, and if I'm not exactly *persona non grata* in polite society, I am only encouraged to involve myself in a limited range of activities. Quite reasonably. I'm no saint and, to be honest, have no desire to become one. If I marry Emily, I will probably lead her into wickedness long before she manages to reform me."

"But isn't that just what I've been saying?" remarked Junia with a trace of impatience. "She needs some wickedness. Teach her to fly wild and free. But if you hurt her, I'll shoot you myself."

His lips twitched. "Another woman said that to me not that long ago. I think she meant it, too."

Despite the lighter tone, he still looked stark, like a man rasped raw. Junia found herself touched far more than was agreeable. "Now go on," she said in a schoolroom tone, "and prepare Henry's very inelastic mind by trying to persuade him that his elder daughter is an attractive and competent young lady. He finds it impossible to believe."

After a hesitation, he left without a word. Junia wondered vaguely whether she should change her dress but reflected that the dining-room chairs were plain wood and washable.

She really felt quite annoyed with Damon Verderan. He had sired a son, and doubtless surrounded him in that careless magic—the inspired impulses, the ready wit, the constant enthusiasm for life. Then he had left him unprotected to be flung from golden warmth into the iron cold of Lord Templemore's jurisdiction.

Of course, no one ever thinks they will die young.

As for Helen . . . Junia had disliked and envied Helen Sillitoe since they were both small—Junia robust, with a mass of dark curls, and Helen softly beautiful and fair. Piers Verderan had his colouring from his father but his elegant bones from his mother.

Helen had always been the gentle lady, with just enough playful high spirits to tantalise. Men had seemed compelled to adore and protect her.

Stupid men, thought Junia sourly, then laughed at her folly after all these years. No one had ever guessed that she'd lost her heart to Damon Verderan and they certainly wouldn't now. But she would have done better by his son than Helen had.

She knew that her meddling, for good or ill, was as much for Damon's son as for her niece. She hoped Damon was looking down from heaven and finally appreciating what he had missed.

7

VERDERAN LEFT GRANTWICH HALL a few hours later, grateful
that his host tired early. He had taken Emily's father in
dislike. He supposed a conventional person might find a
distaste for his beloved's parent a disadvantage, but Verderan merely saw what Junia Grantwich had been talking
about. Sir Henry, while a pleasant enough fellow of the
older school, had irritated him every time the subject of his
daughter had cropped up.

She was "playing" at running the estate and the place
was falling into ruin. She was "an ape leader" and "turning
funny," as women did when they found themselves left on
the shelf. As Sir Henry sank further under the influence of
claret and brandy, Verderan had been slyly warned to
expect some forwardness on the part of the "silly chit" and
asked not to encourage her to embarrass herself.

The urge to tell the man that he wanted nothing so much
as to have Emily be forward with him and encourage her
to do her worst had almost overwhelmed him, but Sir Henry
would doubtless have thought it a joke. He seemed able to
ignore all the things Verderan said about Emily, or to twist
them to fit his preconceptions.

Verderan wondered just what interpretation Sir Henry
had put on his mild warnings about Jake and Felix. He could
see now how they might have been turned into enough to
bring out the virago in Emily. He didn't regret it. Emily in
a fury was a sight to dwell on with fondness.

Sir Henry had hinted that the sale of the hunters was

important to Emily in some way, and there even seemed to be a wager on it linked to the running of the estate and Felix Grantwich, but the old man had been maddeningly obscure. Verderan was pleased, however, that he'd smoothed that road for Emily by bribing Dick Christian.

When the stolid maid showed him out he indulged his weakness and asked after the ladies.

"They're in their rooms, sir," she said.

He thought of asking to speak with Emily, but decided it would be better not. There would be plenty of other opportunities and it would be wise to move slowly and steadily in coaxing this bird into freedom.

As he mounted Beelzebub, however, he could not resist looking up to try to guess which curtained window concealed her. He laughed and shook his head at such lovesick behaviour.

As he trotted down the long driveway he felt restlessly unready for home and bed. Instead, on impulse, he set off for Melton. There was a half-moon, and a three-mile ride would do him good. With luck the company would be pleasant at the club.

By the time he reached there, a light rain was beginning and he wondered if he'd been unwise. He stabled the horse and shrugged. If necessary he'd put up in town for the night.

With hunting starting the next week, Melton was filling fast and the club was crowded with men, mostly young, younger even than he. Once they married, most men followed packs in their own parts of the country rather than spending the winter months in the Shires.

He was greeted affably, for this was a circle in which his sporting abilities outweighed any distasteful stories, and soon settled to a game of whist for the tame stakes of five guineas a trick. His partner was Henry Craven, and their opponents, Lord Alvanley and Quarley Wilson. Alvanley and Wilson were known as men who never shirked a fence, and they were friendly rivals in the field, friends off it.

As the play progressed evenly and was broken by general conversation, Verderan found himself thinking what a bunch of old fogies they were, commenting disparagingly on the younger, wilder set who were playing for high stakes and drinking deeper than they could handle.

It occurred to him, however, that he could do Emily some good here by whetting the appetite for her horses.

"I hear Grantwich is letting his hunters go," he said idly as he shuffled the deck.

"Grantwich?" queried Alvanley. "Who's he?"

"Local squire," supplied Craven. "Always rides a steady animal. Why's he selling?"

"Invalid," said Verderan. "Some kind of accident."

"Poor fellow. How're they being sold?"

"I hear Dick Christian's riding them, but you'll have to look up Sir Henry or his daughter to strike a deal."

"Interesting," said Alvanley as he fanned his hand. "Not sure I'd want to deal horses with a woman, though. And the trouble with Christian is he makes the most vicious animal look like a sweet goer."

There was a general chuckle and Verderan let the matter drop, confident that he'd guaranteed some interest when Emily's horses did appear. He wondered if she'd let him sell them for her. It was surprisingly pleasant to be doing these little things for her.

It occurred to him that he could just go and buy her horses, thus presumably solving all her problems. He would think nothing of losing here the few hundred she would raise from the sale. After a moment, however, he decided she would be unlikely to appreciate such a deus ex machina intervention. If it was a wager, she would doubtless wish to win fair and square; he could always keep an eye on matters in case they grew desperate.

He wondered exactly how the sale of the horses was linked to Felix Grantwich.

Felix was in the club, half under the hatches, playing Hazard with the desperate air of one who is losing. At least none of Verderan's youthful protégés were present to disturb his peace. Felix Grantwich could go to hell in a handcart for all he cared.

His feeling of mellow, tranquil respectability was shattered when George Osbaldeston stalked into the room, angry colour in his cheeks. He looked at no one in particular and sat alone with a decanter of brandy.

Verderan directed an enquiring look at Craven.

The club president shrugged. "He was cock-a-hoop yesterday. Won the bidding for that little elf. Surprised you didn't show."

"No one informed me of the auction," Verderan said, telling himself the fate of Violet Vane's protégée was none of his concern. He'd spoken to her briefly and found her amusing but not as young or naive as she appeared. Titania, which was the name she claimed for herself, was shrewdly determined on a career as a high-class whore and couldn't wait to get her first protector. Shame it had to be Osbaldeston, though.

Wilson chuckled. "You *must* have annoyed dear Violet for her to miss the chance of one of the richest men in town."

"Or she knew I wouldn't be interested. I gave up any taste for children when I ceased being one myself." He deliberately raised his voice a little, hoping Osbaldeston would catch it.

"Now, now, Ver," said Alvanley lightly. "Most of the men here were in on the betting at some point, myself included. Violet showed her off here, nicely togged out in a white silk dress fine enough for Almack's. Have to confess, she's pretty thing. Made even *my* blood tingle, but if I'm bidding into the hundreds of guineas, it'll be for a horse, not a filly."

"I wonder what's eating him, though," asked Wilson, with an idle glance at Osbaldeston. "Think he'd be off riding his new filly."

Osbaldeston's eyes narrowed, and he rose to stalk over to them. "Are you discussing me?" he demanded, looking straight at Verderan.

"We were discussing cattle auctions and riding," Verderan drawled. Unfortunately, Wilson sniggered.

"Suppose you're bitter you missed the sale," snapped Osbaldeston, his face going even redder. "I made sure of it, Verderan. My country, my covert, my vixen."

"Then please go hunt her," Verderan said dismissively, merely completing the hunting analogy.

Osbaldeston's fist slammed down on the table, making the men's glasses bounce. "What the devil do you mean by that!"

The room fell quiet. Verderan looked up coldly at his old enemy and was surprised by the lack of any desire to kill him. He was angry, yes, but not nearly as angry as the same affront would have made him only weeks ago. "Do that again and I'll break your hand," he said flatly. "I meant nothing of significance."

Alvanley moved his glass from proximity to Osbaldeston's fist. "Wondering why you're not off enjoying your new filly," he said. "That's all."

Osbaldeston flicked a glance his way, but didn't reply. His attention swung back to Verderan as if drawn by a magnet.

Verderan couldn't resist. "Been gulled, George?"

He held his opponent's eyes, seeing him long to make another violent gesture; seeing him fight it. Osbaldeston knew that Verderan didn't make idle threats, and if it came to a fight now it would be just the two of them. They were both crack shots. The winner would be in doubt.

With a visible effort Osbaldeston relaxed and took a light tone. "Not at all," he said. "A rare piece of blood. But one has to go easy on a newly broken filly, you know. Can't ride her like a five-year-old."

" 'Course not," said one man who had obviously not been following the conversation. "Mount'd peck at the first in and out."

A gale of laughter broke the tension and Osbaldeston was drawn into another group, but not without a vicious look at Verderan.

"What is it with you two, Ver?" asked Alvanley as he led a three of hearts for the next trick.

"Old history," Ver said. "The gods have been kind and we haven't clapped eyes on each other for years." He put up his king and looked over to see Osbaldeston sitting next to Felix Grantwich at the Hazard table. It was a pairing he didn't care for. Two new arrivals caught his attention, however. They were mere acquaintances, but they were very wet.

"It's bucketing," they gasped as club servants hurried forward with towels. "Roads are rivers of mud and it's dark as Hades!"

"Got a corner for me here, Craven?" asked Verderan.

Henry Craven gathered in the trick. " 'Course, old boy."

When he cantered along towards Hume House at nearly midday the next day, Verderan was feeling at peace with the world. The night at the club had shown him that his taste for the wilder adventures of the younger set was definitely gone and unlamented. It had also, he hoped, shown that his temper was now under control. If he could endure five heated minutes with Osbaldeston without a fight perhaps he was going to settle down to being a quiet, sober gentleman. That would be a nine days' wonder.

The weather, in fact, was not conducive to these mellow thoughts. The rain had stopped, but the sky was grey and heavy and everything was either dripping or soggy. It hardly mattered.

Verderan was merely bothered by the question of how soon he could see Emily Grantwich again, how she would react, and how soon it would be reasonable to ask her to marry him. A few weeks at least.

He rode Beelzebub round to the stables and entered the house through a side door. He was somewhat surprised to hear voices from the library. He wondered who his guests were and what they were making of Kevin Renfrew.

He opened the door and found Chart, Harry, and Cornwallis playing cards and drinking claret, all very much at home. Renfrew was nowhere to be seen.

He raised a brow.

"Hello, Ver," said Chart cheerfully. "Rotten weather. Made a dash over here last night. Corny's roof leaks."

That young man expressed deepest apologies.

"Not at all," said Verderan. "Does this roof *not* leak? It hasn't been tried since I moved in, and it would be the only part of the house in good repair."

"Not in my room," said Chart blithely.

"Hope you don't mind," said Harry, just a little ill at ease.

"Thing is, it's closer to here than to Melton or Oakham, and no guarantee there'd be a vacancy there this time of year. We brought the man that looks after Corny's place and Chart has Quincy with him, so we're helping out."

Verderan wondered what three new guests and two new staff were doing to Mrs. Greely, but couldn't shake his mellow feeling. "I'm glad of the company," he said, and found he meant it. "This is a gloomy house. Where's Renfrew?"

"Don't know," said Harry. "He came down when we arrived about midnight—wearing the most amazing yellow satin thing—fixed up rooms for us, then went back to bed. Haven't seen him since. Strange fellow."

"Always was," said Chart. "Harmless enough, though."

Verderan told them to make themselves at home, which seemed superfluous, and went to check out the situation. To his surprise he found Mrs. Greely in high gig with two new servants to command, though he noticed she was careful in her handling of Quincy, Chart's superior but accommodating valet. He wondered if the woman might not have been soured by simple boredom after years serving the misanthropic Casper Sillitoe.

At least his own man, Ludlow, should now have a crony below-stairs.

He arranged with Mrs. Greely for extra supplies to be brought in, and when she told him "young Mr. Renfrew" had said she should have two extra maids and she'd sent for her sister's girls, he didn't argue.

He then went up to the garrets and discovered the roof did in fact leak, but only slightly in two places, both of which had basins beneath to catch the drips.

He returned to the lower floors, whistling. The place was becoming quite bearable. Hume House was going to make a perfect hunting box with a little refurbishing, and he supposed Emily might like to have a house close to her family home.

When he had changed into fresh clothing he thought he might as well see what his uninvited guests were up to. The trio were trying out the old billiard table and cheerfully announced that the rips in the baize merely made the game more exciting.

"Men after my own heart," said Verderan, and watched in amusement as they calculated shots not only to hit the correct ball but to avoid the hazards.

After a while he said, "Not that I'm trying to throw you out, but do you intend to see to the fixing up of Cornwallis's place?"

"Corny's riding over later," said Chart as he lined up to pocket a red off a side cushion. "Roof leaked in a score of places, though. We'd wondered why the old lady lived on the ground floor."

Verderan saw that Cornwallis was feeling an intruder. "You're entirely welcome here," he said to the portly young man. "I appreciate the company. You may as well take your time and have the roof fixed properly before moving back in."

"That's very kind of you, sir," said Cornwallis.

"Yes," said Harry, and cocked his head. "Hope you mean it about appreciating company, Ver," he remarked. "I hear a coach. Expecting someone?"

"These days I expect anything," said Verderan, and went out to the hall. Deciding he might as well take charity to extreme lengths, he saved his servants' legs and went to open his own front door.

A curricle lurched up to the door over the pitted drive and came to a listing stop in a well-worn depression. It was driven by George Osbaldeston and his passenger was Violet Vane. The groom leapt down from the back to hold the horses and the occupants climbed down.

Verderan waited for them without a greeting. He could see Violet was nervous, which showed she had some sense. Osbaldeston had a nasty expression of self-satisfaction, which usually meant he thought he had someone in his power.

"Good day to you, Verderan," he said.

"And to you exactly the sort of day you deserve," Verderan replied. "Lost your way?"

"Found it, more like," said Osbaldeston, taking Violet's arm and leading her forward to where Verderan stood. Dragging her might be more apposite.

Violet was dressed very smartly in her characteristic shade of purple, a high feathered bonnet on her glossy curls. She still looked unmistakably like a whore.

"I'm sorry, Violet," drawled Verderan. "I thought I'd made it clear that I'm no longer interested in your services. If you need a reference—"

She sucked in her breath. "You scheming Irish bastard," she hissed. "You've stolen my girl. If you want her, you pay for her and you pay double!"

Verderan slid an amused glance to his old enemy. "Oh dear, George. You have been gulled, haven't you?"

Osbaldeston's hands clenched. "We just want the girl back, Verderan," he said.

"I haven't the slightest idea where she is," responded Verderan in a bored tone. "I have no interest in her whatsoever."

"Oh, really?" sneered Violet, her careful accent slipping slightly. "I haven't forgotten you sweet-talking her—straight out of my bed! She begged a lift out of Melton yesterday with a carter and we've tracked her. The last news we have leads her straight here!"

Verderan merely quirked a brow. "Why the heat? If George bought her and she's skipped, it's his problem, not yours." Then he smiled. "Or did you take his note? My dear Violet, I always thought you had a head for business."

Violet was turning puce. "It's none of your affair!" she said shrilly. "I was only doing the chit a favour, introducing her to a better class of gentleman. I was only claiming my expenses back and getting her a cut to set her up . . ." She trailed off and looked over his shoulder. Her eyes grew round and her colour deepened. "You almost had me fooled, you bastard."

Guessing what he would see, Verderan turned. Kevin Renfrew was coming down the wide staircase, chatting amiably to the lady on his arm—a tiny, stylishly dressed female with an aureole of silver-blonde hair and big blue eyes. "I think you'd better come in after all," he said with a sigh, and led the way.

Violet surged forward, "Why, you little slummer—"

Verderan gripped her arm. "We will all behave with

decorum, I think." He looked over at the ethereal couple. "Come here."

Emily spent the morning expecting a summons from her father and fresh recriminations, but nothing occurred. Because of the continuing rain followed by universal wetness she decided to stay at home and attend to domestic tasks and bookkeeping, but unfortunately these left too much time to think.

He had said he *wanted* to kiss her. No matter if he said later it was a mad impulse, for a moment he had wanted to kiss her.

She really shouldn't feel so radiant just because a rake wanted to kiss her, especially with his violent tendencies and his peculiar behaviour to take into account. His mental instability was very sad but probably incurable.

As Emily was sitting at her desk chewing the end of her pen and staring sightlessly at a ledger, Junia scratched and entered bearing a tea tray.

"Are you very busy, Emily?" she asked. "I thought we could have a little chat. Such dismal weather."

"I could welcome a break," said Emily, smiling. But she was wary. It had not escaped her that during dinner the previous night and afterwards, Junia had not once mentioned Piers Verderan or Emily's flight to her room.

They sat beside the leaping, crackling fire and sipped the tea. "I wondered how you were feeling," said Junia. "Last night you seemed a little overset."

I knew it, thought Emily. "Mr. Verderan is a very oversetting person," she said.

"I find him quite pleasant," Junia countered. "But then I have age on my side."

"I am hardly a green girl," Emily said sharply, remembering her father's comments.

"You still seem young to me," replied Junia. "So, what did Piers Verderan say, or do, to overset you, dear?"

Emily took another drink from her cup and thought of all sorts of evasive answers, but then she admitted in a mumble, "He kissed me."

No shock. No outrage. "Was it pleasant?" Junia asked.

Emily almost choked. "Junia!"

"It seems a perfectly reasonable question to me. If you liked it, that means one thing. If you didn't, it means another."

"I liked it," admitted Emily reluctantly. "But that doesn't alter the fact that he's mad and bad. So, what does that mean?"

Junia smiled. "I think it means that you should follow your heart, not what people say." She picked up the pot and refilled their cups. "I knew his parents, you know, and over the years I've followed the family gossip in an idle kind of way. When he turned up here I fired off a few letters and I've had replies. He may be bad but he ain't mad."

Emily stared at her aunt. "Junia, it's almost as if you're trying to push us together. He isn't . . . he can't be *interested* in me in that way. He's just amusing himself."

"Time will tell," said Junia. "And that is for you to work out together. I merely think you should know that he isn't known to be insane, and it's possible he is not as wicked as he's made out to be."

"But you admitted he was bad," Emily pointed out.

"Bad is not so bad sometimes," said Junia cryptically. "Judge him on what you see for yourself, Emily. Not on rumours and old stories."

There was another scratch at the door, and Mary, the maid, came in. "The vicar's here to see you, Miss Emily."

"Oh. Show him into the parlour please, Mary." Emily automatically smoothed her gown and checked her appearance in a mirror. "Excuse me, Junia."

"Of course," said Junia. "But if he proposes, don't say yes, dear."

Emily blushed and protested, "I don't know where you get the notion that all these gentlemen are desperate to marry me."

Junia just smiled.

As a result, Emily entered the parlour nervously. It would be in keeping with the disruption of her orderly existence that Hector choose this moment to offer for her. She would have to say no and then perhaps one day when she had come to her senses she would regret it.

He did not, however, look amorous. He was pacing the room with a weighty frown on his face. "Ah, Emily," he said as he stopped and faced her. "I am on my way to Hume House on a most distasteful mission, but I felt I must stop and warn you."

What now? thought Emily.

"That Verderan man is living up to his vile reputation," Hector said angrily. "I will not stand for it in my parish."

"What has he done?" Emily asked faintly.

"He has abducted a young girl from town to entertain a wild house party he is holding up there."

"*What?* Who?"

"I don't know who. The girl's guardians are seeking her, and your cousin Felix is assisting them. He told me the whole—a young girl cursed by beauty and susceptible to the wiles of wickedness."

"But how do you know she is at Hume House?"

"The news is all over the village that Hume House is full of wild young blades and Mrs. Greely is taking on new staff. And one of the "guests," the gossips tell us, is an unchaperoned child exactly fitting the description given by those poor people. I passed on the sad news to them and they are on their way there now, though since the child has been absent all night I fear the worst. I must follow to throw the weight of the church behind them and reconcile the misguided girl and her family." He gathered his hat and gloves.

"Wait!" cried Emily. "I am coming with you."

"That is out of the question, Emily. That place is clearly no better than the Hellfire Club."

"The child will be frightened. I may be able to help."

Hector looked at her. He was no fool. "You don't believe me," he said, and Emily felt her colour flare. It was true. She couldn't, wouldn't believe it unless she witnessed it with her own eyes, as Junia had advised.

Hector stiffened. "Margaret hinted that your interest in that man was growing, despite all I told you. Even Felix has heard rumours . . . Very well, Emily. By all means come with me and have your eyes opened once and for all."

Emily sent a message for Corsair to be brought round, then rushed upstairs and scrambled into her habit. She had no time to think until they were underway, cantering towards Hume House.

It couldn't be true.

She prayed that it not be true.

= 8 =

WHEN VERDERAN ADDRESSED them, Renfrew and Titania looked over as if they had only just become aware of the group near the door. In Renfrew's case it was probably true, but Verderan would go odds Titania had been aware of them every second.

"Mr. Verderan," she said with a doting sigh and let go of her escort to float down the stairs to his side. She hardly came halfway up his chest, and with her huge eyes she did look very childlike. Her white muslin gown, presumably carefully chosen by Violet, combined fashionable style with charming, youthful innocence—and a very low neckline. She would indeed not have looked out of place at Almack's.

She glanced wide-eyed at Osbaldeston and Violet. "Are they very angry?" she whispered. The "with us" was silent but implicit.

"You should have a career on the stage, my dear," he said, and detached her fingers from his sleeve.

"Oh, thank you!" she gasped meltingly. "You are so kind to me."

Verderan burst out laughing.

"Damn you, Verderan!" snarled Osbaldeston. "You'll meet me for this!"

Verderan knew his right line in this farce was to grit his teeth and say, "Willingly. Name your seconds." He simply couldn't. "For once," he said, "I'm in sympathy with Jake Mulholland. I'm not going to fight over pudding, not even over such a perfect fairy cake as this."

By this time Chart, Harry, and Corny had come out to gawk at the group in the hall. Titania instinctively played to her audience and flashed them an admiring, beseeching smile. They all coloured and preened.

Osbaldeston assumed an air of *sangfroid* and looked over the four young men. "Perhaps we've had you wrong all these years, Verderan,'' he sneered. "Perhaps you ain't in the petticoat line at all. Heard you were very *tender* with your boys at Eton."

Harry coloured up and surged forward. "Damn it all!"

Verderan stopped him with a glance. "He's blustering, Harry, because of grievous wounds to his *amour propre*." He turned back to Osbaldeston. "No one here's in season, George, so go fire your shots elsewhere. As for the girl, as far as I'm concerned she's free to do as she pleases."

Violet glared at her erstwhile protégée. "You'll come with me, my girl, if you know what's good for you!"

"And why should I?" demanded Titania pertly. "You said I'd have some say. I don't like him," she said with a dismissive glance at Osbaldeston, "and he told me he hardly ever goes to London. He prepares for hunting, he hunts, and he recovers from hunting, and I'll give Granny's best stays he never talks of anything else. I don't want to spend the rest of my life in the provinces."

"What airs and graces!" scoffed Violet. "You'll come with me because you won't get your cut otherwise."

"I know that," said the girl. "But I've still got that trinket you gave me to show myself off with, and *he* donated a bit." Osbaldeston looked daggers at her. "I haven't lost much, and now I think I'll do better to act for myself." She swayed to lean against Verderan.

He pushed her gently away. "I hope this doesn't destroy your self-esteem, Titania, but I am not the slightest bit interested in playing Oberon."

She looked at him in sharp surprise, then shrewd assessment. She obviously decided he was speaking the plain truth, for she wilted prettily. "Oh dear," she sighed. "But please, you won't give me back to them, will you?"

"I've already said you may do as you please."

"No, she damned well may not!" bellowed Osbaldeston. He grabbed the girl by the arm and yanked her towards the door. Titania gave an outraged squeal and bit his hand. Verderan got hold of her and pulled her against his chest, out of danger.

"Unhand that child!" declared Hector in ringing tones as he stalked into the hall, followed at a run by a horrified Emily.

Verderan unhanded the child immediately, all amusement gone. "And who the devil are you?" he asked.

"I am the Reverend Hector Marshalswick, vicar of this parish. I am here to tell you that we will not tolerate such rank evil in our midst." He marched over to Titania and took her hand. "My poor child," he said in mellow tones. "What have they done to you?"

For once Titania was utterly at a loss. After a wild look round, she burst into convincing tears against Hector's greatcoat.

Emily came forward to stand beside the couple and looked up at Verderan, white as death. "How could you?" she demanded.

Verderan decided to have done with all this. He put a hand out to Titania to stop the act and get some sense. Emily immediately leapt between him and the girl. "Don't you dare touch her!" she cried.

So instead, he grabbed her. "And don't you dare leap to such unwarranted conclusions!"

"Unwarranted! I can believe my own eyes, you—you libertine!"

"If you have such keen eyesight," Verderan snarled, "who's that?" He physically turned her to face Violet.

Emily stared for a minute and then recognised the woman. "The Violet Tart," she said. "It's an orgy."

Despite his anger, Osbaldeston sniggered at the name. Violet went puce again. "So this is your new fancy piece," she sneered. "Jake Mulholland implied as much."

"Jake Mulholland is a dead man," Verderan said flatly. "I have no profound objection to shooting a woman either."

"Amazing," said Osbaldeston, with an unpleasant smile. "You'll meet Mulholland. You threaten even to meet a woman, but you won't accept a challenge from a man who's as good a shot as you."

"I'll meet you anywhere, anytime, Osbaldeston," snapped Verderan. "Now get out of my house!"

"Not without the girl."

"Go to hell!"

Emily had listened in numb shock, Verderan's hands still on her shoulders, but now she came to life and struggled. "Take your filthy hands off me!" she cried. "You're no better than a slaver!"

"Unhand that woman!" cried Hector yet again, somewhat at a disadvantage as he already had his hands full of a weeping, clinging damsel in distress.

"You let go of my girl!" shrieked Violet and tried to pull Titania away.

"Hello, Ver," said Randal, coming in the doorway, Sophie on his arm. "Staging a theatrical?"

There was a blessed moment of silence.

Verderan let Emily go and she ran to Hector's side.

Titania twisted out of Violet's hands and skipped over to Kevin Renfrew.

Verderan ran a hand through his curls. "Randal, I don't know what cloud you floated down from, but thank God. Perhaps you can return things to sanity. Get rid of those two," he said, indicating Osbaldeston and Violet. As Randal sauntered over to address the matter, Verderan added, "Wait."

He turned to Violet Vane. "What did he bid?"

She looked around uncertainly, weighing it all. "Two hundred. Guineas."

"And her cut?" he asked, indicating Titania, who was keeping shrewd track of the proceedings.

"Fifty," said Violet.

"Titania, is that right?"

The girl nodded.

"What heavy expenses you have, Violet," Verderan said dryly, but he pulled out a card and scribbled an IOU on the back for a hundred and fifty guineas. "You'll have payment tomorrow." To Osbaldeston he said, "Don't be forever expecting me to pay your debts, George."

Osbaldeston's jaw was tight. "But—" He glared at Titania.—"that little bitch stole twenty guineas from me. If you're taking over the lease, you damn well owe me that."

"Nonsense," said Verderan. "It's fair for a night's work. If you have any complaint over this, I will meet you, George, but you'll end up looking the fool."

Osbaldeston obviously decided this was all too true and grimaced bitterly. "There'll come a day . . . ," he muttered. But then he turned on his heel and stalked out, Violet scurrying after with the IOU tight in her hand.

"Hello, Sophie," said Verderan, going over to his newest guest. "I hope you still like madcap adventures."

She was watching everything, bright-eyed from inside a magnificent drab carriage coat, lined and pelerined with sable. She wore no bonnet, but carried an enormous sable muff. She cheerfully accepted a warm embrace and a kiss. "Of course. As soon as we read the letters we just knew we had to come. What on earth's going on?"

"As is usual around here," Verderan said with a sigh, "your conversation doesn't make any sense. Come and meet the other lady present." He led her over to where Emily was standing, dumbstruck. "Sophie, this is Miss Emily Grantwich of Grantwich Hall, my nearest neighbour. Emily, Lady Randal Ashby. The gentleman with her is, of course, her husband, Lord Randal."

Emily had leapt to the worst possible interpretation when this pretty young woman had fallen happily into Verderan's arms. Now, instead of a polite greeting, she found herself saying, "Chloe's cousin, Randal."

Verderan took a little breath. "Chloe's cousin, Randal," he agreed. "You know Chloe Stanforth?"

"Yes, she's my old school friend."

"And did you perhaps write to her and tell her of my arrival in the district?"

"Yes," said Emily, not admitting that she'd told Chloe rather more than that.

"So the letters are perhaps explained," said Verderan to Sophie. "Chloe doubtless wrote to Randal to what? Ask him to save Emily from predators?"

Randal shut the door behind Osbaldeston and Violet, and came to join them. "Of course. Delighted to meet you, Miss Grantwich." He elegantly kissed her hand. "If you get the picture, you'll understand that I am your knight errant, come post haste to stand at your right hand, fiery sword aloft. From whom am I to save you?" His laughing glance took in all the gentlemen in the hall.

Emily was in the now familiar state of total confusion. Chloe had told her that her Cousin Randal was spectacularly handsome and charming, and he certainly was. And here he was, golden haired and glorious, placing himself—a duke's son no less—at her service.

Piers Verderan, dark haired and equally glorious, had just bought a child for his pleasure.

The girl's family had sold her.

Four young men, including the Daffodil Dandy, were watching everything as if they were, as Lord Randal had suggested, the audience at a play.

And Lady Randal Ashby, an earl's daughter, didn't seem to mind any of this a bit.

The ways of Fashionable Society were beyond comprehension and no place for Emily Grantwich.

"Hector," she said. "We must leave. And we will take the child with us. Come along, my dear." She moved towards Titania.

Hector, however, was clearly flustered. "Emily," he said. "This girl is not what I thought."

Emily stopped and looked at him. "What do you mean?"

Hector went red and searched for words.

"She's a whore," supplied Verderan kindly.

Emily looked in horror at the delicate creature, who smiled apologetically, then rounded on Verderan. "Is that your excuse, you vile man? She's a *child!*"

"She's seventeen."

"If you had a seventeen-year-old daughter, would you think her ripe for any man with a guinea or two in his pocket?"

"If I had a seventeen-year-old daughter," Verderan retorted, "I'd have been a remarkable prodigy!"

"I don't go for a paltry few guineas!" declared Titania in outrage. "What do you think I am, a dolly-mop?"

"Titania," said Verderan chidingly, "there are ladies present."

"There is one lady present," said Hector sternly, "but not for long. Come, Emily!"

He grabbed her arm, but his proud exit was stopped abruptly by a hand in his cravat. "I think," said Lord Randal gently, "you missed being introduced to my wife. Sophie, my dear, apparently this is the local vicar." He let Hector go. "My wife, sir. Lady Randal Ashby."

Hector was red in the face and almost speechless. "My deepest apologies, my lady. This whole business . . . disordered my wits . . . It cannot but be a shock to you to find yourself in this—this warren. I am afraid the vicarage is too small to accommodate you, but I am sure Grantwich Hall would offer you hospitality."

"That's so kind of you," said Sophie, eyes twinkling with amusement, "but there is obviously the need of a lady's gentle touch here. However," she said, turning to Emily, "I hope I will be welcome to visit tomorrow."

"Yes, of course," said Emily blankly. "But Hector, we cannot just go and leave this child with all these men."

Hector had clearly lost his crusading spirit but gained some diplomacy. "I'm sure we can leave the matter in Lady Randal's hands, my dear."

At this point, however, Lady Randal raised an objection. "I think you should take her away, vicar," she said bluntly. "It will be exhausting to try to keep track of her in a house of bachelors."

Hector looked as if he was going to choke. "I—I am not exactly sure where I would put her just at this moment . . ."

"Well really, Hector," said Emily in disgust. "You should have thought of that before you came charging up here!" Emily was desperately trying not to be aware of Piers Verderan observing everything with a cynical smile; of how hurt she was to have finally discovered the kind of man he was; of how jealous she was of the ethereal Titania and the beautiful Sophie . . .

"Emily, we will discuss this later," Hector said forbiddingly, and tried to take her arm again.

"What is the point of that?" she replied, wrenching it free. "We must make a decision now." She turned to Titania and tried to be kind in spite of her bitter and unworthy jealousy. It wasn't the girl's fault that she was just the sort of creature to appeal to a rake. "You may come home with me for a while, my dear," she said, "and we will discuss your future. I am sure I can find you a suitable situation."

"Do you have a brother then?" Titania asked.

Both Randal and Verderan appeared to suffer a choking fit.

"I have, yes," said Emily, confused. "He is not at home at the moment."

"Oh," said Titania. "It's very kind of you to want to help me, ma'am, but exactly how do you intend to go about it? I'm quite happy here, and it doesn't bother me a bit," she added, with a naughty twinkle, "to be in a house full of bachelors."

"Emily, we are leaving!" declared Hector angrily, and yet again grabbed her arm.

"Unhand that woman," said Verderan quietly but in a tone that created a shocked silence. Emily found herself free and looking at Piers Verderan for the first time, as it seemed, in eons.

"Emily," he said, "I wish to speak to you. In private." He indicated a room. Emily took a step before realising she was being a fool.

She took the step back. "We have nothing to say to each other," she said coldly.

"Unless you come and hear what I have to say, you will never know, will you?"

"Emily," barked Hector, "I am leaving and you will come with me!"

At that moment, Emily disliked all men intensely. "Hector, stop—stop *hectoring*! You have no right to order me around. If that little—that little *tart* can do as she wishes, I don't see why I can't!"

Sophie gave a cheer and applauded. Hector looked at Sophie with outrage and clearly thought of a sermon on

ladylike decorum, then glanced at her amused and indul-
gent husband and gave up the idea. After a thwarted glare
around the hall, he said, "With or without you, Emily, I am
leaving this sink of iniquity!" When Emily made no move
he stalked away and slammed out of the house.

Emily, however, was not watching his exit but looking
with distress at Titania. "I do apologise," she said. "I'm sure
you aren't really . . ."

" 'Course I am," said the girl cheerfully. "I only squawked
earlier because you seemed to imply that I'm *cheap*, which
I definitely aren't, or not anymore. Don't you worry about
me, ma'am. You look after yourself. If he," she said with a
cock of her head at Verderan, "invited me to a private room,
you wouldn't find me hanging around jawing."

That merely linked her with Verderan in Emily's mind.
"Very well, sir," Emily said with a glare. "I will come and
hear what you have to say, and you will hear something
from me. But I will take my knight errant!" She summoned
Lord Randal and stalked off to the room indicated, which
proved to be a dingy, unused parlour, dusty and damp. The
curtains actually billowed under the steady icy draft from
the windows.

Coming to a halt, Emily realised that she had just ordered
around the son of a duke. She turned to apologise to Lord
Randal, who was following with his wife. He put a finger
gently on her lips. "Don't," he said with a smile. "Apologising
is a bad habit if you're going to move in these circles. Brazen
it out. Consider us your jury." He then led Sophie to a frayed
sofa and helped her off with her coat. They then sat there
side by side, cuddling under the sables, waiting to be amused.

Emily turned dazedly to Piers Verderan.

"Speechless?" he said, with a little smile. He caught hold
of her hand and swung her into his arms. Her faint struggles
were ignored, and Emily found all her anger transformed
into a burning need to kiss and be kissed. Her arms went
around his neck, and her lips found fire against his. The
flames rippled along her nerves bringing feverish heat.

She gasped and opened her lips and discovered the spicy
warmth of his mouth, was lost in the taste and savour of him

as she caught fire and burned free. She heard a moan and realised it was her own but her only need was to press ever closer and burn hotter until she was utterly consumed . . .

He pulled away, lingeringly, at last, and Emily moaned a faint protest. As she rested her spinning head against his chest, his hand came up to cradle it protectively.

He shuddered as he murmured, "Emily." His cheek came down to rub against her curls, and she felt the deep unsteady movements of his chest as he breathed. They matched her own. She had discovered that passion which had no truck with decorum and morals . . .

Then it all came back—the child, the money, their audience . . . She pushed away, horrified, and Verderan let her go, though his darkened eyes held hers for what seemed like eternity.

When she broke that bond and looked at Lord Randal and his wife, however, they were lingeringly finishing a kiss every bit as passionate as theirs. "Dashed awkward to just sit and watch," said Randal, utterly relaxed, a tender, possessive hand still curled around his wife's neck. "You didn't seem to need rescuing yet."

"You're all mad!" said Emily, hands to flaming cheeks.

"Then come and be mad with us," said Verderan, gently drawing her hands down.

"You expect me to join your orgy?" Emily exclaimed in outrage.

"No one is having an orgy here," he reassured, then glanced humorously at Randal and Sophie. "At least, if there are any orgies, they'll be private and monogamous. Which," he added, with a look which made her toes curl, "seems like a very good idea."

"Indeed," said Emily. "And what of your little Tit—I mean *Tart!*"

Emily hid her flaming face on the nearest surface, which happened to be his chest. His arms came around her like angel wings. She heard laughter from Randal and Sophie at her jumbled words, but all he said was, "Little Tit is perfect. Violet Tart, Daffodil Dandy . . . You'll have to christen everyone else in the house."

Emily pulled away, though it was the hardest thing she had ever done. "I'm not staying here," she said fiercely. "I don't know what's going on here and I don't want to—"

"That's all right," said Verderan, wrapping an arm around her again. "I don't know either."

"Stop doing that!" she gasped, feebly pulling away.

"No."

"Why not?"

"Because I want to, and I always do what I want."

He'd trapped her eyes again. She couldn't look away. "We've had this conversation before," she whispered.

"How boring for you," he said softly. "Let's have a new one. Marry me, Emily."

"No," she said instinctively, then instantly regretted it. Then knew it was the right thing.

"Why not?" he asked, undiscouraged. "I can think of a hundred reasons myself, but I had begun to hope you were as mad as I am."

"I've given you no reason to think I'm insane," Emily protested. "I have always been totally sane and rational until you and that powder—"

"*Poudre de Violettes*," he said understandingly. "I know. But I'm sure the effects are permanent and Renfrew's advice is to just enjoy them."

Renfrew. The Daffodil Dandy. Felix's friend. Emily looked over at Lord Randal. "I want to go home," she said desperately.

With a slight smile, he instantly rose to his feet and came over. "Very well."

"Randal," said Verderan in an ominous voice.

"I'm Emily's knight errant," said Randal lightly. "If she wishes to leave, she leaves."

Emily wondered for a terrible minute if a new fight was going to break out over her, but Verderan smiled. "Of course. She's probably getting rheumatism just standing here. My wits must be addled to try to make love to a woman in such surroundings."

The last thing Emily had been aware of was cold.

He raised her hand to his lips, and this time there was a

speaking look to go with the gesture. "I love you, you know."

"You can't," she protested

"Of course I can," he said calmly. "Meanwhile, I give my angel charge over thee, 'lest at any time thou dash thy foot against a stone.' " Seeing her confusion he said, "Something biblical, which seems to be a theme of ours. Didn't you know that Randal is the Bright Angel to my Dark? You don't have a knight errant, my darling, you have a guardian angel. Two, if you want to count me."

Emily looked up at the Bright Angel in question. "I am not going to marry him," she said firmly.

"Not if you don't want to," he agreed amiably. "But I wouldn't marry the vicar either."

"When I finally come to my senses," said Emily darkly, "he will probably seem a very desirable *parti*. At least Hector doesn't shoot people who serve him sago pudding!"

She heard a groan from Verderan as Lord Randal broke into an incredulous grin. "He did what?"

"I did no such thing," said Verderan.

"You threatened to," said Emily, swinging around to face him.

"No, I didn't."

"Are you going to deny," she demanded, "that you shot Jake over pudding?"

Verderan sighed. "No. I admit that one. Emily, you're right. It's time for you to go home, but I'll escort you. Randal's not dressed for riding."

"I will go alone," declared Emily, feeling as if the wind had gone out of her sails. She had been making a grand exit, but now she was being dismissed like a schoolroom miss. She expected a fight and looked forward to it. She would show him she was not to be pushed around.

She wasn't even to be given that. "Very well," he said. "I'll come to speak with you tomorrow."

"I'll be out," said Emily uncompromisingly and finally managed to sweep out of the room.

Crossing the hall she heard merry laughter from another room and hesitated. It was clear Titania was in there with the young men and should be rescued. But Emily couldn't fight that battle at the moment. The girl would obviously be in no significantly lower state tomorrow than she was in today and Emily had more urgent problems to tackle.

Such as convincing herself that marrying Piers Verderan would be a very bad idea.

= 9 =

EMILY RETURNED HOME to find Junia out on one of her nature walks—unlikely as that seemed on such a blustery, soggy day—and so not available to be told just what evidence had been presented to Emily's own eyes as to Piers Verderan's true nature.

Even as she paced her room, shredding a lace handkerchief, seething with frustration at having no one suitable to talk to, Emily was haunted by the lingering heat of that kiss. And the simple way he had said, "I love you, you know."

How could she know anything so ridiculous? Especially when he had just bought an exquisitely beautiful young woman.

Emily skulked in her room, unable to do any meaningful task and unwilling to risk an encounter with Mrs. Dobson. At dinnertime, however, she went down so as not to appear too peculiar. Junia swept in late and windblown.

"Got caught up," she explained as she attacked her soup. "Some lovely grasses over near the river. And gossip everywhere. What did Hector want?"

"If you've been listening to gossip," said Emily, "you know just what Hector wanted."

Junia chuckled unrepentantly. "Let's see. When I first went out, Mrs. Ferryman told me there was a wild party up at Hume House, full of Meltonians and Cyprians. When I passed Greenwood Farm I heard a couple from town had been pursuing their daughter, who'd been lured up there with promises of heaven-knows-what rewards. When I stopped at the Belvoir Arms I heard their drayman had dropped a girl yesterday evening at the drive to Hume House. Pretty little thing and he was sorry to leave her to walk the rest of the way with the rain coming on. How am I doing?"

Emily scowled. "Does the whole county know everything?"

"Don't they always?" Junia spooned up some soup then continued. "What next? A bit of a dry patch—nothing but rumours, which appear incidentally to have been spread by our Felix—then I hear you and Hector were seen galloping towards Hume House *ventre à terre* and that later the town couple were seen heading back to Melton at a fancy pace without their daughter, if daughter she ever was . . . ?"

"Daughter indeed," said Emily, pushing away her scarce-tasted soup. "She's a whore. A tartlet. Junia, he *bought* her for a hundred and fifty guineas, then had the nerve to ask me to marry him!"

"Hmm," said Junia. "I did get a garbled tale to that effect. That's what caused me to be late. Betty Wrigley is Mrs. Greely's niece and she's only in day service. Just as I was passing she arrived home with a tale of Piers Verderan paying the girl's parents for her. And you, apparently, sending the vicar off with a flea in his ear when he tried to intervene. Then you stayed in the place and disappeared with the author of all evils."

Emily hid her face in her hands. "I'll never live it down."

"Oh, I don't know," said Junia. "On the whole, people think it's fine to have some excitement and Hector's not very popular, you know. He disapproves of so many country amusements. In fact the greatest impression on Betty Wrigley's mind seemed to have been made by a fur worn by some other young woman."

Emily looked up. "Sables," she said wistfully. "Absolutely ravishing sables. Lord Randal Ashby turned up with his wife. I thought she was a whore too, at first. He's Chloe Stanforth's handsome cousin, younger son of the Duke of Tyne."

Junia ignored most of this ramble. "If you marry Piers Verderan, he'll doubtless deck you in ravishing sables too."

Until that moment Emily had not admitted how Randal and Sophie had affected her. They so clearly adored one another and their love had set them free. Randal delighted in his wife's every action; Sophie moved through life, his care a golden shield between her and all unpleasantness. Emily just knew carping criticism and improving guidance had no part in their lives. But she could not believe such magic was for her.

She couldn't face food. Even as Mary came in with the next course, she stood up abruptly. "You can't expect me to marry a man who buys children."

Mary stopped dead, mouth agape.

"It depends what he does with them, I suppose," said Junia. "Put that tray down, Mary, before you drop it." The maid did so and left in a hurry. "More gossip," murmured Junia. She eagerly investigated the food beneath the silver covers.

"I would have thought it was obvious what he was going to do with this one," snapped Emily.

"Doesn't do to leap to conclusions," said Junia. "You should eat. The pork chops are done as you like them."

Before Emily could respond, Mrs. Dobson stalked in, working apron on and stirring spoon in hand. "Miss Emily," she declared, "I hope I know my place, but I can't and won't stand by to see you throw yourself before swine! Mary says you're going to marry Casper Sillitoe's nephew. Him as has all those loose women up there. And children too, Mary says."

"It's not true, Dobby," Emily protested.

"What isn't?"

"Any of it. At least," she admitted, "there's one loose woman. But no children and I'm not going to marry him."

With that, she fled to the miserable privacy of her room and thought longingly of being wrapped in the angel-wings of Piers Verderan's love.

And, it must be admitted, of being wrapped in sables and kissed whenever and wherever the mood took them.

As the hours chimed away on the hall clock, she imagined the progress of the evening at Hume House, coming to the time when she could no longer delay the thought of Verderan leading his purchase upstairs to finally earn her keep.

In fact, Verderan had provided Titania with a room with a lock and key, but beyond that he had no intention of interfering in her life. He hadn't even tried to find out what she and Kevin Renfrew had been up to since her arrival late the previous evening.

It should have been obvious; yet with Renfrew one never knew, and Titania's behaviour to the young man made it clear she did not regard him as a potential protector, more as a brother.

Despite the sudden influx of visitors, dinner had been surprisingly adequate. Mrs. Greely had merely produced enormous quantities of well-cooked plain food, which was exactly to the tastes of the six healthy young men. With the addition of Casper Sillitoe's excellent cellar and the presence of two pretty, charming, and undemanding women, the meal had been a roaring success.

Verderan had suggested that Titania be asked to dine elsewhere, but Sophie would have none of it and Randal raised no objection, so he had merely kept an eye on her to make sure she behaved. In fact, she did very well, so perhaps Violet had earned her commission.

He had no intention, however, even if Randal's tolerance stretched that far, of having the ladies go apart after dinner. He initiated a game of loo for penny points, which most of the company were still young enough to enjoy, after which he sent Titania to bed.

He hadn't noticed any assignation being made.

Shortly after, Sophie went up to the room allocated to the Ashbys and Randal escorted her. Verderan abandoned the young set at that point and sought his own room. He had a fire, some brandy, and books, and at last an opportunity to think of Emily.

Just how disastrous had the whole scene been? Despite her outrage, despite her blunt rejection of his suit, there was that kiss.

God, he'd known there was passion in her, but he'd never

dreamt they would come together like pitch and flame. If it hadn't been for Randal and Sophie, inadequate chaperones though they were, he might have surrendered to the fire then and there. . . .

As if summoned by the thought, Randal knocked and entered, dressed in a cream and gold banjan.

Verderan grinned and said, "You'll be putting Renfrew's nose out of joint."

"Impossible to do," Randal said, subsiding elegantly into a chair by the fire and accepting a large glass of brandy. "You appear to have the only truly habitable room in the house, you know."

"Are you complaining? What else can unexpected guests expect?"

"I'm not complaining. The standard of entertainment so far has been excellent. I've come to report on Marcus Grantwich."

"It necessitates a midnight tryst?"

"After a fashion. Took a bit of doing, sorting all this out . . ."

"Is he alive?"

"As far as anyone knows. Stop interrupting, and let me relate the great efforts I expended on your behalf. Government circles ain't my usual milieu, you know. In fact," he confessed, "if Chelmly hadn't turned up to speak on some agricultural bill, I'd have been stumped."

"How is he?"

"Pretty good and reassessing his life busily. The mere thought that I might have inherited if his injury had proved fatal has given him a new enthusiasm for marriage. The trouble is that he can't seem to find anyone to his taste. Even attended a few 'do's, but the sight of all those wide-eyed ingenues salivating over his future coronet panicked him."

"Don't blame him. But what about Emily's brother?"

"Chelmly turned a few rocks and discovered amazing things. Captain Marcus Grantwich, you'll be pleased to hear, is not missing in action at all, Ver. He's been involved for the past year with something mysterious."

"Undercover work?"

"Very undercover, probably underhand. Something to do

with smugglers and highwaymen on the south coast and definitely not to be recorded in dispatches."

"Oho. But he must have had word of his father's accident."

"Apparently not. Whatever he's been doing was going so well that his commanding officers thought it best not to disturb him with trivialities. They've been persuaded otherwise by now—one gathers his project was coming to a natural end anyway. You can expect him, I would think, any day."

Verderan leaned back with a smile. "Good," he said. "Thank you for your efforts."

"Are you sure?"

"What do you mean?"

"About it being good," said Randal. "Talking to people, I got the feeling Captain Grantwich is a fire-eater who'd defend his womenfolk to the death. He may not take to his sister marrying you, and today's little drama isn't going to raise your reputation in the neighbourhood."

"Emily's of age. He can't stop her from marrying me if she decides to do so."

Randal raised a skeptical brow but made no further comment. "Care to relate the background history to all of this?"

So Verderan told him the events leading up to the day's histrionics.

"I didn't realise you had a mind to settle down," commented Randal.

"Nor did I until the *Poudre de Violettes* addled my brain," said Verderan dryly. But then he added, "I think it's all your fault, actually."

"*I* didn't fix you up with Violet Vane."

"No, but you inveigled me into polite society for your wedding," said Verderan, lounging back in his chair and watching the dancing flames in the hearth. "It was strange, but I found I liked it. Out of consideration for you, I suppose, I was accepted. I met young women who didn't shrink in horror or throw themselves at me"—He flashed a look at Randal—"or anyway, not as much as usual. I saw you and Sophie . . ."

He laughed, and refilled their glasses. "I must admit that

at first I thought any man must be mad to let a woman tangle him in such a coil. Now, however, I find it has its own masochistic appeal. Especially with the hope of better days to come."

"And do you have such hopes?"

Verderan slanted him a humorous glance. "Do you doubt me?"

"I was wondering," mused Randal, "when you were going to explain all about pudding."

Verderan laughed. "Not until my wedding night if I can help it. And I'll make sure there are no lethal weapons to hand." But then he sobered and rose to his feet. "I have no doubt I can snare her, Randal. I've all the tricks of seduction, God knows, and she's so vulnerable—both naive and passionate. But should I? I'm ready to settle down, but that can never change what I have been. Nor will it wipe out what people think I am."

"Perhaps you ought to sort out of your grandfather once and for all."

Verderan went to lean against the window frame, to look out at clouded dark. "That's a book better left closed."

There was a silence broken only by the tick of the clock and the crackle of the fire.

"I decided to marry Sophie," said Randal at last, "because I realised I could never trust any other man to love her as I would love her, to keep her safe and at the same time set her free. Is there another man you can trust to do the same for Emily Grantwich?"

Verderan turned sharply and met his friend's eyes. "No," he said. "There isn't." He stood in thought for a moment then shrugged. "So be it."

Randal rose and put down his empty glass. "So be it. And speaking of love, Sophie awaits." At the door, he kissed his fingers to Verderan. "Sweet dreams, my friend. I, however," he added, "have the reality. Envy me."

Verderan laughed. " 'A brave man or a fortunate one is able to bear envy' " he quoted. "And I am brave and hope to be fortunate. Go away before you tax my tolerance."

As soon as the door closed he leant his head against the

cold window glass and relived that extraordinary kiss, cursing softly. He'd not felt such burning frustration since his schooldays.

After a restless night Emily arose the next day clear about one thing only. She must be out of the house when Piers Verderan called. She knew it would be no good to merely deny herself. A man like that would ride roughshod over poor Mary.

The sun had returned and the outdoors beckoned. She would go to High Burton and attend to the matter of the broken hedge. Surely after that she could think of other business to keep her away from home. She chose to ride Nelson since he would so soon be sold.

At least that was one matter which was in order. Griswold would want his money by the middle of the month, but by then all three horses should have been ridden by Dick Christian in a hunt, and hopefully sold well. Next Monday would see the first run of the season, a Quorn meet, and that would be Wallingford's turn.

She didn't feel easy until she was on Nelson and well away from the house. She wouldn't put it past that man to turn up before decent folk were through with their breakfasts. It wasn't so much that she was afraid to meet him, but she had said she wouldn't be in when he called, and was determined to keep her word.

As she galloped across a field she saw the red flash of a fox, late home to its earth.

"Enjoy the day," she said to herself. "By next week you will only be amusement."

At High Burton, she found the sheep mostly in their proper places and inspected the fence with the shepherd. It was a simple matter and couldn't be stretched out to take the morning, even with a prolonged chat about the flock's illustrious breeding lines.

Next she remembered a minor problem to do with a tenant farmer four miles away and set off at a gentle pace to attend to it. Hopefully, as it was in the opposite direction to Hume House, the gossip wouldn't have reached there.

The farmer's wife, Letty Edwards, had an outstanding claim against the Cottesmore Poultry Fund for chickens lost to foxes nearly a year ago. As landlord, Emily promised to take the matter up with the fund manager. She also accepted an invitation to eat, and shared a hearty steak and kidney pie with the family. As she hadn't eaten dinner or breakfast, she enjoyed this thoroughly.

Until Farmer Edwards said, "Hear tell you're to marry that Lunnon man, as has taken over Sillitoe place, Miss Grantwich. Take you away, I reckon. Sir Henry put in a manager, you reckon?"

"No," said Emily, reflecting that at least the man only seemed interested in the matter as it would affect him. "I mean, I am not planning to marry anyone, Mr. Edwards. I will manage the estate until my brother comes home."

She saw the skeptical look flash between the man and his wife, but nothing was said other than a noncommittal grunt. Did they not believe Marcus to be safe? That was reasonable. Emily's sensitivities, however, were all turned towards Piers Verderan and she was sure they were skeptical about him.

After that stop, she could not think of another errand, so she merely took a long way home and took her time about it.

She was trotting along a lane down to the village when she heard a shout. She looked up and saw three riders on a rise—Lord Randal, his wife, and Piers Verderan. Verderan set Beelzebub into action to canter down towards her.

In a spurt of pure panic, Emily hauled Nelson around and urged him flat out in the opposite direction. After a little while she glanced back, half hoping that Verderan would have taken the hint and gone his way. He was hard in pursuit.

Was it fear she felt now? Or was it challenge? Whatever it was, it burned in her blood like a fever.

"Right, Nelson," murmured Emily. "We can take that black devil." She turned the horse towards a gate into a field, cleared it, and set across towards the next fence. Nelson stretched, and the horse's thrill of the race seemed to surge through into her. Emily leant forward and encouraged him on.

Another glance showed her Verderan clearing the fence with elegance. Beelzebub was a fine mount and probably fresher than Nelson, but Emily knew this land like her own back garden. She rode Nelson fast at a hedge and cleared it ready for the unexpected dip in the ground beyond. As they flew on through a field of cows to the next barrier she glanced behind her and saw Beelzebub peck on landing and be masterfully collected.

She felt a twinge of guilt at putting the horse in such danger, but hoped it would teach Piers Verderan caution and slow him down.

The next barrier was an oxer—two fences with space between. An in-and-out. Nelson took it in style and then set off up a gentle slope. Emily had to ease him a little, for this was the end of a long day for him. A worried glance showed her Beelzebub cruising up the hill as if it was the flat.

Once over the top, though, she raced down towards an unusual obstacle—a hedge with a ditch on both sides. It could be jumped from this side by clearing both ditch and hedge at the precise spot where the latter was low, then taking precarious footing on a bit of firm ground to leap the far ditch. She and Marcus had mastered it once, and she knew she could do it again. Verderan would have to go a quarter mile to the gate.

She set Nelson firmly at the barrier despite his doubts, and he cleared it. The horse faltered slightly at the far side when he saw the second ditch, but she held him steady and took him over it.

"Good boy," she praised the fidgety horse once they were on firm ground. Nelson was obviously having grave doubts about her sanity.

She turned to wave a cheery goodbye to her pursuer.

And saw Piers Verderan setting his horse at the jump.

"No!" she cried.

He'd obviously watched her technique. Beelzebub hopped over the fence short, which was the only way to land right on the far side, then tried to jump the ditch. His footing slipped and he pecked badly, sending his rider crashing to the ground even as the horse recovered and found firm ground.

Verderan lay still. Beelzebub stood close by, head lowered as if apologising.

Emily cantered Nelson down, flung herself off, and ran to Verderan's side.

"Oh, my God," she whispered, as she searched his body with her eyes and hands for broken bones or swellings.

His blue eyes opened, smiling, his arms came around her, and he dragged her on top of him. "There's no place you cannot get over with a fall," he said with a grin. "Tom Assheton-Smith definitely knows his stuff."

Emily struggled. "You crazy man! You could have killed yourself!"

"Then I'd have died for love of you," he said.

Emily stopped fighting and lay plastered over him, head to foot. "You can't really love me," she protested.

"And you can't be such a widgeon. Love isn't rational or ordered, Emily. It's mad and wonderfully crazy."

"Then you don't want to love me," she said sadly.

He kissed her. "I didn't sit down one day and say 'I want to fall in love with Emily Grantwich.' But I am in love with you, and it is utterly delightful. Are you in love with me?"

"No," said Emily, instinctively keeping her head down on his chest. He said nothing and she eventually had to peep at him.

He raised a skeptical brow. "I'm the world's most conceited fellow," he said. "You'll have to work hard to convince me of that."

She struggled again, but the angel wings had turned to bands of iron. "I don't want to love you," she said, collapsing once more onto his chest. With a smirk she added, "You're going to be awfully muddy."

"I'll doubtless get rheumatics," he agreed. "Will you minister to me, Emily? Rub liniment into my shoulders . . ." His hands moved to massage her shoulders, sending a shiver of pleasure down her spine. ". . . My poor aching back . . ." His hands moved down to press and rub in the small of her back.

Emily took a deep shuddering breath and wriggled. He took a deep shuddering breath beneath her.

"And lower?" he murmured, moving his hands lower to cup her bottom.

"What are you doing?" she whispered.

"Getting carried away," he admitted softly. "One of us is going to have to put a ruthless stop to this, or take the consequences. And you're on top."

Emily began to scramble off him, but then she looked and saw his darkened eyes, the touch of colour in his cheeks, saw the way he breathed. A sense of power came over her that she could do this to a man, to this man. Slowly, against the screaming of her conscience, she lowered her lips to his.

His hands came around her again, and the fire burst into flame. He rolled them halfway, and her hands sought the lines of his back, the smooth skin of his nape, the crisp edge of his hair. She felt a hand slide around her and up to her breast . . .

Then he was up and away from her, breathing as if he'd run a race. He went a few steps and leant on his horse. Emily scrambled to her feet and looked down helplessly at the muddy mess all over her habit.

He turned to face her. "When are you going to marry me?" he asked.

She looked up helplessly. "I'm not," she said. "I can't. I don't belong in your world."

"I will make my world whatever you want it to be."

"Respectable?" asked Emily with an edge.

He sucked in a breath. "That's a low blow, Emily. I think I can create a degree of respectability for you if you wish. Though why you'd wish, I don't know. Think of all the people you'd have to spend your time with. Respectability's like heaven. The big problem with heaven is the people who are so certain they'll be there. Hell has always seemed more promising to me."

"There you are, see," said Emily in despair. "I can't marry someone who wants to go to Hell."

She walked blindly over to Nelson and looked up, unable to mount such a big horse without some kind of aid.

He came over and offered his linked hands. She put her foot in and was tossed up. She settled into the saddle.

"I could give you heaven on earth, Emily," he said.

She looked down and knew he could. "That's blasphemy."

"Religion again." He put his hand up and covered hers on the pommel. His face was serious; his eyes dark and intense. "I can show you delights of mind and body, and learn them from you, too. I will set you free to explore the world, and yourself, and me. And I'll be a secure haven when you need one. Marry me, Emily."

It was as if he truly laid heaven on earth out before her as temptation, but a heaven she could hardly believe in. Life wasn't like that. Life was duty and responsibility and trying to live up to other people's impossible standards.

"I can't," she whispered.

She saw the pain wash briefly over his beautiful face and that made it worse. She'd believed, despite the evidence of her senses, that this was a game for him, a passing fancy. Now she saw the truth . . .

Then he masked it with a smile and ran his hand down Nelson's neck. "A fine horse. I'd like to match him against Beelzebub, both fresh, one day. And," he added pointedly, "over a fair course."

"All's fair—" Emily stopped herself completing that saying.

"—in love," he supplied.

"You'll doubtless be able to match Beelzebub against Nelson," she said quickly. "He'll be hunted at the first Quorn meet next Tuesday."

"I rarely ride Bel in a hunt," he said.

"But you were the one who lectured me about keeping fine horses to tame work!"

"I was, wasn't I," he admitted ruefully. "I'm too fond of Bel to risk him in a rough field, but I take him along as a second horse and run him if it's not too wild."

Emily patted Nelson's neck. "Do horses get injured often?" she asked.

"It depends a lot on the rider, how many risks he takes and how skilful he is." He went over and swung up onto his horse. "I'm the only one who ever rides Bel these days, and I know I sometimes ride wild, so I protect him from my baser nature."

Emily wondered if there was a message there for her.

140

He walked Beelzebub over to her side. "I purchased him for a mistress who believed a fine black horse would set off her colouring. She proved to be unworthy of him, so I bought him back with a diamond parure. She was so delighted by the exchange that I knew her to be unworthy of me too. Do we take the hedge back?"

This was showing her his baser side with a vengeance. After a moment Emily found her voice. "It can't be jumped from this side. There's not enough ground on the other side between the hedge and ditch."

He rode over and studied it, then came back and said, "Nonsense."

As he turned to ride at the obstacle Emily shouted, "Mr. Verderan, no! Don't!"

He swung his horse back. "My name, among friends, is Ver."

"Your name is Piers," she corrected.

"I don't like to be called Piers. Ver."

"Ver's a silly name. It's French for worm."

"I know. Do you find it appropriate? People don't seem to make much of it, somehow."

"Because you'd shoot them," she pointed out tartly.

"Very likely," he replied and turned back to the hedge.

Emily tightened her lips, but as he urged Beelzebub forward she shouted, "Ver, for God's sake, stop it!"

He turned back, eyes bright and laughing.

"Damn you," she said. "Would you have tried it?"

"Yes, and your language is becoming less ladylike by the day. I live in hope."

"You live in your own portable Bedlam," she retorted, and set off for the gate at a canter.

He came to ride alongside her. "Haven't you ever realised how much fun it is to be mad?"

"No," she said repressively, though she knew what he meant.

"Let me teach you," he said seductively.

Emily just urged Nelson to greater speed.

He rode alongside her all the way home without saying another word, and Emily was aware of him as if he were a fire burning there, heating her without touching. This was impossible.

At Grantwich Hall he rode into the stables with her and introduced Beelzebub to Haverby.

"My, he's a fine one, sir," said the groom appreciatively.

"Yes, he is. Just water him when he's cool."

He strolled around the stalls, assessing the horses. "Sound hunters," he said at last. "Nelson is the best, I'd say. Worth a fair bit."

"Yes," said Emily. It reminded her that he had paid a hundred and fifty guineas for Titania, which was more than she expected to get for any of her horses. She set off briskly for the house.

When he came up with her she heard herself say sourly, "And how is the girl? Worth what you paid?"

He stopped her with a hand on her arm. "Emily, I didn't pay for Titania to set her up as my mistress."

"Just a temporary convenience, is she?"

His lips tightened. "Your language is becoming a little too unladylike. I have no interest in the girl at all."

"It seems to me," she declared, "you have a hundred and fifty guineas' worth of interest."

"For a determinedly decent woman, you have a decidedly *tart* edge to your voice, my dear. She's free to do as she wishes, and I haven't touched her. Do you believe me?"

Emily looked at him, feeling slightly ashamed. "Yes."

"Good. I'll never lie to you."

"So," said Emily. "If I find her a suitable position, you won't stand in my way?"

He gave a little sigh. "No, of course not, but, Emily, Titania's views on suitable positions and yours are not exactly in harmony."

Emily nodded. "I see she's ambitious and I admire her for that. She has pretty manners when she tries. Perhaps I can find her a position as a companion."

"I doubt it, but even if you could, a companion will not make the kind of money Titania stands to make plying her trade."

"Whoring? She can't *want* to do that."

"Yes, she can," he said. "With the right protector it's as

good as being married. She'll have a house and carriage, servants and jewels. Look at Harriette Wilson. And with luck she'll get to keep most of it when she changes hands . . ."

"Changes hands!" protested Emily.

"Usually when the man marries. It's not good form for a married man to keep a regular mistress, especially when newly wed. She'll have a say as to whom she goes to next and it's not beyond reason that she marry one of them. Emma Hamilton did, after all."

"But it's wrong," protested Emily doggedly.

"So conventional morality says, but it's marriage without the church and a far better marriage than a girl like Titania could ever dream of. Not as permanent as Holy Wedlock, I'll grant you, but generally a good deal more honest."

"And you have the nerve to ask me to marry you?" Emily snapped.

He reached out and cupped her cheek. "If you marry me, Emily, I'll never take another woman to my bed."

"I can't," she said blindly, pulled away and marched on towards the house. He attempted no further persuasion.

There she found Randal and Sophie being entertained quite conventionally by Junia in an old grey round gown with a tear in the skirt.

Junia stared. "My goodness, Emily, you must have had a fall!"

Emily looked down at her habit and flushed. "Yes, I did. I'll just change if you will excuse me, Lady Randal, Lord Randal."

As she stripped off the muddied garment she wondered how Verderan would explain his soiled clothing. He wouldn't even bother to try, and anyway, Junia, Randal and Sophie would all guess exactly what had occurred.

He was like water on a stone—or more likely, fire at a pile of kindling. He was destroying her will and the standards in which she had been reared. Each time they met he made the idea of marriage to him seem a little less ridiculous, and a great deal more pleasant.

But could she live with a man who thought whoring an honest profession and hell more attractive than heaven and who shot people who did not share his taste in food?

= 10 =

WHEN SHE WENT downstairs, Emily found Verderan had already left, making his damp and muddy garments his excuse. She was alarmed at how much she missed him. The rot was already deep.

After tea, the four walked out into the garden and Junia went ahead with Sophie, while Emily followed with Lord Randal. She was aware of a desire, a craving, to bring the conversation around to Verderan. He did it for her.

"My considered opinion," he said bluntly, "is that you should marry Ver, you know."

"Why?" Emily asked.

"Apart from the fact you love each other?" he queried, bringing heat to her cheeks. "Ver needs you." He flashed her a charming smile. "I know I'm supposed to be your protector, but my friendship with Ver goes back a long way. I have to take his needs into account too."

"Do you think such a marriage would be to my benefit at all, my lord?" Emily demanded.

"Of course. It does no one any harm to be loved. Of course, if you set tremendous store on pattern-card respectability there would be problems. I don't think Ver will settle to that any more than I am likely to."

"I have always thought respectability to be very important," said Emily. She tried to make it sound like a declaration of faith, but he caught the cavil in it.

"And now?" he asked.

"And now," she admitted, "I don't know . . ." Emily

quickly turned to another subject. "Lord Randal, do horses often get injured in the hunt?"

"Assuredly. Some men regard it as an exercise in derring-do and will fly at anything."

"What of Dick Christian? Do you know him?"

"Of course. He's a fine rider and a good judge of horse and obstacle. Still, his job is usually to make the horse look like a prime hunter, to push it. If he thinks a horse could really shine he'll challenge it. Why do you ask?"

"I need to sell my father's hunters," she admitted. "I have hired him to ride them."

He looked slightly startled. "Is that wise—selling them, I mean?"

"There is no one to ride them," she pointed out.

"But still. Your brother . . ."

"My brother is almost certainly dead or badly injured, Lord Randal. My father wants them sold." She found herself adding, "The successful sale is the price for me keeping control of the estate out of Cousin Felix's hands." What was it about Lord Randal Ashby that broke through her natural reticence?

"Hm." He seemed very thoughtful. "And the one you rode today. Is he to be sold first?"

"No," Emily said. "I wanted to see how Christian worked out. He is to ride Wallingford next Monday—a good sound hunter, then Nelson the next day. Will you be at the first meet? It's the Cottesmore, I believe."

"No. I'm not hunting this year." The tender glance towards his wife told Emily the reason. She envied Sophie that kind of devotion and wondered if Piers Verderan would give up hunting for her.

"That's a shame," she commented on his decision. "I need someone to negotiate for me. I can do it, or father—though he's so tetchy these days. A Meltonian would be better."

"Ask Ver."

It was the obvious solution, but one her instincts screamed against. "That wouldn't be wise."

Randal let the matter drop. He found this eagerness to sell the horses amusing, considering the imminent return of the son of the house, but he wasn't supposed to tell anyone about Marcus Grantwich's goings-on.

Later that day, however, he reported the conversation to Verderan.

"I had the impression the sale of the horses was some sort of wager," said Verderan. "It sounds a dim-witted one. Typical of Sir Henry, I suspect."

"What do you think is going to happen when Captain Grantwich comes back to find his stables bare?" Randal asked with amusement.

"Serves him right," said Verderan callously. "I've taken the man in dislike in absentia. He never seems to have valued Emily as he should and has shown a callous disregard for his family in the past year. Even if his activities were secret he could have assured himself of their well-being. In fact, I'll be happy to do my best to sell all the horses as quickly as possible."

"Then Emily will need someone to handle the sale for her."

Verderan smiled. "Indeed she will, and it will give substance to rumours of closeness if I do it. As well," he added wickedly, "as giving me an excellent reason to visit her tomorrow."

Thus Emily was brought the news at the breakfast table that Mr. Verderan wished to see her. As she was alone— Junia was breakfasting in bed—she indulged in sheer bravado and had him brought to her at table.

"You're about so *early*," she said meaningfully, "you are probably hungry. May I offer you anything?"

He sat down opposite her, completely at his ease. "Anything?" he queried, causing her to blush. "I have eaten," he went on smoothly, "but I would like some coffee if there's any left in the pot."

Emily prayed for cool cheeks as she rang for an extra cup. "A little early for a call, is it not?"

"You're such an *active* young lady," he riposted. "I was afraid you'd be out again. I'm getting too old to be always haring around the countryside after you."

Emily choked on a piece of toast at such an obvious bouncer.

Instead of Mary, Mrs. Dobson stalked into the breakfast room with a cup and saucer in hand. She banged it down on the table dangerously hard and surveyed Verderan, tight-lipped. He flashed Emily a questioning, even alarmed, look. She had to fight a case of the giggles. How exactly did one introduce a rakish suitor to an overprotective housekeeper?

"Eh, Dobby, this is Mr. Verderan. Casper Sillitoe's heir. Mr. Verderan, this is Mrs. Dobson, our housekeeper. She's been with us forever," she explained.

He turned on one of his most charming smiles and rose to his feet to bow. "Mrs. Dobson, I'm delighted to make your acquaintance."

Dobby actually blushed. If it wasn't a flush of anger. Her words made it clear she was no more immune to his invei-gling than any other woman. "Well, I never. Pleasure I'm sure. Not but what it's a mite early . . . but then again . . ." She looked around at a loss and grasped her true business with relief. "Perhaps you'd like some toast, sir. Or ham. I've lovely fresh eggs . . ."

"Having tasted your cooking recently I'm very tempted, Mrs. Dobson, but I've already breakfasted."

"Yes, well," said the woman hazily. "I'll be on my way, then." She showed she was not totally bamboozled by adding, "I'll just leave the door open, Miss Emily."

"Well," said Emily, as she poured coffee into his cup. "What a disgraceful exhibition."

"You shouldn't be so harsh on the poor lady."

"I was referring to you, Mr. Verderan," said Emily frostily. "Have you no shame?"

"No," he said with a smile. "I like this."

"What?" Emily asked warily.

"Sitting across the table from you in the morning."

Emily smiled tightly. "And you without a hangover. How remarkable."

"Emily, darling, put some sugar in your coffee. I never have hangovers."

She suppressed all awareness of the "darling" and raised a skeptical brow.

"I told you I'd never lie to you. I don't get hangovers.

These days I rarely drink enough to even get bosky."

"Next you'll be telling me you don't gamble."

"Certainly I do, but that's one reason I don't drown my wits. If I gamble I keep my head straight."

Emily remembered some of the stories her brother and father told of their nights at the tables. "Isn't that a little unsporting?"

He chuckled. "Doubtless. But I don't force others into the fourth bottle."

Emily was finding this all too beguiling. She too could imagine the joys of regularly taking breakfast with him. "So, Mr. Verderan," she said firmly, "what is your reason for this early visit? If you are concerned about the sheep on High Burton, I have arranged for the repairs to be made."

"I don't give a damn about the sheep on High Burton," he said amiably. "For all I care, they can eat the covert and the foxes too."

Emily gasped.

"I came for the simple pleasure of seeing you, my ruling passion, my all-consuming flame."

Emily felt a proper lady would flee, but it seemed foolish to flee mere words. Some words, however, did not merit the description "mere." She heard herself gasp a pathetic, "Please don't!"

"Emily," he chided gently. "Throw off this dull conformity. You don't want or need it any more than you want your grandmother's stomacher. I'm taking pleasure from just sitting here across the table from you. Can you deny you are pleased to have me here?"

She pushed away from the table, away from him. She put the width of the room between them. "You confuse me," she complained.

He stayed at the table, cradling his coffee cup. "That's because you are confusing yourself. The part of you that's been raised to be good, to be modest, to be meek, is fighting with the part that wants to be bold, adventurous, and free." He put the cup down. "I'm offering freedom, Emily, so unfortunately I can't, or won't, force you."

She looked at him, her gaze level and uncompromising.

"What are you doing now, then?"

"Persuading," he said with a smile and rose to come over to her. There was something in his eyes which made her take a few steps back until she bumped against the wall.

"Don't."

"What?" He stopped an arm's length away.

"I don't know," she whispered.

"I do, and so do your senses." His voice was as soft and mellow as a fine instrument. "I could seduce you here and now, Emily, and you know it. I could touch you," he said softly, and his eyes began to wander caressingly over her body, "and flames would run down your nerves . . ." She felt those flames come from his gaze and burn on her skin. "Flames that would join together to fill you with heat and send you shooting into the sky like the sparks from a Guy Fawkes bonfire."

Emily was lost in the fire and in his deep blue eyes. "I could stretch out my hand," he said steadily, "and you would put yours into it . . ."

Belatedly, Emily realised she had done just that. She tried to tug free, but he drew her slowly towards him. ". . . and I could do with you whatever I would wish. . . . That however," he murmured, when she was nestled in his arms, "would be forcing, no matter how cunningly done."

His voice took on a more normal tone. "You're too vulnerable to this sort of thing, my dear." He let her go and moved away. Emily wrapped her arms around herself, feeling vulnerable and frighteningly bereft. "So I can only persuade," he said laconically. "I came to offer to handle the sale of your horses."

"What?"

"Wallingford et al., he gently reminded her. "Christian is riding them. If there's interest, and I'm sure there will be, I will handle the sale at the club. Do you have a minimum?"

She shook her head, still struggling to make the transition to business.

"You should. Let's say eighty. If he runs well you'll get a hundred. You'll get more for Nelson. Possibly up to two hundred. Will that be enough?"

"Lord Randal told you?" she asked.

"Of course. How much do you need?"

She disciplined her mind. "Three hundred in all," she said.

"That should be possible," he agreed and prepared to leave.

"Mr. Verderan," she said sharply, and he turned.

"I thought we'd progressed to Ver," he complained.

"Only when you're risking your life over impossible obstacles," she retorted.

"What an interesting marriage we're going to have, my smoldering ember. Are you going to marry me?"

The question was tossed out so casually that it took a moment to register. When it did, Emily fought insanity and shook her head.

He sighed, but did not seem to be crushingly discouraged, which in view of his recent demonstration of power was not surprising. "What were you going to say?" he asked.

"What?" Emily couldn't remember. Then she gathered her wits. "You are not to buy my horses," she said.

"Why not? I like the look of Nelson."

"It's a wager. It wouldn't be fair to fix it that way. You are not to buy them or arrange for them to be bought. I have to do this fair and square."

He looked at her for a moment, then shrugged. "As you will." He came back to her and touched her cheek gently. "Think hard about freedom, Emily. It is not always easy to claim our liberty, but the pains are worth it. 'Freedom has a thousand charms to show, that slaves howe'er contented, never know.' "

"I am not a contented slave," she protested.

He chose deliberately to misunderstand. "Then there's all the less reason to remain one."

Then he was gone.

Emily couldn't think of a single reason not to run after him and throw herself into his arms and into his keeping except a lifetime of proper behaviour and restraint.

Proper behaviour and restraint seemed a damnable business all in all.

For the first time the idea began to root that the next time he asked her to marry him she might say yes. That she might marry him and follow the whim of the moment. Might marry him and be cherished. Might marry him and let the passion in them both burn free.

It was terrifying.

It was exciting.

It was, just possibly, inevitable.

Junia came in and looked at her. "Why are you grinning like a simpleton? Ah," she said after a minute. "Excellent."

Emily didn't see Piers Verderan for days. She took to riding out more often than was necessary and heading in the direction of Hume House. She never encountered him.

She found herself listening for any scrap of gossip about him and his house-party, and there was certainly plenty of that but all very tame. From the local point of view it was rather disappointing, but Emily found it comforting.

Titania had apparently left the house along with the Daffodil Dandy, who was apparently a Mr. Renfrew. The rumour was that she'd gone to London to become a famous actress, but Emily could easily think of simpler explanations. She was very relieved to think the girl was away from Verderan.

As for the young men, they ate, rode, ate, gambled, ate, drank, and ate. Mrs. Greely was having a wonderful time, one gathered, catering to such healthy appetites.

On Saturday, Sophie came over to visit, accompanied only by a groom. Randal and Verderan, she explained, were off shooting, which she found very unpleasant.

"So I thought it would be enjoyable to have some female company for a change. If you're not too busy."

"Of course not," said Emily, taking in Sophie's elegance with some envy. Her blue habit was very stylish, but it was her short burnished curls and a general air of polish which were utterly unprovincial. Emily would not have the slightest notion of how to achieve such an effect. All her doubts seeped back. Titania and the Violet Tart were Verderan's type of woman; Sophie was doubtless his type of lady.

Emily had neither the style nor the beauty to compete with either.

She rang for tea. "If you and Lord Randal would find it more comfortable to stay with us here, Lady Randal, we would be delighted to have you."

"Oh no, Miss Grantwich," said Sophie merrily. "It's great fun at Hume House. I'm sure you would enjoy it tremendously, too. In fact," she confessed with a wrinkle of her charming nose, "it's wonderful not to have *ladies* disapproving of me all the time. Gentlemen are generally more relaxed about things. And I would like it if you were to call me Sophie. Lady Randal always sounds like someone much grander and older than I."

"I would be pleased to. And I hope you will call me Emily."

Thus relaxed, they were soon engaged in chatter over tea and Mrs. Dobson's most buttery tea cakes. Emily sought extra news of Chloe and was amused by the stories of Verderan and Chloe's young son, Stevie. When, however, Sophie related how Verderan had stripped almost naked in the middle of a picnic to rescue the child's wooden horse from the river, she couldn't help but be shocked.

"You mustn't look so," said Sophie. "It was so hot he was an object of envy, not horror. Next year, Randal's going to teach me to swim." After a moment, she added, "I hope you don't think this impertinent, but I do hope you can bring yourself to marry Ver."

"You too? Everyone in the world . . . well," said Emily, incurably honest, "not Hector, I'm sure."

Sophie chuckled. "Is he the outraged vicar? I wouldn't marry him," she advised. "He'd want to improve you."

Emily sighed. "I always thought improvement to be desirable."

Sophie cocked her head. "Self-improvement. Perhaps even mutual improvement. But does he think you're going to improve him?"

Emily's mind boggled. "I hardly think so," she admitted. "Have you improved Lord Randal then?"

Sophie frowned slightly. "Sometimes too much. It's hard

not to coddle someone one loves so very much, Emily. He's not hunting because of me. I've decided the only thing is for us both to hunt. I'm going to work on it."

"But ladies don't," Emily protested.

"If I hunt and anyone tries to claim I am not a lady," said Sophie with unconscious arrogance, "they'll receive short shrift from many quarters. There are ladies who follow the hounds, you know—the Marchioness of Salisbury is Master of the Hatfield Harriers, and both Queen Elizabeth and Queen Anne were very partial to the sport. If I persuade Randal," she said with a twinkle, "will you come too?"

Emily felt a flash of panic at the thought. "I couldn't, Sophie."

"Why not?"

"What would people say?"

"Why should you care?"

"I have to live here."

"Not if you marry Ver."

Emily found her hands gripped together. "It's not the sort of thing I do," she admitted. "I never make a scene, or shock people. It—it would be like throwing oneself in the river in the belief one would float."

"Or find a solid raft," said Sophie. "Ver's already out there, Emily. He'd look after you."

"How solid a raft has he got?" Emily asked dubiously. "Has he done all the things they say?"

"I don't know," admitted Sophie. "Probably. But the ones I've heard of aren't so very terrible—"

"Shooting people?" Emily queried.

"Nasty people. I heard quite a bit about Brightly Carstock, for example, because one of his victims was at school with me. He persuaded her to elope, then let her father buy him off. But he'd already had his way . . . to be honest, he'd raped her violently. I don't think she ever recovered. I gather she wasn't the only one, and he used to fleece innocent young men out of their money. I don't know why he and Verderan finally came to dueling, but you can see why people were willing to pass the whole thing off."

"I suppose so," said Emily, but a part of her said it wasn't right, any more than killing Jake Mulholland would be right.

"Anyway," said Sophie, "Ver's changed too. He's more—more relaxed these days. Less acidic. He's floating in calmer waters. It would be a shame to see him back among the shoals."

She leant forward, suddenly more serious and sober. "I want Ver to find happiness, Emily. I really do believe he deserves it but"—she shrugged and frowned as she sought for words—"it's as if he and Randal are part of each other. Until Ver is settled, Randal will never be. I don't mean settled in a boring sense, but just at ease in their hearts. In some way it's Randal's finding me that's calmed them both, but Ver has to find his own love to complete it. You are that love."

There was something frightening about this intensity, this complexity. "How can you be sure?"

"How can I not be?" Sophie said. "It's like looking in a mirror."

"You were reluctant too?" asked Emily.

"I?" said Sophie with a laugh. "I pursued Randal relentlessly from the schoolroom, probably from the nursery. But it's the same. You can no more get rid of Verderan now than you could cut out your heart and live."

To Emily this sounded terrifyingly true.

Sophie rose and drew on her gloves. "I don't think I can work on Randal by the first meet. But by the time the Quorn meets on Tuesday I hope to have done the trick. Will you come with us?"

"What will Verderan think?" Emily asked as she stood.

"Tsk, tsk," said Sophie. "If you think he'd object, then you don't know Ver. If you care, you have a long way to go."

"Oh really," said Emily sharply, resenting this tone from a girl a good eight years her junior. "Well, if I don't know Mr. Verderan, I'd be a fool to marry him, wouldn't I? And if I go hunting, I'll be the talk of the area for years to come and I'll *have* to marry him."

"Good," said an unrepentant Sophie. "So, shall I tell Ver that if you join the hunt on Tuesday next, you'll marry him?

If he objects, I wouldn't marry him anyway."

Emily gaped. "I—I can't . . ."

Sophie's bright blue eyes challenged her. Emily remembered other darker blue eyes challenging her to take risk, taste danger . . .

"Yes," she said harshly. "Let the challenge stand. This can't go on forever. But I still don't know which I'll do, Sophie, and you still have to get your husband's permission."

"Not permission," pointed out Sophie. "Agreement. And he'll be sure to agree with such a tempting situation as a reward."

With that Sophie was off, leaving Emily aware that she had been cleverly manipulated into a do-or-die situation come Tuesday.

Back at Hume House, Sophie greeted Randal and Ver on their return with the news. "Emily Grantwich says that if she turns out with the Quorn next Tuesday, she'll marry you, Ver."

Randal for once looked slightly bemused. Verderan looked nearly as dangerous as his old self. "What have you done, Sophie?"

"Are you threatening to whip me again?" she asked saucily, but moved closer to Randal just in case.

"You're a married lady now," Verderan said. "I'll leave such matters to your husband."

"How stuffy you sound," Sophie retorted. "I'll report this back to Emily," she warned, "and then she'll never marry you."

"What have you done, Sophie?" asked Randal, but more gently.

Sophie began to feel slightly uneasy. "Emily admitted she needed to take a plunge. She's going to teeter on the edge forever if someone doesn't give her a push. I said I wanted to ride with the hunt next Tuesday and asked her to come along."

"I think Ver can do his own pushing," said Randal with a look in his eye she didn't much like. "And we're not hunting."

"Emily won't go without some support," Sophie said. "I promise not to take risks."

"You're taking quite a few at the moment, minx. Why do you think we should hunt?"

"Because you want to really, and so do I, and if we always stay safe it's going to be a long life but boring, Randal."

"I'm sorry you're finding it tedious," he said with an edge.

Sophie coloured. "Randal!"

Verderan cleared his throat. "If this is going to turn into a domestic dispute with the predictable reconciliation, I think I should leave. On the whole, I think Sophie's manoeuvre is masterly, Randal. Emily does need to be pushed. I think I can also—not being above devious devices—give the situation a few twitches of my own. The first is to draw it to your attention that a certain Mr. Sadler of Nottingham intends to launch a balloon on Monday from a site this side of Leicester. Keep an eye on the winds, my friends. I'm sure Emily could be persuaded to ride out to watch for such a sight. My other piece of meddling I can handle for myself." With that he left them.

Sophie watched him leave, then turned to Randal with a mixture of belligerence and nervousness.

After a second he laughed. "Disputes are so tedious, aren't they? Let's skip that part. Come and be reconciled, love."

= 11 =

VERDERAN WENT INTO Melton in search of Dick Christian. He was fortunate enough to run his man down without too much trouble in his favourite haunt, the Blue Bell.

Christian nodded when Verderan sat down beside him. "Taken by another charitable urge, Mr. Verderan?" he asked hopefully.

"In a way," said Verderan, ordering ale for them both. "You're to ride Wallingford for the Grantwiches on Monday?"

Christian nodded.

"What sort of horse is it?"

"Neatish, sir," said Christian readily. "Good rump and hocks. Forelegs well afore but perhaps a little thin in the shoulders. Responds well. None of those horses seems to have been handled rough like."

"I have a feeling you won't have to ride any of the others," Verderan said and took a pull of his ale. "What I'd like, without any injury to the horse, is for you to make your run on Wallingford to look dangerous, particularly if there should be observers about. Particularly," he added, "if one of those observers should happen to be Miss Grantwich."

The man looked at him shrewdly. "Dangerous to me or the horse?"

"To the horse."

The roughrider drank his ale. "I could probably bring him down without hurting him, sir. That kind of thing?"

"Yes. But not to break his spirit."

"I wouldn't do that to a horse, sir. Not for a thousand guineas."

Verderan took the hint and passed over another twenty.

"And you don't think I'll be called on to ride the others?" Christian asked as he pocketed it. "I have plenty would take up the spot."

"I don't think so, but I'm sure Miss Grantwich will send word."

"Fair enough, sir," said Christian. "And," he added with a grin, "you know where to find me if you need me again."

Verderan continued his waiting game, knowing it would be more effective than pressure. He saw Emily only when he and the whole party at Hume House went to Sunday service in the village. The Reverend Marshalswick was decidedly cool, though his sister was friendly when not under her brother's eye.

Verderan got to shake Emily's hand, which was better than nothing. "You are looking a little peaked," he remarked. "Working too hard?"

"How very unflattering," she retorted sharply. "And you know it is decisions which prey on me, not labours."

"I never flatter," he countered. "You stir my senses to delirium even when peaked, dear one. And I didn't force you into accepting ultimata. Renege if you wish."

It was delight to watch the sequence of emotions pass over her face. He'd known from the first she would be delicious to fluster. She latched onto his last challenge. "Of course not," she snapped, as he had intended.

"If you join the hunt on Tuesday, will you ride Nelson, Emily? If so, you should let Christian know soon enough to allow him time to settle for another ride. It's his livelihood."

"You do not need to lecture me on proper behaviour, Mr. Verderan."

"Of course not," he said, fighting down an urge to fold her into his arms and soothe her cares away. "I merely wanted to offer to ride Nelson myself on Tuesday, if necessary. That way, you could release Christian now. And since Randal will probably ride, he could take the other horse— Oak-apple, I believe."

She was flustered and perplexed again. "That's very kind

of you, Mr. Verderan," she said with a frown. "I'm just not sure—"

"If it's fair? You're more meticulous about these things than most men. As I understand it, you can sell the horses any way you wish. You could even accept five hundred guineas for the whole string here and now."

"Five hundred!" she gasped.

"Yes."

"No."

"As you will. Do I get to ride Nelson, then?"

"No, I do," Emily snapped.

He smiled, feeling the distinct possibility of winning her spread through him like brandy. "Excellent," he said. "You're going to make me very happy."

She went bright pink , but made no attempt at a rebuttal and beat a hasty retreat. He watched her until she was out of sight.

Emily set a blistering pace during the walk back to Grantwich Hall until Junia protested. "Emily! I consider myself in prime case for someone my age, but I'm winded."

Emily immediately slowed almost to a crawl. In fact, crawling into a hole for a month or two seemed very attractive.

"Piers Verderan," guessed Junia. "I wish you would make up your mind and either put the poor man out of his misery or make us all happy."

"I don't even know why everyone is so set on the match. A less likely couple is hard to imagine."

"The Violet Tart and Hector Marshalswick," said Junia promptly, startling a spurt of laughter out of Emily.

"I give you that, but truly, it's like an eagle and a dove. We have nothing in common."

"You will grow together," Junia said. "You will learn to fly high and he will learn to enjoy the comforts of the dovecote."

Emily stopped and looked at Junia. "That doesn't make any sense. Eagles eat doves."

"Doesn't, does it? But it's a pretty fancy. So, what are you going to do?"

"Wait until Tuesday. It all comes down to the first Quorn

meet. If I ride the hunt, I'll marry him. If I do," she added morosely, "I'll have to."

Junia demanded an explanation and as soon as she had it she looked very pleased. "Admirable. By luck or genius, Lady Randal has hit upon the very thing. If you don't ride the hunt, you don't deserve him, anyway."

"It is hardly a proof of moral value," Emily protested.

"No, but it's a test of courage."

"And what test is he to pass?" Emily demanded.

"He's already passed, I think. Why do you assume," demanded Junia with unusual severity, "that it's easy for a man like him, or any man, to lay himself open to a woman, to be vulnerable? Just because he puts on a bold face, do not assume that he cannot be hurt."

"I never asked him to," Emily protested.

"No, but you could appreciate the way he's trying to handle fate. I think it is time for me to tell you more about Piers Verderan."

On Monday, the first of November, Verderan, Chart, Harry, and Corny set off to the first meet of the season, a meet of the Cottesmore pack. The four men were on hacks, their favourite hunters having gone up at first light so as to be rested and fresh for the run. Lacking the grooms to ride spares, the trio were depending on one horse each for the day, but Verderan had sent three horses ahead. He would start out on a grey called Thorwick. In case of a particularly hard run he had Ulysses to change to and, in case of an easier day, Beelzebub. The grooms who rode them would keep in touch with the hunt without pushing the horses and would come up if summoned.

It was the sort of day hunters dream of, clear and sunny but without any frost. There was only a light breeze and the sky was virtually cloudless.

At the meet they found all the excitement of the first real day of hunting. The black, white, and tan hounds were milling ready, tails wagging, controlled by their huntsman and whippers-in.

The greats were there—Lord Lonsdale, of course, as he

was the Master of the Cottesmore; a party from Belvoir including Beau Brummell; Alvanley, Sefton, Jersey, Althorpe, and Quarley Wilson; Assheton-Smith was there, though his hounds wouldn't have their first run until the next day.

There were a number of Blackcoats, or parsons, and many Browncoats, or farmers, and local professionals. There were, of course, the usual body of graziers and tradesmen in their blue coats, led by their longtime leader, John Marriot. But the vast majority were in the traditional gentlemanly pink.

There was even the famous chimney sweep, in his tall black hat and waving the symbol of his trade, a brush. He was hailed and welcomed by all. Hunting, after all, was a sport for anyone with a horse, and on the field only riding counted.

Dick Christian rode easily among the throng on Wallingford. As he had said, it was a promising horse if a little narrow in the shoulders. As he worked his way around he would drop a word as to who to approach if anyone thought the beast promising. There were always plenty of people interested in a horse ridden by him, hoping that by purchasing such a horse they would magically be transformed into such a gifted rider.

Among the high spirits, someone started to sing of the famous Billesdon-Coplow run of 1800—twenty-eight miles which weeded out the men from the boys and left Thomas Assheton-Smith famous for being first in at the end, even though in the end the fox had won free. Soon all joined in:

The Coplow of Billesdon ne'er witnessed I we'en
Two hundred such horses and men at a burst
All determined to ride, each resolved to be first . . .

But Lonsdale cut short the chorus and moved his hounds out. The nearly two hundred riders followed after, making their way to the first covert, where they hoped to find a fox. It was now nearly noon, but early that morning the earthstoppers had been all around this area, stopping up the entrances to the foxes' holes, in the hope that at least one charley would take refuge in this covert.

At the chosen spot, a spinney with plenty of ground cover, the hounds were thrown in and eagerly began to draw. The riders waited. Some dismounted and took a little liquid refreshment. Others hovered around the covert, hoping to see the fox break and call the halloo to alert the Master and the hounds.

Then suddenly, a red flash, a halloo, and the dismounted hurry into the saddle. The hounds are gathered at the spot where the fox broke and are cast to find the scent. Soon the best of them have it. Baying, they stream like a cream and gold tide across the field after the fleeing fox.

Immediately the horsemen follow, keeping behind but up. The fox slips under a brush fence. The hounds push through. The riders must leap or search for a gate.

The hunt is on.

There was no direct evidence of the hunt at Grantwich Hall, but everyone was aware of it. Sir Henry was in a terrible mood and Emily was obsessed by the morrow's decision.

What Junia had told her of Verderan's childhood had both shocked and touched her. She could imagine all too well the running battle between the spring-steel nature of Verderan and his despotic grandfather. Old Lord Templemore would have started with bluster but gone on to harsher and harsher measures, determined in the end to break what he could not mold.

And perhaps in some way he had succeeded in that, for the man today was surely not the person who would have grown from a happy youth. The flaunting of Society, the anger, the killing—these, she was sure, were all Templemore's work.

On the other hand, she had to admit that he had exhibited little of his harsher side to her. He was unconventional. He challenged where others would accept. But he was kind and, in his own way, thoughtful.

Which was the true Piers Verderan? Which side of his nature could she expect to dominate in the coming years?

For she knew now that she wanted Piers Verderan, wanted what he could give her, but also wanted to give him the warmth that had all too often been lacking in his life. But now she had allowed herself to be worked into this corner where the only honest way to claim him was to do something outrageous—something totally against her nature and her upbringing. It was not so much that she thought it wicked to hunt, but she would have to make a spectacle of herself.

She remembered their first meeting. She had doubtless made a spectacle of herself then, but in his company it had not seemed to matter. Would that magic work again?

She had taken the first tame step by cancelling her arrangement with Dick Christian. She had still paid his fee, however, as she wasn't sure he would find another ride at such short notice. That still left the major step to take and though her spirit was willing, her conventional sense quailed.

But she was sure Junia was correct. If she couldn't do this, she wasn't ready for the rarefied air of life with Piers Verderan.

It was a relief when she was told that Lord Randal and Sophie were calling, even though she expected further pressure.

It appeared not to be so.

"Emily," said Sophie, bouncing up as soon as Emily entered the parlour. "There's a balloon ascension!"

"Where?"

"Oh, over near Leicester, but the wind is blowing this way. I'm convinced it will come this way, so we're out to give chase. Since we are not after foxes."

Emily looked from Sophie to Lord Randal. "And tomorrow . . . ?"

"We ride," he said, but did not ask her intention.

"Will you join us, Emily?" asked Sophie. "It should be fun to try to track the balloon if it should come this way."

Anything was better than sitting around the house fretting. "Of course. Just allow me a moment to change."

They were soon out, Emily on Corsair, scanning the sky for any sign of the balloon.

Emily hardly expected that they would see it, for there must be any number of factors in the direction of such machines, but it was a glorious day for a ride and she enjoyed showing Randal and Sophie some of the local sights.

Then, up in the sky, there was a flash of colour.

"My God!" exclaimed Randal incredulously. "It's coming."

"Not exactly," said Emily after a moment. "It's heading towards Wymondham. Let's go!"

She set her horse along a lane, choosing a route which should intercept that of the balloon. Soon they passed through a gate and across the fields.

The coloured shape became larger: red, blue, and gold. Soon the tiny basket underneath could be seen, and perhaps a person waving.

They stopped to check their angle.

"Randal," Sophie asked, bright-eyed. "How does one get to ride in a balloon?"

"Sophie," he said with a groan, "have pity on my poor grey hairs."

"You don't have any, silly."

"Little you know. Blonde hair disguises them, you know."

Then they became aware of other sounds. A horn. A baying.

"The hunt," Randal said. "It's coming this way."

"And the balloon's coming lower," pointed out Emily. "I do hope it doesn't crash."

"They have to come down somewhere," said Randal. "It'll be the devil to pay, though, if it comes down in the middle of the hunt."

They immediately set off again at full speed, trying to anticipate the landing place of the beautiful object decorated with pictures of sailing ships and sea monsters.

Suddenly a red flash alerted them to the fox, hurtling desperately across the field, the hounds audible a mere few fields back.

"Keep out of his way," warned Randal. "Give him his chance. And watch for the hounds. In fact, I judge this to be as good a place as any to watch both hunt and balloon descension."

The hunt swept over a rise to their right, hounds in the lead, followed closely by the Master and his men, and with some of the field not far back.

"There's Ver!" cried Sophie.

Emily looked to see him leap a fence.

"There's Wallingford," said Emily, seeing the horse close behind. Then she gasped. As the horse landed, he seemed to miss his footing and went down, rolling. Christian was clear but never lost the reins. In a moment he had the horse checked and settled, remounted, and chased after the leaders.

"Surely he should take him out after such a fall," Emily exclaimed.

"The horse looks well enough," said Randal. "Christian won't stop for such a little thing."

Emily watched Wallingford with concern as they came closer, but could see no obvious damage. She was glad, however, that she, not Christian, was to ride Nelson. She would definitely sacrifice some flashy performance to save her horses from such a fall.

Such thoughts were broken off, however, when shouts signalled the sudden dropping of the balloon. The huntsman blew on his horn in a futile attempt to send the monster on its way.

The hounds gave up their proper prey to circle and bay at the descending object. Lord Lonsdale was red in the face, Verderan was laughing, and the rest of the hunt began to ride up, exclaiming at the sudden wonder in their midst.

"Come on," said Randal, and they cantered over to where the balloonist was throwing out ropes to people to fix his craft. "We'd better make sure the purists don't award someone his brush and mask!"

By the time they reached the balloon, however, the general spirit was one of good humour.

"By God, man," said Lonsdale, slapping Mr. Sadler on the back. "If you're so set on following the hunt I'll lend you a horse next time!"

"Not at all, my lord," said the man, not much abashed at the company he found himself in. "I'd be scared to death to be riding one of these mettlesome steeds."

This was greeted by a gale of laughter.

By general consent, it was accepted that the hunt was over for the day. It had been a fine run of over ten miles and if the fox escaped this time, well, he'd be around to provide sport another day.

The whippers-in collected the hounds and started them on the long walk back to their kennels. The field gathered around to investigate the balloon.

Verderan rode his handsome chestnut over to Emily. "Here you are with the hunt and the sky hasn't fallen," he remarked.

"No, merely an object from the sky," she responded.

"You think your outrageous behaviour brought down the balloon?" he queried. "We must convey this novel view of science to Mr. Sadler."

His words were almost sharp, but his expression wasn't. It melted her bones. She was a sad case and almost totally lost. "If you keep looking at me like that," she murmured, "I'm going to fall out of the saddle."

"If we went just a few fields away," he murmured back, "I could take advantage of that admirably."

"Growing bashful?" Emily asked sharply to cover the longing and confusion that swelled in her. "Sophie told me how you stripped virtually naked and went swimming at a public affair."

"But not that I've ever made love to my future wife at a public affair," he countered gently.

Emily took a deep breath to steady herself. "You're too strong a wine for me," she said.

"You underestimate yourself. And anyway, one develops a strong head after a while. A stolen glass of port will turn a boy tipsy. A man drinks a couple of bottles and can make his own way home."

"And how am I to take that? A few words with you turns me giddy," Emily translated. "So after a while, all day and night with you will leave me hardly affected at all?"

He grinned. "Unlikely, thank God."

With that he left her, which seemed an ungentlemanly thing to do, though she hadn't the faintest notion what to reply to such a statement.

If she pursued him brazenly through the crowd and said, "I will marry you," would he ride with her into the sunset and teach her the pleasures of love?

Probably. But she knew that for her own satisfaction she had to pass the test of tomorrow.

She turned Corsair and began to ride home. Hooves thundered behind her and she paused hopefully.

It was Lord Randal. "It was worth the chase, wasn't it?" he said. "Lonsdale's even invited Sadler for dinner. I know you're accustomed to riding about alone, but I think I should escort you. Not all Meltonians are true gentlemen."

"I will be perfectly safe," said Emily, gesturing about at the country people come to see the spectacle. "But thank you."

"Very well." Lord Randal pulled out a piece of paper. "When he left this morning, Ver asked me to give this to you if we should see you. It may not be necessary now you've spoken."

Emily looked at her name in smooth, strong writing—the first written communication she had ever had from him. She thanked Lord Randal and headed for home. She wanted to be in the peaceful privacy of her room before she opened this letter.

It was doubtless just to do with High Burton, or the horses . . .

She hurried into the Hall and up to her room, stripped off her gloves and broke the seal.

My darling Emily.

In case you have any doubts, I still want, in fact need, to marry you. If you falter, please think of the consequences for both of us. If you refuse me, I will never rest easy knowing you are languishing in bondage. Will you rest easy, knowing I do not handle reverses graciously? If you should marry another, can you make him happy? If I should marry another, I know I cannot.

Blackmail, I know, but I am not too lofty for any trick that will win you.

Remember, this test is not of my making. If you don't wish to hunt it is of no significance. I will give up hunting immediately if that is your desire. All I need is for you to put your hand in mine and say you will trust me with it forever.

As for the hunt, if you still wish to sell Nelson, it would go better if I were to ride him as I could then sell him as "my horse" at the club, which always brings the best price. If you wish to take part, I would like you to ride Beelzebub. He will take care of you, and you must allow me a little foolish, doting protectiveness.

I will send him over this evening for you to ride if you wish.

Emily thought of the horse he said no one but he was allowed to ride. Proof of devotion indeed. And, truth to tell, she had nothing against a little foolish, doting protectiveness.

There was little more to the note.

I am not an earthly paragon, and certainly not an angel. My desires are all too earthly. Make no doubt about it. That, however, is a subject for another letter which you have not yet given me the right to send.

It is written, though, and scorching a hole in a nasty old walnut desk here at Hume House. I hope tomorrow to give it to you, and perhaps demonstrate some of the finer points therein.

For now, my love, be of good courage. A daring deed, once done, becomes a commonplace. There is very little in life truly worth fearing.

It was signed simply, "Ver."

It all clicked together. The need to see what was happening to Nelson out in the field, the fact that she'd been present today without the sky falling in, and Verderan.

He wanted her and was willing to lower his hard-won guard almost to nothing before her. Surely she could do her part.

═ 12 ═

IT WAS, HOWEVER, no easier than she had expected.

A Hume House groom walked Beelzebub over. Emily sent back Nelson and Oak-apple.

The man also brought a note from Sophie saying she and Randal would come by to collect Emily. It would be too easy, though, to allow herself to be swept up and carried along by the self-assured Ashbys, and so she replied gratefully but declined, saying she would make her own way to the meet.

Then, after the man had gone, wished she had taken the easy way.

Emily spent quite some time in communication with Bel, but the horse did not have anything to say about Verderan that she did not already know and seemed to have little sympathy with her predicament.

Just before dinner, Emily visited her father. She occupied the time with a lively account of the balloon descension. Sir Henry was in one of his better moods and laughed along with her, only once saying, "Damme, I wish I'd been there!"

As a visit it went very well, but Emily had intended to warn him of the next day's events. If she was, in effect, going to accept an offer of marriage, her father should know. Her courage failed her, however, and she left to go to the dining room with the carefully planned words unsaid.

If she couldn't even tell her father, could she go through with the deed?

She remembered her one disastrous foray into theatricals. Sir Arthur and Lady Overbrook had proposed a production of *The Unfortunate Couple* during Christmas some years back, and Emily had been reluctantly conscripted to play Lady Lydia's maid. Though she was not thrilled at the opportunity she had managed the rehearsals well enough and had truly believed she could go through with it.

When the night came, however, and the Overbrook's ballroom began to fill with the local gentry, she had peeped through the makeshift curtain and panicked. Her throat had seized up and she had been unable to utter a word.

Frantic reassurances and even a drop of brandy had achieved nothing. It had been fortunate that Miss Hardesty, who played Lady Lydia, had always brought her maid to the rehearsals, for that young woman proved to be word-perfect in the part and able to step into the breech admirably.

Could something equally ridiculous happen again? How could she be sure it wouldn't?

After dinner she determined to have done with all this foolishness and prove her nerve. She marched along to her father's room to reveal all. She knocked briskly and entered, finding him playing a desultory game of Patience.

"Care for a hand of Piquet?" she asked impulsively.

He brightened. "What stakes?"

"Father," said Emily. "Are you trying to chouse me out of my pin money? A thousand a point is the highest I'll go." When he'd taught her this game years ago they had played for such fanciful high stakes.

With a laugh he agreed and the game progressed in great good humour, tallying-up, despite the outrageous stakes, close to even at the end.

Emily realised how much their relationship had deteriorated since his accident, and how much she had neglected him of late. Certainly, Sir Henry had become unpleasant about business matters and misunderstood her in so many ways, but he was a well-intentioned father for all that and she had become so caught up in other matters that she had almost forgotten him.

As she put away the cards and he reminisced about other games and other times, she wondered if one could hire a male companion. Something was needed, especially if she were to marry . . .

She stopped, remembering why she had come here in the first place.

She even turned to speak.

Sir Henry smiled. "You're a good daughter, Emily. I'm a fortunate man to have you and know you'll never leave me. Come give me a kiss."

Emily kissed him and left, a failure again, and now with a new burden. How could she leave her father to the care of strangers? And was this a genuine dilemma or just an excuse not to have to make a public spectacle of herself on the morrow?

She went up and sat by the window of her room, brushing her hair. She watched the breeze stir the trees in the moonlight and send the falling leaves whirling and scudding. Then she saw the figure.

Someone was making his way from the drive across the lawn towards the side of the house. It was Lord Randal Ashby. What had happened?

She flung up the window, leant out, and gave an unladylike whistle. He turned and came quickly over, miming that she should come down to speak to him. Emily flung her red woolen cloak around her shoulders and slipped down the backstairs to the kitchen.

The stove was already banked and the room deserted. She unlocked the back door and crept out into the night, her heart thundering with fear. Something terrible must have occurred.

Lord Randal met her at the corner of the house. "What is it?" Emily gasped.

He took her hand. "Did I frighten you? I'm sorry. Nothing too terrible . . . I don't think, but Ver's mother's turned up."

"Helen Sillitoe?"

"As was," he agreed. "We were at the club—Ver sold Wallingford for eighty-five by the way—when his man came with the message. Osbaldeston somehow got wind of it, probably listening behind pillars again, and started making comments about Ver finally facing up to his Irish responsibilities, about his mother's reaction to the debauch going on at Hume House . . . Ver hit him before your name could come into it."

"Oh, heavens," Emily moaned. "Will there be a duel?"

"I doubt it," Randal said with a grin. "Osbaldeston was making fiery noises, but I pointed out that if he survived Ver he'd have to fight me, since he'd implied Sophie was taking part in a debauch. He decided to consider it a mill and forget about it."

"So where is Ver?"

"At Hume House. After I'd dropped him off, I gave into impulse and came down here. I think he'll need you."

Emily gathered her cloak more firmly around herself. "Why?"

He looked away and frowned. "I don't know how much you know about Ver and his family . . ."

"Quite a lot, actually."

"Well, then, perhaps you can guess. I don't think I know the whole of it, but for all he's grown a tough shell, it's like a wound inside. I don't know what's going to happen, but I don't see how his mother turning up can be pleasant for him."

"But what can I do?"

"Be there."

"Lord Randal," Emily protested, "It's eleven o'clock at night."

"I know."

Emily looked back helplessly at the house then up at the man. He was disquietingly serious. "Very well. Did you say you'd driven?"

"Good girl. Yes, I've got the curricle. Come along."

So when Mrs. Dobson, alerted by some noises in her kitchen, peered out of the window, she saw Emily and a gentleman sneaking down the driveway. "Lord love us," she muttered. "She's eloping!" She hurried off to tell Miss Junia.

When Randal brought the curricle to a halt before Hume House, delicately avoiding the worst depressions, all seemed quiet and normal. Candlelight shone in a number of rooms but there were no sounds.

Emily got cold feet. "Lord Randal, are you sure . . . ?"

"I'm sure."

Emily climbed down and went with him into the house. The hall was deserted, but Kevin Renfrew came out of the billiard room in shirt sleeves, cue still in hand.

"Oh good," he said, and it particularly seemed to be addressed to Emily. "They're in the library."

"In you go," said Randal, indicating a door.

"But what about you?" Emily asked in panic.

"I'll do vigil out here. This is, I think, family business."

"But I'm not . . ."

"Emily, you're the closest thing to family Ver's had since he was eight years old." He gave her a little push and Emily went.

Her hand was sticky with sweat as she turned the knob and opened the door.

Verderan was standing by the fire facing a woman seated in a chair. Helen Sillitoe. Her hair was grey and some had escaped from it's bun to straggle in wisps down the sides of her haggard face. She was no longer a beauty and looked much older than her contemporary, Junia, but the bones were still there, the bones she had passed on to her son.

She turned, startled and even frightened, to face the new arrival. She looked wounded and exhausted. Emily quietly shut the door behind her. She searched desperately for something to say to cut through the heavy painful atmosphere of the room.

She glanced at Verderan and saw the stark lines of his face. She wanted to run to him, but instead she went to his mother.

"Mrs. Verderan," she said, drawing on a lifetime of training in correct behaviour. "I am Emily Grantwich of Grantwich Hall. You doubtless remember my father, Sir Henry, and my aunt, Junia. You must have had a tiring journey. I'm afraid this house isn't in the best repair—Ver's only been here for a few weeks. We would be pleased to have you come to stay at the Hall for a day or two if that would be more comfortable."

She cast a quick glance at Verderan, trying to judge if she

was doing the best thing, but he was looking down at the fire and she could not read him.

"Comfortable!" repeated Helen with a half laugh. "Comfortable! I've forgotten what the word means." She looked up at Emily, wild-eyed. "We ate gruel. I turned my dresses. I scrubbed the walls with my own hands . . . *He left one hundred thousand pounds!*"

Emily looked to Verderan in bewilderment. He met her eyes. "My grandfather is dead."

"Crushed!" declared Helen. She smiled feverishly at Emily. "You've heard of people being crushed by debts? Well, old James Verderan was crushed by miserliness. These last years he wouldn't even spend to keep the place in good repair, and in the end the arch into the courtyard collapsed on top of him and did for the old bugger."

Emily gaped at this sudden burst of vulgarity and flashed another look at Verderan. He, however, seemed to be plagued by his own devils. "You're Lord Templemore," she said blankly.

"Damnable, isn't it?"

Emily hadn't the faintest idea what to say or do. Had these two been here in silence ever since Verderan had arrived home? No, Helen must at least have told him the news.

"It's late," she said at last. "Everyone is tired. You need your bed, Mrs. Verderan, and it is your choice as to whether you stay here or at the Hall."

Helen looked down at her roughened hands. "He hasn't asked me to stay."

Emily looked up at Verderan. "You're his mother. There's no question of asking."

Verderan met her eyes, but there were depths behind his gaze that she could not begin to grasp. "Given an alternative," he said, "I am not sure she would want to stay here."

"She has an alternative," Emily responded. "She may also stay here." It was a statement and she meant it. No matter what had happened between these two in the past, she could not marry a man who would refuse his mother a bed for the night.

"Of course she may stay," he said with a sigh. "This is her old home, after all."

It was something Emily had forgotten, but it put a grudging edge on the invitation she did not like. She did not presume to judge too quickly, however. She had no idea what was going on beneath the surface.

"Mrs. Verderan?" she prompted, catching on Helen's face a yearning look at her son which tore at her heart.

"I will stay here," the woman whispered. "Just for a day or two," she added hastily.

Without prompting, Verderan said, "You will stay here as long as you wish. Or at any other of my homes. You may wish in a while to set up an establishment for yourself, but there is no hurry. I'm afraid Casper let this place fall to rack and ruin too, but I'll see what can be done."

With that he walked out of the door and Helen watched him. Emily was horribly aware that he had not once called Helen "mother."

"No matter what happens," Helen said with a sigh, "never let yourself be estranged from a child." She turned to Emily curiously. "I never thought to wonder where you had come from like an angel of mediation."

"From the Hall. Lord Randal Ashby brought me to see if I could help." At Helen's blank look she added, "He's Ver's friend and he's staying here with his wife."

Helen sighed again. "I didn't expect him to have friends. I believed it all, you see, that he was a thief and a libertine. I knew he was living richly, but I thought . . . I thought it would be seedy somehow, and full of low characters."

Emily smiled wryly. "You should meet my cousin Felix." She took Helen's rough dry hand. "Many people believe it, and in truth Ver's not exactly a saint, but he is a good man at heart and so he has friends."

"You love him," Helen said.

"Yes."

"Does he love you?"

Emily thought of hedging her answer, but simply said, "Yes."

Helen smiled faintly. "I'm glad, but a little jealous. I find myself foolishly hoping that we might get back a little of the time we missed. But now he will have someone else to absorb him."

"There will be time for you too," Emily promised. "But I think he needs time now to accommodate himself."

Helen stood, proving to be quite tall. Her travelling cloak was stained, worn, and patched; the gown beneath was so faded that the print could scarcely be distinguished. How many years had it been since Ver had left for Eton, never to return? About sixteen.

Sixteen years of scrimping and slaving for tyrannical Lord Templemore, believing her son had stolen the family money and left her in penury.

"He feels guilty," Helen said. "I should have thought before I fled here, and not turned up as quite such a waif. The old man took my money, though. I don't understand these legal matters, but somehow my annuity died with him . . ." Her fingers plucked at a loose thread in her cloak. "He feels as if he abandoned me, but it was I who abandoned him."

The thread broke in her fingers and she looked down with a frown. "I was lost without Damon, you see, and awed by the fact that Piers was heir to a title. I let Lord Templemore bully me . . . and I let him . . ." She shuddered. "So many nights I have thought of the things I could have done . . ."

She turned suddenly to Emily. "Can you make him happy?"

Emily felt no doubts. "Yes," she said. "And you too, I think."

Helen's lips turned up in a quizzical smile, and for the first time she showed the ghost of her younger beauty. "You can make me happy, too?" she queried. "Or I can also make him happy?"

Emily smiled back. "Both."

Verderan came back in and caught the smile. He looked startled. "I'm afraid the spare beds are all damp," he said. "You will sleep in my room tonight. It is aired and comfortable."

Helen looked as if she would protest, but then accepted.

Verderan looked behind him and Sophie came into the

room. "This is Lady Randal Ashby, Mother. She will take you up and see you have everything you need."

The word "mother" sounded in the room like a deep bell. Emily caught her breath; Helen looked at him, startled, and a little colour came into her cheeks. She did not look quite so old.

He took her hand and drew her closer for a cool kiss on the cheek. "You are welcome, Mother, and will not be in need again."

Watching, Emily silently begged Helen to draw him in for a warm hug. The woman hesitated, obviously tempted, but then just touched his face gently, said, "Good night, Piers," and left with Sophie.

Verderan turned to Emily and gave a sigh that was close to a shudder. "I wonder how long it will take for her to stop calling me that," he said brittlely. Then he held out a hand, "Thank you for coming."

She went straight to him to give him the hug his mother had not. He clung to her.

"All these years," he said bitterly, "I've sat on my grievances and ignored her situation."

"You could not have known . . ."

He pulled away and paced the room. "Oh yes I could. If I hadn't been able to guess, I had plenty of people willing to drop hints. I sent her a curt invitation to come and live in England and when she refused, I abandoned her."

"She did refuse," Emily pointed out.

"You didn't know my grandfather. He could make a starving man refuse food." He turned to face her. "I was punishing her. She didn't stop him, you see. I don't know what I expected her to do, but she was my mother . . . and she didn't stop him."

Emily walked over to Verderan and raised her hands to his face, which was scarred with old horrors and new guilt. "She feels she abandoned you and you feel you abandoned her. I think you'll find your tallies wipe each other out. Start afresh, Ver."

His arms came around her. "With you?"

She rested against him. Angel wings. Michael, not Lucifer.

"I still have to pluck up the courage to ride the hunt," she teased. It suddenly seemed a matter of small significance.

"Would a kiss encourage you?" he asked.

"No," she said and moved away, "It would seduce me, and well you know it. Wait until tomorrow."

He grinned. "To seduce you? I haven't got a Special Licence, you know."

"How very unthoughtful of you. We probably could have been married on the field by one of the Blackcoats."

"You are developing a taste for the unusual, aren't you?"

Emily blushed. "I'm developing a taste for you." She eyed a large walnut desk. "Is that . . . ?"

"Yes," he said. Adding, "Not till tomorrow."

"I think you should give me the letter as fair warning of what's to come."

"I'm not so foolish."

Under this banter he was already looking better, more himself. Emily was aware of a temptation to stay and improve upon her work—

The clock struck midnight and Emily started. "I must go home."

"Of course," he said, and kissed her gently. "Thank you again." As if impelled, he added, "You are going to come to the hunt tomorrow, aren't you?"

The vulnerability of it brought tears to her heart. "Wild horses wouldn't keep me away," she said. "Even if it means I'm going to be, God help us, Lady Templemore."

The words brought all that starkness back to his face. "Don't make it an excuse to renege," he warned. "If I can bear to be Lord Templemore, when the name makes me feel sick, you can damn well bear to be Lady Templemore."

She soothed his face again with her hands. "We'll make it a name to be proud of," she promised. "It will mean love and happiness and charity. And lots of happy little Verderans to carry on the tradition."

He hugged her tight. "I'll hold you to that. If you don't come to the hunt, I'm going to come and kidnap you."

"Good, but it won't be necessary."

He drove her back to the Hall in the moonlight and talked

a little of his mother as they went. It was mostly his faint memories of his younger life before the death of his father, when his mother would take over the kitchen to bake special treats, and let him help. And sit by his bed when he was sick. And sing duets with his father in the evening.

"She was made to be happy," he said, "but not to fight. My father would have expected me to preserve her happiness."

Emily didn't point out that he had only been eight years old. From adult hindsight that perhaps did not matter.

She had him stop at the end of the drive so she could slip back into the house unobserved.

They shared one, quick, searing kiss before parting.

"Till tomorrow," were her parting words.

=== 13 ===

MRS. DOBSON IMPARTED the terrible news to Junia Grantwich. Junia sat up in bed and stared at the woman. "You must be dreaming. Why would she do such a thing?" But these days Emily was capable of anything.

She immediately pulled on a wrap and led the way to Emily's room, where Emily clearly was not. Even worse, there was no sign of her having gone to bed at all.

The two women searched the house—quietly for fear of waking Sir Henry—but eventually had to admit that Emily was nowhere within Grantwich Hall.

"The stables!" exclaimed Junia with relief. "Of course, with the hunt tomorrow, she's probably gone to visit the stables."

"At nearly midnight?" queried Mrs. Dobson in disbelief.

"These young people. I'll just put on some clothes and fetch her."

She pulled on the simplest garments—loose trousers, Cossack shirt, and boots—and hurried out of the back door.

The stables, however, were depressingly quiet. All the horses which should be present were there, including Beelzebub.

"Well," said Junia, eying the handsome black thoughtfully. "If she and Verderan were eloping they wouldn't leave you here." She went slowly back to the house, considering the possibilities.

It was possible a lovesick Emily had taken a moonlit walk, though it was cold and breezy and not particularly pleasant. If so, she was nowhere in sight.

It was possible she had slipped away for an assignation with her beloved, but such behaviour seemed extremely unlikely from someone who was having the tremors over hunting, a less heinous crime.

If one was given to gothic flights of fancy it was possible to imagine Emily being lured away from the house by some other lustful male. But the only possibility was Hector Marshalswick, and even Junia's imagination could not stretch that far.

By the time she reached the warmth of the kitchen again, Junia had persuaded herself that Emily was a grown woman and able to take care of herself. She set herself to convince Mrs. Dobson; an altogether harder task. They shared a cup of tea, and she gradually brought the woman around to the idea that Emily had voluntarily gone about her own business and would soon return home safely. She also persuaded her that alerting Sir Henry could do no good and would only agitate him.

Just as they were draining the pot, there was a loud rap on the front door-knocker.

"Lord save us!" exclaimed Mrs. Dobson, clearly fearing the worst.

"I'll go," said Junia, "since I'm decent." She had to admit to a tremor of alarm herself. Who could be calling at such an hour except someone with bad news? She lit a candle from the one on the table and left the kitchen. There was another sharp rap. "Wait, wait," she muttered as she hurried across the hall, shielding the flame from the draft of her own movement. "You'll wake the whole house."

A shouted query from Sir Henry's room showed the damage was already done. She popped her head in to tell him she was attending to the matter and put her candle on the hall table. Then she swung open the door, fear in her heart, a tart comment on her lips.

Both died.

"Marcus!" she cried, swamped instantly with delight. "Praise the Lord, my dear boy! Where have you come from?"

She grasped the tall young man by the sleeves of his

greatcoat and dragged him into the house. Then she realised the vicar and his sister were behind him. "Come in! Come in!" She took in her nephew, safe and glowing with health, with all his wits and limbs. It was more than she'd ever dared to hope. At another frustrated bellow from the library, she pushed him that way.

"You must go to your father. Have you heard . . . ? Yes, of course, Margaret would have told you." She pushed him into the room and then turned to the other two. She hugged Margaret. "I'm so happy, I'm likely to cry. You tell me, where has he come from?"

Margaret returned the hug ecstatically. She was glowing, and not a little teary herself. "He's not very clear in his accounts. I think it's secret. But I don't care a scrap. He's home. He's home for good!"

Junia hugged her again. Then, for good measure, she hugged Hector, who suffered it.

Mrs. Dobson appeared shyly, her nightgown covered by a shawl, bearing a candle. As soon as she heard the news she started to cry. Then she staggered off to make more tea.

"What of Emily?" Hector asked. "She will want to be woken, I'm sure. Marcus could not help stopping by the vicarage to see Margaret, and we came up to share your joy."

"Yes, indeed," said Margaret. "It is the middle of the night, but such a night can only happen once in a lifetime. I'll go up and wake her."

Junia looked around frantically. "Er . . . I don't think she's there."

"Oh?" said Margaret. "Where is she?"

"Staying with friends in town," Junia said, then knew it was foolish. She saw Hector give her one of his narrow-eyed looks.

Marcus came out of Sir Henry's room, looking a little sobered by the state in which he found his father. "Come along in," he said. "Did I hear Mrs. Dobson mentioning tea? We will all have some in here, but father wants to toast my return with champagne. I'll just go fetch some. Did you say Emily is in town?"

"What's that?" shouted Sir Henry. "Come in here, the lot of you!"

They crowded into the room and Sir Henry looked them over, already seeming more alert, more like his old self. "What's this about Emily?"

Junia couldn't think of a sensible thing to say.

Hector said skeptically, "She is apparently visiting friends in town, sir."

"Since when? She played Piquet with me after dinner." He glared at Junia. "Where the devil is she?"

"Gone for a walk, I think," Junia said.

"At midnight? And why did you say she was in town?"

Junia sighed. "I haven't the slightest notion where she is. There."

Marcus frowned. "It's not like Emily to do anything so strange. Is she ill?"

"She's turned damn peculiar, if you want the truth," said Sir Henry. "Got above herself once I had to let her help me with business, and then she took to chasing men."

"Henry, really!" protested Junia.

"What men?" asked Marcus.

"Piers Verderan," said Hector primly.

Marcus flashed an startled look around the room. "The Dark Angel? How . . . ?" It was clear the news that Boney was at the door would have been more believable.

"He's Casper Sillitoe's heir," said Sir Henry. "Living at Hume House for the hunting, and he's got Emily so she doesn't know up from down." He glared suddenly at Junia. "Is that where she is? Eh? Eh? My God, Marcus, get up there and save her!"

Marcus looked stunned. "Emily?" he queried blankly. "Surely, sir . . ."

"I am afraid it is quite likely true," said Hector. "I have seen her demonstrate a decided partiality for the fellow."

Marcus shook his head but turned towards the door. "I will certainly go and look into things, though I can hardly believe . . ." He walked into the hall. Junia followed to try to explain some of what had been going on. A movement on the stairs alerted them and they looked up to see a wide-eyed Emily.

She stared as if she was seeing a ghost. "Marcus?" Then

her face lit up with joy. "Oh, Marcus! Thank God, thank God!" She ran down to fling herself into his arms.

But he held her off. "Where have you been?"

Emily was too shocked to speak. The surprise of her brother's return, delightful though it was, after the intensity of the situation at Hume House, on top of days of anxiety . . . And now, instead of shared joy, her brother was looking at her with cold suspicion.

"At Hume House?" he asked harshly.

Dazedly, she nodded, and became aware of Junia, Margaret, and Hector staring at her from her father's door. She saw what they all thought and was filled with fury.

"Bring her in here!" demanded Sir Henry.

Marcus did so with a hand on her arm, but Emily wrenched out of his grip and marched in under her own steam. Once there, she faced them all boldly.

"Have you no shame?" demanded her father.

"I have nothing to be ashamed of."

"What? You admit to sneaking up to the Dark Angel's house in the middle of the night and expect us to believe you were up to no harm?"

Emily looked him straight in the eye. "Yes."

Mrs. Dobson came in with a loaded tray, took in the atmosphere, put down her offering, and left.

"Very well then," said Hector, in the tone of a peacemaker but with unendurable smugness. "Why not tell your father why you went up to that place."

Emily looked around them all. "Mr. Verderan's mother arrived this evening. I went up to help." Despite her firm tone it did sound remarkably feeble even to her own ears.

Junia asked, "Helen's come over from Ireland?"

Hector asked, "After all his cruelty, she would come to him? I find that impossible to believe."

Marcus asked, "Why the devil should you be helping? Can't he afford maids?"

"Because I'm going to marry him," Emily said, silencing the room.

Margaret's eyes brimmed with delight, and Junia said, "Good." But the men reflected horror.

"You are lost to all decency!" declared Hector.

"You can't be serious," said Marcus.

"She's addled," said Sir Henry. "She probably went up there, crawled into his bed, and as a result of what happened, thinks he'll marry her. I warned you, my girl."

Emily glared at her father red-faced. "You have a disgusting mind!"

"Emily, guard your tongue," said Marcus sharply.

"If you are going to marry him," asked Sir Henry unpleasantly, "why hasn't he come talking to me about it?"

"He will," said Emily, fighting tears and struggling to keep her dignity. "Thus far it has been between the two of us."

"I'll go odds it has," growled her father. "Oh, damn it all, Emily, I warned you."

"And I told you I could be trusted," she cried. "Trust me. For once, Father, will you trust me to run my own life!"

"No," he shouted back. "You're a woman, and as foolish as the rest of the species! Thank God I've got Marcus back and can have done with this farce. Marcus, my boy, lock her in her room while we consider what is best to be done." He cast a significant glance at Hector, who was looking rather smug.

"Father," warned Emily.

"No more of your nonsense."

"Henry," said Junia. "You are making an utter fool of yourself."

"You should know," he said nastily. "You've been making a fool of yourself all your life. Someone should have fixed you up with a man before you turned funny. Marcus."

Thus prompted, Marcus came over to Emily. "Come along," he said, not unkindly. "We'll fix things, Emily."

There was nothing to be gained by staying, so Emily allowed her brother to escort her up the stairs. "Marcus, I am willing to make allowances," she said. "You've been away for a long time and you don't know the half of the situation . . ."

"I bumped into Felix when I got off the coach in Melton," he said bleakly. "He filled me in remarkably."

"You'd believe *Felix*?"

"Not at the time. I obviously owe him an apology for knocking him down." He sighed. "Emily, how could you let yourself be used like this by a man of Verderan's stamp? Men like that don't marry. I always thought you so sensible."

At her door, Emily turned to him. "Did it ever occur to you, Marcus, that I might not want to be sensible?" She took the key from the inside of her lock and handed it to him. "Welcome home, brother." Then she slammed the door.

Marcus Grantwich looked at the key and the solid door. He was very tempted not to lock it at all, but decided it was better to do so for now. He really couldn't handle the rampant lunacy that seemed to have taken over here. He was tired from the rush of tying up his military work and racing home to face his family catastrophe. In fact he was exhausted.

But his work during the past year—behind the scenes, undercover, and mixing with people whose principles were quite different from his own, yet principles all the same— had taught him some things.

Was it just that which had made Emily look quite beautiful tonight—with her hair long and loose and that red cloak framing her face magnificently?

Or perhaps it was the way she held herself so she looked a good few inches taller, and the proud spirit that shone in her eyes, and the way her eyes had met those of her accusers . . .

As he walked slowly downstairs he recollected that it had never been wise to believe anything Cousin Felix said. On the other hand, he'd heard about Piers Verderan and even met the man once or twice when he was still home to hunt.

Remarkably handsome, sharp as a blade, and as hard. Hard and cold, with fire underneath. The thought of such a man and Emily was ludicrous until he called to mind the new Emily. The one who had confronted their father so boldly.

Was this really a match or was she being duped? If it was

a match, was it permissible? If it wasn't, what was a poor tired brother to do about it?

And he'd thought he was coming home to peace and rest from strife.

He found Hector and Margaret sitting in Sir Henry's room, but Junia was nowhere to be seen. Margaret looked up at him miserably and he went to her. "I'm sorry, love. This isn't the joyous party you wanted, is it?"

She shook her head. "That doesn't matter, Marcus. I have you home. But what about Emily?"

"We'll work it out for the best. I think it would be better, though, if you went home now. I'm tired to death and not up to a great scene at the moment. We'll sort things out tomorrow."

The Marshalswicks rose and took their farewells. Hector said, "I will return first thing to discuss what is to be done."

As he saw them off, Marcus discovered he did not like Hector very much. Emily was really none of his business, and he had never once, since Marcus had knocked at their door, left him and Margaret alone for a fond reunion. Over-propriety or simple thoughtlessness?

He rubbed his forehead and went back to his father, who was looking weighed with care. "Don't know where I went wrong," he muttered. "She's changed. She's not my little Emily any more."

Marcus collapsed wearily into a chair by his father's bed. "She's brave," he said.

"Bold," countered Sir Henry.

Marcus smiled. "A little, but more brave than bold. You frighten me, Father, so I'm sure you frighten Emily."

"Fat lot of good it does, when I'm stuck here. All I can do is shout."

"We'll have to find some way of getting you about a bit," Marcus said. "Perhaps consult some other doctors . . . But be kind to Emily, Father. If by any chance Piers Verderan does want to marry her, should we stand in their way?"

"No, of course not," sighed Sir Henry. "In fact, I like the man, for all his reputation. But he won't. There's nothing to her except good sense and a sound head. If he's given her a slip, though," he said anxiously, "don't you go challenging him. The man's a killer."

Marcus understood now why his father had made such a scene. "I'm supposed to ignore it?" he asked.

"What use to us all are you, boy, brave but dead? I've just got you back," Sir Henry said, perilously close to tears. "I can't bear to lose you again."

Among the things Marcus had learned recently was that there were many kinds of courage and his had been tested in all of them. He no longer felt the need to prove himself to anyone. "Very well, Father," he said. "I give you my word it won't come to a duel."

With that he left, almost too tired to walk, and made his way up to his old room. He assumed it was as he left it, and though it would be cold and damp, he'd known worse conditions than that. He just needed a place to collapse.

When he arrived at his door, however, he found it open and Junia and Mrs. Dobson busily making the bed with sheets warmed before the kitchen stove and setting hot bricks in it. Warm water stood in the jug and a decanter of brandy and a glass were by his bed.

"It's nice to be home," he said mistily.

Dobby beamed. Junia kissed him.

"Rest. Everything will be fine tomorrow."

Emily awoke, and the sun told her it was later than her usual time for rising. She also remembered it was the day she was to go hunting. She wondered what Marcus and her father would have to say to that but didn't much care for her mind was full of Verderan and their future together. She hummed happily as she dressed in her habit and went to the door, only remembering when it refused to open that it was locked.

Really, she thought with a frown, this was ridiculous. She'd been so tired last night after all the excitement that she hadn't been able to work herself up about it, but now she felt irritated. She wasn't a schoolgirl, after all.

She knocked, and called genteelly. After a little while she

heard Junia say, "Henry's got the key and he says they're not ready yet."

"They?" asked Emily. "Who's they?"

"He, Marcus, and Hector."

"Well, how ridiculous," said Emily. "Do they think I'm going to meekly fall in with whatever mad plan they come up with?"

"In a word, yes. Shall I go and get an ax?"

"Only as a last resort," said Emily. She looked around her room and found a large brass tray and a hard-heeled shoe. "If you want to help, Junia," she said through the door, "you could ring that old gong in the dining room." Then she applied shoe to tray.

It made a satisfying crash.

In a few moments the resonant sound of the old gong joined in. Just to add to the mayhem, Emily took to marching around her room in her boots, stamping in time with the crash of the tray.

The gong stopped.

After a moment her door was opened by a laughing Marcus. "You're utterly mad!" he declared.

Emily looked at him, saw he wasn't the enemy, and fell into his arms. This time she wasn't repulsed.

"Oh, Marcus. I really am glad you're home," she said, half crying.

"And I'm glad for whatever it is has happened to you, Emily. But be gentle with Father. He's confused and afraid."

"Why afraid?"

He came to perch on the corner of her bed while she restored her instruments to their proper places. "He can't believe that a man like Piers Verderan wants to marry you," he said simply. "Don't blame him. You used to be a meek little sparrow and you've turned into . . . I don't know. An eagle?"

"Thank you!" Emily declared.

"My pleasure," he responded. "I realised it almost as soon as I saw you again. But it's crept up on him and he can't quite grasp it yet. He's worried that you're going to cause a scandal, and get hurt. He's also terrified that I'll call the man out for it and get killed. He seems to think he kills at the drop of a hat."

"Not quite," said Emily. "But he has killed two men in duels." She was determined not to try to whitewash Verderan.

Marcus looked startled, but said, "I've killed a few myself. One does in a war. Perhaps he had reason."

Emily smiled and gave him her hand. "I think you'll like him. Truly. Now, I'd better come down and sort things out."

He raised a brow at this decided utterance and looked her over. "You're dressed for riding roughshod. Tread softly, Emily."

"I'll be as soft as I can and still get my way," she replied. "And I am dressed for hunting." She swept out and down the stairs before he could ask the startled question on his lips.

In her father's room, Hector sat looking sanctimonious. But he held his tongue.

Sir Henry said, "What in Hades do you think you're doing, girl?"

"Getting out of my room," said Emily pleasantly. "Good morning, Father. Hector."

Her cheery normalcy dumbfounded them, but Sir Henry rallied. "It's just possible that Hector here will make you an offer, Emily, if you promise—"

"How kind of you," Emily said to Hector, keeping up her smile. "But I'm afraid I am already pledged to another."

"Nonsense," said Hector, growing flushed. "Even if he was to offer you marriage, would you really marry a man who has a loose woman installed in his house? One he paid for?"

"I'm sure you'll be delighted to learn," said Emily, "that Titania is in London, learning her new trade as an actress."

Hector didn't look delighted. "I would if I believed it," he scoffed.

"Believe what you want." She turned back to Sir Henry. "Father, I am going hunting, and there I will formally become engaged to marry Piers Verderan, who is, incidentally, now Lord Templemore."

Her father gaped. "Hunting!"

"So she says," supplied Marcus, leaning against the door and looking amused.

"Oh Lord!" gasped Emily.

"Finally come to your senses?" barked Sir Henry.

"No, but Father, we've sold Wallingford!"

"What!" asked Marcus, ceasing to be amused.

"And Verderan and Randal are riding Nelson and Oak-apple. We'd best make sure they don't sell them too!"

"You're damn right!" exclaimed Marcus. "Why are you selling the hunters?"

"To pay for the sheep . . ." Emily started to laugh at the look on his face.

"The world has gone mad," he declared.

"I know," she gasped. "It's *Poudre de Violettes*. I must have brought enough home on my clothes to influence everyone!"

"Sir Henry," said Hector. "It distresses me to have to say this, but Emily is undoubtedly unbalanced."

"Oh, stubble it, Hector," said Marcus. "This business with the horses is serious! I'm coming with you, Emily. No one is selling the hunters."

"Hold on," said Sir Henry. "You're not leaving me here! Hector, you've got your gig?"

Hector allowed that to be so. "Give me a ride," demanded Sir Henry.

"Father—" Emily protested, but then stopped herself. If Sir Henry could get about, it would do him a world of good.

"Go away," Sir Henry said, "and send Oswald to dress me. Then he and Marcus can carry me out."

Emily waited in the hall, fretting a little at the passage of time, but not able to disappoint her father if he were truly willing to make the attempt to leave his bed. Marcus had rushed off to change into riding gear. Hector merely stood, looking offended.

Emily tried to think of something healing to say to him, but suspected anything she said would only bring on a new diatribe. She decided it was charitable, if conceited, to believe he was suffering from, not a broken, but a slightly bruised heart.

Junia appeared and asked, "Why are you hanging about? Not turning chicken-hearted, are you?"

"No," said Emily with a rueful shrug. "But Marcus wants to come and make sure no one sells the horses and Father's decided to come too. Why don't you join us," she asked facetiously, "and make it a family gathering?"

Junia looked much struck. "And Helen Sillitoe's up at Hume House?"

"Yes," said Emily, confused.

"I think I'll go riding too."

"But you haven't ridden in years!"

"I still have a habit somewhere," said Junia and hurried off.

Emily just shook her head and eyed the clock.

Soon Sir Henry was ready and was carried on linked hands out to the gig, without apparent pain, though he grumbled and cursed at his useless legs. Hector continued to voice disapproval of the whole business.

"Shut up, Hector," said Sir Henry, "and drive. No, wait. Marcus, fetch me a loaded pistol."

"What on earth for?" asked Marcus.

"Impudent cub! Do as you're told." When his son still hesitated, he said, "If that fellow hurts my girl, *I'm* going to shoot him. There's not much they can do to me for it, is there?"

Marcus shook his head but went on the errand.

Emily looked at her father, quite touched. "Just you be sure, Father," she warned, "that I have some complaint before you fire."

Soon Marcus was back, and the gig set off down the road at a steady pace. Emily and her brother hurried down to the stables to find their own mounts.

There they realised they had a shortage of good horses. Marcus went straight to Beelzebub, a bright light in his eye.

"He's mine," said Emily firmly. "You can ride Corsair, or one of the three-year-olds."

"Yours? How could you afford a horse like this?"

"He's Ver's," she said softly, and stroked Bel's velvety nose. "He never lets anyone ride him, but he's letting me today."

Marcus looked at her, and the horse. "He really is going to marry you, isn't he?"

192

"Yes," she said. "Unless, of course, I'm late and he shoots himself from grief. Choose a horse, for heaven's sake."

When Haverby told her Junia had ordered Venus saddled up and had headed out at a bouncing canter, Emily felt it was in keeping with the way the world was these days. She had thought she was going to ride out lonely and nervous to make a spectacle of herself. Now she was going with her whole family in train and didn't feel strange at all.

Just impatient.

Soon they were ready. They set off at a gentle pace, and soon caught up with the gig.

Emily slowed to match the vehicle's pace, though she longed to race to Verderan. She consulted her small fob watch. "If we're going to be late, I'm riding ahead," she warned them.

"Emily," said Hector, "your forwardness astonishes me."

"Hector," said Marcus. "You're turning into a prosy bore. A vicar doesn't have to be a dull stick, you know. Kirby Gate?" he asked Emily.

"Of course. Always is for the first meeting of the Quorn. Hector, I'm sure you could go a little faster without hurting Father." Hector reluctantly urged his horse to more vigour.

"I'd give my right hand for that horse," Marcus said, looking Bel over enviously.

"Make do with Nelson," she said. "He's turned out very well."

"If Verderan's going to be my brother-in-law, perhaps he can put me in the way of some good horseflesh."

"Perhaps. He does have a place in Ireland now."

"Good Lord," he said. "You're going to be 'my lady.' Will I have to bow and scrape? And you'll outrank Anne. That'll put her nose out of joint!"

"Marcus," said Emily, "Stubble it."

At the meeting of the Quorn hunt Sophie was almost unaware of the notice her presence was attracting. She was too concerned over Emily's nonappearance.

"Where is she?" she asked Randal. "There's only ten minutes to go. After last night I can't believe she'd fail now."

"Anything could have happened," said Randal and eyed Verderan. "I'm just not sure what Ver's going to do if he's stretched too tight. At least Osbaldeston's not here."

Verderan was sitting like a statue, watching the road down which Emily would have to come. Nelson moved occasionally under him and was controlled instinctively, but the horse too seemed to be still and focussed.

The Master of the Quorn passed by. "Ashby!" exclaimed Assheton-Smith. "Good to see you out. Heard you weren't going to hunt this year." He smiled dryly at Sophie. "If we have to accept Lady Randal as the price of your presence, so be it."

"Mr. Assheton-Smith," said Sophie pertly, "there is no reason a lady cannot hunt."

"Certainly there is," he said. "You are designed by God to distract men."

"Then perhaps men shouldn't hunt," offered Sophie with a twinkle.

"Take her away, Ashby," said the Master with a groan. "I'd rather have balloons any day! Good day, Ver."

Verderan looked around briefly with a slight smile that didn't reach his eyes. "Tom."

He immediately looked back to the road, and Assheton-Smith raised a brow. Before Randal could explain, Verderan stiffened. They all followed his intent gaze.

Down the road came not a lone rider, racing to be on time, but a slow cavalcade—one gig, one curricle, and a whole bunch of riders. One was Emily.

Randal grinned with relief. Verderan relaxed. "Care to see what's going on?" he asked Randal and Sophie. "Don't start the hunt without us, Tom!"

"I will start the hunt when I see fit," Assheton-Smith called after him. "And don't create any fiascoes. I'll have no sideshows with the Quorn!"

Verderan raced Nelson towards the procession, registering blankly that Sir Henry was in the gig, but with eyes only for Emily.

When he was halfway, she set Beelzebub forward and raced to meet him. They ended, unsatisfactorily, feet apart.

"I suppose I can do without kissing you for a little while," he said, smiling brilliantly.

"I suppose," said Emily, equally besotted. "And don't you dare think this was simple."

"Has anything ever been for us?" He looked over at her entourage. "Moral support? Protection?"

Emily gave a look of exasperation. "Just family," she said. "And friends. I hope you're prepared for this after years of doing without. Your mother's here too."

"What?" he looked in surprise at the curricle driven by Junia Grantwich and containing his mother and Margaret Marshalswick.

"Junia decided your mother should witness this momentous event, then she thought she might as well pick up Margo."

Randal came up. "That's my curricle," he said blankly, and rode off to see the damage.

"And your father?" Verderan asked.

"He's risen from his sickbed to shoot you if you reject me," said Emily with relish. "The tall strapping fellow is my brother Marcus, who has promised not to call you out, even if you do reject me, but who will doubtless beat you to a pulp."

He smiled at her. "I'm utterly cowed and in your power."

"I know," she said.

He dug in his pocket and produced a square-cut ruby. "Are you prepared to wear this?"

She took off her glove and held out her hand. "When did you buy that?" she asked as he slipped it on.

"About a week ago. I told you I was a conceited fellow. Is it safe now to go closer to your protectors?"

They rode over.

"You're supposed to ask my permission," said Sir Henry gruffly.

"Ah, but I'm such a stiff-necked fellow I couldn't think of it until I was sure she'd accept me." He held out a hand to Marcus. "Welcome home."

"Welcome to the family, my lord."

"Don't start that," said Ver firmly. "I'm keeping it a secret."

"You can't do that," Marcus protested.

"I can try. At least until I'm on my honeymoon. By the time we return, hopefully I'll have grown accustomed."

"I'll 'my lord' you morning, noon, and night," promised Emily cheerfully. Verderan gave her a look that raised a blush.

Hector spoke up. "It appears I may have been mistaken in some of my views of you, Mr. Verderan. I apologise."

"That's very handsome of you, vicar. If I'd lost Emily to you, I'd have been somewhat disgruntled, too."

They moved on to the curricle before Hector could work out a suitable response. Margaret admired the ring, and said to Verderan, "You see, I knew what I was doing when I left you two alone."

"I don't know how you ever came to be a vicar's sister," he said sternly. She dimpled at him.

Then he turned to Helen Sillitoe, who was no less shabby but considerably less haggard. "Mother, I hope you are happy for me."

"Very happy," she said. "You have found a pearl, and also a woman of warmth and strength."

Ver and Emily instinctively reached for each other and held hands. Both Nelson and Beelzebub looked round to wonder at this strange state of affairs and then tossed their heads as if despairing of human peculiarities.

"I do think they talk," said Emily.

Verderan looked at her. "Spare me. I've just got my life onto a precarious piece of level ground. Don't cast me into new insanity just yet."

"Aye," said Marcus, "But talking of horses, you're riding mine. And I don't want it sold."

"I don't suppose you do," said Ver, and immediately swung off.

"I say, that's not necessary . . ."

Ver waved and a distant rider began to come over. "I have three here. My groom will ride that one. It looks a little raw and you don't want to miss the run."

"I certainly don't," said Marcus with a grin and mounted. "Nelson's always been a promising beast, and I can see he's coming into his own."

Verderan looked up at Emily, and she obediently slid off
Bel and into his arms.

"Here now," said Sir Henry. "There's people watching!"

Neither Emily nor Verderan paid any attention and when
they finished the thorough kiss, the friends and neighbours
who'd come along broke into applause.

"Do you still want to hunt?" Ver asked.

The promise in his eyes of other things they might do
sent a shudder through her, but she said, "After the trouble
I've been to to get here? Of course I do!"

He took a letter out of his pocket and gave it to her. "Very
well, but I wouldn't read that until you're safe home again."

"Is it going to burn a hole in my pocket?" she asked.

"More than likely. The old desk went up in smoke in the
night."

She was laughing as he tossed her into the saddle. His
groom rode up on a rangy dun, and he swung into the saddle
just as the horn blew and the hounds started out.

"Then let's hunt," said Ver and they turned to join the
field.

Author's note

MY SISTER LIVES near Melton Mowbray and I have often stayed with her, so it was natural for me to think of setting a story in the "Queen of the Shires." After all, if the young ladies of the regency dreamed of waltzing at Almack's, their brothers dreamed of riding to glory with the Quorn.

In fact, since nearly all the rich, well-born young males of England spent November to April hunting in the shires, I began to wonder why the "husband-hunting mamas" didn't move into the area along with them. But then I decided those wily matrons (also wives and mothers) knew that even a "diamond of the first water" would not receive so much as a glance when paraded next to a "bang up bit of blood and bone."

Horses, not ladies, were the true passion of the regency male.

Hunting has always been popular with the English, but until the eighteenth century, the quarry of choice was the deer. With increasing population and agricultural land-use, however, deer became scarce and the fox came into its own. It is said that in 1762 the Duke of Beaufort was returning from a disappointing day's hunting when he threw his hounds (a technical term, not an indication of brutality) into some rough growth and drove out a fox. The subsequent chase was memorable and hunting foxes slowly gained in popularity.

There were still two factors which prevented the development of fox hunting, however. One was that the hounds lacked the speed and endurance to stay with the fox. The other was that foxes are nocturnal, and if one wants to catch them out of their earths, one has to rise before dawn—not much to the liking of the aristocracy.

It was the great Hugo Meynell, who inherited the position of Master of Fox Hounds of the Quorn in 1753, who solved both problems. First he began to copy some of the famous breeding experiments of the agricultural revolution and thereby improve the hounds. Then he employed earth-stoppers. These men would go around a selected area before dawn and stop up any earths they found. Some foxes would be forced to seek hiding above ground in gorse or thick undergrowth (called a covert) where, if the hounds were lucky and the fox was not, one of them would be found.

Not to be killed there, I hasten to point out. That is called "chopping a fox in covert" and is considered a terrible waste. The aim is to have the fox break and run, and hopefully run for hours over challenging country so the riders who follow the hounds will have an exciting ride. After all, when Oscar Wilde described fox hunting as "the unspeakable in full pursuit of the inedible," he summed it up pretty well. The fox is not hunted for food, but for the sport it gives.

Regency hunters claimed that the purpose of fox hunting was to kill vermin, but this is exposed as spurious by the great trouble they went to to preserve the foxes for their enjoyment. Tom Assheton-Smith believed that to kill a fox other than by hunting was a heinous crime. If worse came to the worst, some Masters would even resort to bag-foxes—those purchased from other areas, or even from abroad.

For the hunting enthusiast, such as a Meltonian, the ride was everything; he didn't mind if the fox finally won free and lived to provide a run another day. (Lord Alvanley is reputed to have remarked, "What fun hunting would be if it were not for the damned hounds.") If the fox was caught, however, the hunter's greatest wish was to be in at the kill, to show that he could keep up with fox and hounds over twenty to thirty miles and many hours of the most challenging riding imaginable. Many fell. Many horses and men were injured. Many died. It was an exercise in machismo.

Perhaps Wellington and the other senior officers on the Peninsula were not so eccentric as it seems when they encouraged their cavalry officers to hunt, even allowing them furlough to return to England during hunting season. If Wellington truly said that "the battle of Waterloo was won on the playing fields of Eton," he may well have added, "and on the rolling fields of the Shires."

There are any number of interesting characters from the world of regency hunters, but I have used only Assheton-Smith and Osbaldeston in this book.

George Osbaldeston was probably as unpleasant as I portray him here, but he was also a great sportsman. He once shot 100 pheasant and 97 grouse with 197 shots, and rode 100 miles in 10 hours to win a bet of 1000 guineas. He did achieve his goal and became Master of the Quorn in 1817.

The Meltonians of the regency were fairly civilised men who took their hunting seriously. Things got out of hand as the century progressed and wild pranks were common off-field amusements. In the 1830s the Marquis of Waterford and some friends took it into their doubtless drink-sodden heads to daub a large part of Melton with red paint. This is the origin of the phrase, "to paint the town red."

The development of the railway system changed hunting as it changed the whole of England. Now people could come and go more easily and were less likely to turn to foolishness when there was no hunting. Now the more sober elements of society, who were unable to dedicate months to the sport, could come up for a few days. Ladies, even, began to accompany their men and join the field. The Shires entered a more respectable, and even more glorious phase of their history.

But the Melton hunting society of the regency has its own special character and charm and I found it an ideal setting for the story of Piers Verderan and Emily Grantwich. After all, in what other location would such a quiet, conventional person as Emily be likely to encounter the Dark Angel and actually find they had something in common?

I hope you have enjoyed their story as much as I have enjoyed writing it. I love to hear from my readers and invite you to write to me, care of the publisher: Walker and Company, 720 Fifth Avenue, New York, NY 10019.

(Incidentally this, like all novels, is a blend of fact and fiction, but the incident of the balloon descension into the Cottesmore hunt on November 1, 1813 occurred just as I have described.)

—Jo Beverley

If you would like to receive details on other Walker Regency Romances, please write to:

The Regency Editor
Walker and Company
720 Fifth Avenue
New York, NY 10019